D1321340

Mirror mirror

Mirror mirror

CARA DELEVINGNE

with Rowan Coleman

First published in Great Britain in 2017 by Trapeze,
an imprint of The Orion Publishing Group Ltd
Carmelite House, 50 Victoria Embankment,
London EC4Y 0DZ

An Hachette UK company

1 3 5 7 9 10 8 6 4 2

A CIP catalogue record for this book is
available from the British Library.

ISBN (Hardback): 978 1 4091 7274 1
ISBN (Trade Paperback): 978 1 4091 7275 8
ISBN (eBook): 978 1 4091 7277 2

Book design by Janette Revill
Printed at Clays Ltd, St Ives plc

MIX
Paper from
responsible sources
FSC® C104740

www.orionbooks.co.uk

To my family and friends who helped
me through my teenage years.

And to anyone who feels lost; I hope this
book inspires you to follow your dreams
and to never give up hope.
Anything is possible.

Introduction

Growing up and making the transition from childhood to adulthood is one of the most interesting times of our lives: the chaos, the madness, the hormones, the constant changes and extremes. It's a crucial time filled with drama and high emotion that shapes us into the adults we are destined to become.

Most people refer to the teenage years as the best time of your life, and it's true that it is a carefree time, full of adventure and joy. But it can also be incredibly challenging and difficult, especially if you are the sort of person who doesn't easily fit in.

With social media playing such a large part in our daily lives, it's even harder to be a young person now than it has ever been, especially with the increasing pressure to appear to be perfect. It's a world where people are quick to judge others without taking the time to fully understand them, or consider what might be happening in their lives.

When I set about writing *Mirror, Mirror* I wanted to tell a story that gives the reader a realistic picture of the turbulent rollercoaster teenage years, and to create characters that everyone can relate to. I wanted it to be a book about the power of friendship, and how surrounding yourself with people that you love and trust makes you strong.

Above all I want to tell my readers, that it's OK if you don't know who you are yet. It's OK if you are different and unique because you are already perfect. As long as you learn what it is that makes you happy, and follow your heart everything will be OK. Be yourself, no matter what. Recognise your strengths and realise that within you is the power to change to world.

With love
Cara

Acknowledgements

There have been many people involved in the making of *Mirror, Mirror* and my deepest heartfelt thanks go to the amazing Rowan Coleman who made the writing of this book such an incredible experience. At Orion special thanks go to Anna Valentine, Sam Eades, Marleigh Price, Lynsey Sutherland, Elaine Egan, Lauren Woosey, Loulou Clarke, Lucie Stericker and Claire Keep. At HarperCollins US thank you to Lisa Sharkey, Jonathan Burnham, Mary Gaule, Alieza Schivmer, Anna Montague, Doug Jones and Amanda Pelletier. Thank you to my team at WME: Sharon Jackson, Joe Izzi, Matilda Forbes Watson, Mel Berger and Laura Bonner. Thank you to my good friend Storm Athill for the wonderful artwork on the cover.

Eight weeks ago . . .

The sun was rising as we were coming home, our arms interlinked, feet dragging, the heat of summer building in the air. Rose's head was on my shoulder, her arm around my waist. I can remember the feel of it exactly, her hip and the mismatched rhythm of it bumping against mine, her skin on my skin, warm and soft.

It was just before five; the early light fierce and golden, making every dirty street gleam like new. We'd seen this sunrise a lot on our way home after long nights out, making each moment together last until we closed our eyes. Right up until that night, life had finally felt golden, like it belonged to us and we to it, filling every second with something new, something that felt like it mattered.

But that night was different.

My eyes ached, my mouth was dry, my heart pounded. We didn't want to go home, but what could we do? There was nowhere else to go.

'Why now?' Rose said. 'Everything was good, man. She was good, happy. So why now?'

'It's not the first time, is it?' Leo said. 'That's why the

pigs don't care. She's done it before. Money, backpack full of food from the fridge, her guitar. Disappear for a couple of weeks. It's her M.O. '

'But not since Mirror, Mirror,' Rose said. 'Not since us, right? Before she was into all that cutting and shit, and running off. But not since the band. She was . . . we were all good. Better than good.'

She looked at me to back her up and I had to agree, everything had changed in the last year for all of us. Before the band, we were all lost in our own way, and then somehow we happened. And together we were strong, and cool and rock hard and in-your-face awesome. We all thought Naomi was in that place too, that she didn't need to run away any more. Until last night.

That night, we were out all night, all over town.

Every place we ever went to with her, we went to again without her.

The places we told our parents about, the places we didn't.

The clubs we should have been too young to get into, hot and stinking of sweat and hormones, battling our way through a heaving mass of dancers, trying to catch a glimpse of her.

We slunk in the shadows, in alleys down the back of pubs where you could score, talking in low voices to nervous kids with shadows for eyes, who offered bags of skunk. That night we said no.

We visited places behind unmarked doors where you have to know someone to get in. Dark basement rooms, where people still smoked inside until the air was thick with it, and the music was so loud it made your ears ring, your chest vibrate and the floor jump to the beat under your feet.

We went to all of those places, and everywhere else. The park on the estate where we go to muck around. The riverside, alien and overlooked by millionaire apartment blocks. Vauxhall Bridge, our bridge, the one we've walked across so often, shouting to make ourselves heard over the traffic, that it feels kind of like a mate, kind of like a witness.

Finally, we went to that empty betting shop with the broken door and a mattress in the back, where some kids go when they want a place to be alone. Some kids, but never me because one of the things I really hate is being alone.

Hour after hour of that night went by, and we were sure with every moment that passed we'd find her, that she was pulling one of her stunts, the kind of thing she did when she was hurting and needed to be noticed. We were sure our best friend and band mate, Naomi, would be somewhere in a place that only we knew. She would be waiting for us to find her.

Because you couldn't just exist one day and vanish the next. That makes no sense at all. No one just disintegrates into thin air, without leaving some kind of trace behind.

That's what we told ourselves that night we looked, and the night after that, and all the nights that followed until our parents told us we had to stop, that she'd come home when she was ready. And then the police stopped looking, because she'd run away so many times before.

But it never felt like that to us, it didn't feel the same as before, because she wasn't the same as before – not that they listened, with their bored expressions and blank notebooks. What could they possibly know?

So we looked and looked for Naomi, long after everyone else stopped. We looked everywhere.

But she wasn't anywhere.

All we could find were the spaces where she used to be.

1

Today: Life goes on, that's what everyone says.

We have to keep getting up, going to school, coming home, thinking about shit like exams that are happening soon. And 'hope, pray and trust' and a load of other bullshit nothing they keep saying to us.

Life goes on, but that's a lie, because the night Naomi vanished she pressed a big fucking pause button. Days tick by, and weeks and seasons and all of that shit, but not anything else. Not really. It's like we've all been holding our breath for eight weeks.

Because I'll tell you what they don't say any more; they don't say she'll come home when she's ready. I see her older sister Ashira at school, head down, closed off like she doesn't want anyone to get near. And her mum and dad wandering around the supermarket, staring at stuff without really seeing it. Even though it's Nai who's gone missing, they're the ones that look lost.

And yes, once she would have run away to make everyone look for her, she would have, because once she thought that kind of psycho-drama was a big deal. But she hasn't for a long time, and never like this. She'd never want her mum and dad to be so twisted up with worry for her, or for Ash to look like she is always holding her breath, braced for bad news. Nai is complicated, but she loves her family and they love her, it's like this beacon that draws the rest of us round them, love-hungry moths to a flame. Theirs is a family that actually gives a shit about each other.

You see, Naomi wouldn't do this to them, or to us. But no one wants to hear that, not the police, not even her mum, because the thought of Naomi being a hardcore bitch is better than the thought of her being simply gone.

Which is why sometimes I just wish they'd find a body.

That's how much of a dick I am. Sometimes I wish she was dead just so I could know.

But they haven't. They haven't found anything. And life goes on.

Which means today is the day that we audition for a new bassist to replace Naomi.

For a minute, it looked like we might break up without her. The rest of Mirror, Mirror – me, Leo and Rose – we met up for a rehearsal and wondered if we should just call it quits, we even said that we should. And then the three of us just stood there, no one leaving, no one packing up, and we knew without having to say it out loud that we couldn't let go. Letting go of the band would be letting go of the best thing in all of our lives, and it would be letting go of her, for good.

Naomi founded the band, or at least she's the one who turned it from some lame-arsed homework project into something real, something that mattered. Nai is the reason we all found something we were good at, because she was so good at her thing. I mean, she was a great bassist, legendary; you'd hear her lay down the beat and you'd be shook. But even more than that Naomi can write – I mean really good songs. I'm not bad and together, her and me are great, but Nai has that thing, that special thing that takes something leaden and grey and makes it shiny and special. Before Mirror, Mirror she never knew that was her superpower, but now she does, because we told her. And the more we told her, the better she got. And when you've got a superpower like that, you don't need to run away.

The day we nearly split, our music teacher Mr Smith, came into the rehearsal room. It was the summer holidays, school was mostly empty except for us. We were only allowed on site because of him, he'd got us permission and spent his holiday sitting and reading a paper while we fought and played. But this time he came and sat down, and waited for us to stop talking and look at him. It hit me how different he looked right then. Mr Smith is one of those people who fills up a room, not just because he's tall and kind of built, like he works out and stuff, but also because of the way he is; he likes life, he likes *us*, the kids he teaches, and that's rare. He makes you want to do stuff, makes you want to learn, and it's all because of this kind of energy you just don't see in adults that much; it's as if he really does give a shit.

That day though, he looked like someone had let the air out of him, like all the energy and good vibes he usually brings with him had disappeared. And it was frightening to see him that way, because he's one of those people who is always so strong. It got to me in a way I can't really explain; it made me like him even more. It meant a lot to see how much he cared that Nai was missing, really cared. Outside of her family and us lot, it seemed like he was one of the few people who did.

I don't know how the others felt but the moment I saw him that day, I wanted to help him, as much as I knew he wanted to help us.

'Are you guys really thinking about splitting up?' he said.

We looked at each other, and for a second it felt like it did before we were friends, lonely and awkward and the idea of being back there again was terrifying.

'It feels wrong without her,' I said.

'I get that,' he said, running his fingers through his hair so that it stood up in blonde spikes. 'But listen to me when I tell you that if you do split up now, you'll regret it. You four . . . you three . . . I'm so proud of you, and everything you do together. I don't want you to lose that, not for you, and not for Nai. Now there's not much that you can do for Naomi, but what you can do is make sure people keep remembering her name until she is found. Make sure they never stop looking for her. I've had this idea – we'll stage a concert, here at the school. Raise funds to help her family keep up the search, keep her story in the public eye. Make the whole world look at us, at you guys, and see how much we care about her. That's what I want to do, kids. But I can't do it without you. Are you in?'

And yeah, of course we said we were in.

It's the only thing we could think of doing.

We kept going, just the three of us all summer, but the concert is nearly here and we've realised what we have to do. We have to find a new bassist. Fuck's sake.

Naomi was . . . is . . . the best bassist I've ever played with, which is weird because she is a girl, and girls aren't normally good at that shit. That's not sexist, it's just a fact. It takes a sort of single-minded determination to be invisible to really play the bass, and girls – well, normal girls – like to be looked at.

But today must go on. I've got to get my shit together. Dragging myself out of bed, I look at the crumpled pile of clothes on the floor.

It's all right for Leo, the dude just gets out of bed and he looks on-point.

He picks up his guitar and he might as well be God; girls worship him as if he is. It doesn't seem fair, really, that at the age of sixteen, he can be so together, like he came fully formed and deep voiced, tall and muscular.

Me, though, I'm still in that awkward phase. I live in that awkward phase, I *am* that awkward phase. If there was an emoji for awkward phases it would look like me. I fully expect to still be in the awkward phase when I'm forty-five and almost dead.

I *want* to look cool, but Leo cool; plain white T, jeans, hoodie and immaculate white high tops isn't the sort of cool that I can do. There isn't any sort of cool I can do, except the cool I borrow from being Leo's mate.

Rose has also nailed looking good, but she is legit beautiful, and beautiful never really has to try. Dark brown hair, dyed blonde, but not all the way to the top; not skinny like some girls, Rose's boobs and hips keep the boys of Thames Comprehensive in her thrall.

But that's not all, she wears a fuck ton of make-up, even though she looks prettier with none – maybe because of that. She backcombs her hair and puts holes in her tights on purpose. Rose knows what her look is and she makes it happen, charging the air with static electricity and detonating millions of little explosions all around her wherever she goes.

Other girls try and copy her, but there aren't any other girls like Rose, because I swear to God, Rose is the only girl I have ever met who really gives zero fucks.

And when she sings . . . walls vibrate. Eyes turn green. Boners harden.

Out of the four of us in our magnificent misfit family, Naomi was . . . *is* the one who is most like me. If Leo and Rose are the fuck-that-shit-prom-king-and-queen of the school, me and Nai are the Overlords of Geek.

And when I think of Naomi in her thick-framed glasses that swamp her heart-shaped face and hide her soft brown eyes, I feel proud of her. The way she wears shirts, buttoned all the way, and pleated skirts a totally different length to anyone else. Her sensible shoes, laced up and polished. Behind it all, the deliberate mismatches and the odd choices, she is a completely take-no-prisoners, accept-no-bullshit original.

Sometimes Naomi and I used to go to the library at lunch and just sit and read. We'd be quiet and still. It was peaceful. She'd catch my eye over the top of her book, and raise an eyebrow at me when some year nine try-hard went past and we'd smirk at each other, two disbelieving super-nerds who had somehow lucked out into pole position.

And when she played . . . it was just as good, in fact better than the best bassists in the world. With me on the drums we were the heartbeat of the band, carving out the groove with rare precision.

I can't be arsed to think about my band look, so fuck it: checked shirt, jeans, white T-shirt underneath, that's my usual uniform. Lumberjack-pro, Rose calls it.

At least I don't have to think about my hair any more since I shaved most of it off.

Carrot Top.

Ginger Nuts.

Dickhead.

All names I've got just for being a redhead, and not just any old ginger, no, a curly haired redhead, at that. Jesus, I grew up looking like an invitation to kick my head in. There are things I could do about it, Rose likes to tell me. She's desperate to put product on my hair and straighten it. And I'm like, er no. And about every three days or so she offers to dye it black, but again I say no, I'm ginger, OK, deal with it.

Besides, if my hair was black they couldn't still call me Red, and my nickname is the coolest thing about me.

What I did was to have it cut really short the day before Nai disappeared. Didn't tell anyone, just went to a barbershop, told them shave it round the sides, long on top, long enough to flop in my eyes and bounce and freak out like mad when I'm sitting on the rig. Mum screamed at me for a solid hour when she saw it. I'm not even joking, she said I looked like I came out of a maximum security prison.

When Dad came in from one of his 'all night council meetings', she screamed at him for not screaming at me.

It was worse than when I had my ear pierced four times, so after that I don't bother telling them about the things I do that help me feel like me. It's not worth the aggro.

And long before that I had realised that my parents

weren't going to be the ones to save me, fix me or help me. They are both so caught up in their own self-destruction, me and my kid sister Gracie are pretty much nothing more than collateral damage. Once I realised that, life seemed easier, believe it or not.

Sure, it's hard to ignore that my mother hates me and my dad's a sleaze. But I give it a good go.

Mirror, Mirror Lyrics

Where Did She Go?

There was always sunshine in her step,
Power in her smile.
She never lived with one regret,
But she only stayed for a while.

Where did she go, the girl I want?
Where did she go, the girl I haunt?
Where did she go, I can't find her.
But I won't stop looking, I'll keep on looking until . . . .

I find out.

2

Rose owns the room, shutting down the pricks that thought they could learn bass in a week with a single death stare.

'Jesus, Toby, the way you mangled that bass puts me off you for life, mate,' Rose tells her latest victim. 'Do you finger your girlfriend like that?'

'Sorry, mate.' Leo shrugs. 'Maybe stick to . . . not playing an instrument?'

As Toby leaves, his pink cheeks blazing, I peer out into the corridor and look at the queue. There is a queue. Once I was that awkward twat in the corner that everyone ignored, and now people are queuing to be in my band. It feels good and bad at the same. Nai helped us build this band, she's the best songwriter out of all of us, the heart of it all. It was her tunes, her words that made people stop and listen. And now these people are queuing to replace her.

I want this band, I need it. I think that's what makes me a fucking bastard.

They fall one after the other and I watch them go, safe behind my kit until there are only two contenders left.

This girl called Emily, pretty and cool. Not so sexy she might eat you alive, but sexy enough that you could look at her all day long, and dream up poems about her hair and shit.

The second Emily walks in the door, I can tell that Rose is having none of it. She doesn't have to say anything, you can just see the lightning flash in her eyes. She's the hot girl in our band, there isn't room for two.

Which is a shame, because as she starts to play, I can feel that Emily is good, I can sense her moving in close to my rhythm and inserting herself between each beat of my sticks. It feels good, really good, intimate. I find myself meeting her blue eyes and smiling at her – because playing drums is the one time letting a girl know I like them doesn't make me want to kill myself. She smiles back and before I know it one of my sticks slips out of my hand and clatters to the floor.

'Sorry love,' Rose says, not even looking at Emily. 'Not really working, is it. Nice try though.'

Emily doesn't react, she just shrugs super cool, smiling at me again before she leaves.

'I liked her,' I say. 'Can't I have her?'

Rose punches me hard in my bicep, and pain shoots into my shoulder. That girl can hit.

'Jesus, Rose! Lay off the guns!'

'They aren't guns, they're water pistols more like.' She shakes her head. 'Fuck's sake, Red, keep it in your pants. This isn't your chance to pull any old slut that walks in.'

'Emily's not a slut,' Leo says. 'I liked her.'

'Jesus, you simple-minded fuckheads. Really, all it has

to have is tits on it and you're like sheep.'

Leo and I exchange a glance, repressing a smile.

'Isn't that how you basically rule the school?' Leo mutters and Rose cuffs him across the back of the head.

Next up is Leckraj, this random kid from year eight. He reminds me of me aged thirteen, no idea how to handle the jungle of Thames Comprehensive. His bass is almost bigger than him, but at least he can play up to grade five. Not as well as Emily, nothing like Naomi, but he'll do. It looks like he'll have to, because he's all that's left.

'So, Leckraj, I'm going to take you through the bass line for "Head Fuck", OK? And then . . . '

'Kids, can you stop a minute?'

Mr Smith is suddenly in the middle of the room, and he looks like a current of electricity has glued him to the spot, forcing him upright. I've never seen an expression like the one on his face right now, like he's just heard the end of the world is coming. It frightens me. My gut is twisting and churning. This is bad, it's going to be bad.

No one says anything.

No one has to.

It's like the air around us thickens and slows time to a standstill, sticky in my lungs. I can't breathe.

We all know what he's come to tell us.

'They've found her?' It's a whisper that comes from inside me though it sounds like I'm hearing it from light years away.

He nods, unable to look any of us in the eye.

'Is she . . . ?' Leo this time, eyes fixed hard on Smith, waiting for the axe to fall.

'She's . . . ' Mr Smith seems to choke for a second, shaking his head. Finally he looks at us, there are tears in his eyes, his mouth is twisted and it takes me a moment to realise . . .

. . . he's smiling.

'She's alive,' he says.

3

The world falls from under my feet. For a moment I see her face, the way it was the last time I saw her, and how she smiled, her eyes lit up from the inside, and all I want to do is be with her.

'Well, where is she, then?' Words rush out of Rose. 'We need to go and see her now, *right* now. Where is she? Is she at home? Here? Is she here?'

'St Thomas's,' Mr Smith says.

'Shit.' Rose shakes her head.

'The hospital? What's happened to her?' Me.

'Did someone hurt her?' Leo, jaw clenched. 'Who the fuck hurt her?'

'Listen . . . ' Mr Smith raises his palms like he's trying to quieten down a room of rowdy kids. 'I know this is a lot to take in, that's why I wanted to make sure that I got to tell you. But I've spoken to all of your parents, and they've agreed I can take you there now to find out more. But there's something you have to know.'

'Where's she been?' Rose asks, before he can get another word out. 'She must have said where she's been.'

'Did she say why?' Leo's voice is low, full of anger. 'Did she say why she ran away?'

'What happened to her?' Me again. 'Did she say what happened?'

Mr Smith's shoulders slump as he sinks down onto the corner of the platform stage, staring hard at the floor. I can see him figuring out how to say what he has to say next, trying to make sense of it all himself, with every carefully chosen word. He's trying to protect us. That's bad.

'Something . . . something happened to her in the last few hours. Some rivermen found her tangled up in the ropes used to moor the river tour boats around Westminster Bridge. In the water. She was unconscious, breathing but barely. The rope kept her head out of the water . . . but she's injured, badly. A head injury and . . . no one knows how serious it is yet.'

'What does that mean?' Rose takes two steps towards him, so fast that for a moment, I think she's going to hit him. Slowly he looks up at her, holding her gaze.

'It means there is a very high chance that she won't make it.'

From joy to despair in a heartbeat. I see her face again, and wonder how it can be possible to find someone and lose them in the very same moment.

There was this one year when I was ten that I was in hospital so many times, social services came to check up on me. The first time I broke my wrist playing with next-door's puppy; it jumped up, I fell backwards and hit my hand on a stone flowerpot as I landed. Crack; the sound of it made me throw up. Then I did my ankle playing footie when Kevin Monk came in with a two-footed tackle. That hurt like a mother-fucker. And finally I bruised a couple of ribs when I fell out of a tree, in a dare to see who could get the highest, quickest. Won the dare, though.

Funny thing is, I liked those trips to A&E. I liked the long waits, because it meant either Mum or Dad were sitting next to me, and I got them for however many hours it took to be seen. Even though Dad was always missing something important and Mum, who was pregnant with Gracie, would be uncomfortable and tired, for as long as we were there I had them. They'd really listen to me, and we'd talk, laugh, and they'd let me play games on their phone. After I fell out of the tree, I had to stay in overnight, because they were worried about my head. Mum rented a TV for us to watch and she sat next to me all night, balancing a massive bag of Doritos on her baby bump, holding my hand.

When the social worker came round, they talked to me at the kitchen table with Mum sitting on the edge of her chair, biting her nails. I couldn't figure out why Mum looked so worried, but I didn't want her to be, I didn't like that look on her face. I wanted to make it go away. So I told the woman about each accident, one after the other, in great detail; dog, football, tree. And then I had to tell her again, and one more time while Mum was out of the room before she finally packed up and left.

'What are you like?' Mum had said, when she'd come back in, putting her hand on the top of my head, running her fingers through my hair. 'My little daredevil.'

She made me a hot chocolate with marshmallows and I

remember sitting at the table, wondering what it was that I'd done right.

The last time I was here was when Gracie was born; Dad leading us through a maze of corridors into a room full of curtains where Mum was sitting on the edge of her trolley bed with my tiny crimson little sister screeching her lungs out. When I'm really down I think of that day, the four of us round the bed, a unit. A family, the smell of Gracie's hair, the smile on Dad's face. The way Mum looked so tired and so happy. I always think of that day, because that's the last time I remember feeling like a family.

Yeah, that was the last time.

As we follow Mr Smith through the hospital, it all slides past like some low-tech VR, the shiny floors and long corridors. Something sharp scents the air, catching the back of my throat. The silence in the lift, the sound of our rubber soles squeaking when we walk, the flickering lights overhead.

And then there is a room, and we know our best friend is in it. And maybe she is dying.

Standing outside the room, I see Nai's mum and dad, arms wrapped around each other, heads buried in the other's neck. I see Nai's mum clawing fistfuls of her husband's shirt, like she's afraid that if she lets go she will drown.

'Mrs Demir?' It's Rose that steps forward leaving Mr Smith standing by the lift. Normally we'd just call them Max and Jackie, but in this moment it doesn't seem right somehow.

The second that Nai's mum sees Rose, she reaches out

to her, pulling her into the middle of their embrace. Leo and I follow, one after the other, our arms around the people who always let us into their home at all hours and never made us feel unwanted or unwelcome.

I'm lost for a moment in the dark, hot embrace of people, gluing my eyes shut against the threat of tears, determined not to let anyone see how scared I am. Then the moment disintegrates as we let go of each other, and I'm blinking under the strip lights again.

'How is she?' Mr Smith has been standing a few steps away from the five of us, watching.

Jackie shakes her head and Max turns to the window, looking through the slatted blinds at the person lying perfectly still on a bed. I'm used to seeing Max full of laughter, dark eyes sparkling, belly shaking, always another terrible joke on the way. To see him like this, shadows in the hollows of his face, thin and weak; it's hard to look at.

I feel like I should go over and stand next to him, but I can't, I'm afraid. Afraid of what I will see.

A head injury, what does that mean? Will she look different, will there be blood? Nai and I, when it was just us two, would find the worst possible horror movie on Netflix, chainsawing slashers and vengeful demons, the bloodier the better. But this is real. *This* is horror. And it scares the fuck out of me.

I keep my eyes fixed on Jackie, her banana-yellow dyed hair with the deep dark roots, her long thin arms, and skinny legs in skinny jeans, dressing like a kid twenty years younger than her, something that always drives Nai mad. My mum thinks Jackie is trash, but then again she thinks that about me, too.

'Did she talk to you yet?' Rose is holding Jackie's hand.

'Did she wake up?'

'Max,' Jackie whispers to her husband, who shakes his head, reaching out for a passing medic.

'Doctor?'

A woman in a white coat stops, frowning at us.

'These are my daughter's friends, really more like her family. Will you explain what's happening to them please? I'm still not sure I understand myself.'

The doctor presses her lips together thinly, showing just a trace of impatience, but folds her hands together and starts talking.

'Naomi was discovered by a tugboat crew on the Thames, caught up in some mooring ropes . . .'

'Only a few minutes from home.' Rose looks at Leo. 'She was nearly home. Did she fall?'

'It's not clear how she got in the water, only that the moorings she became caught up in probably saved her from drowning, her head trauma certainly would have rendered her unconscious. That, and the severe cold from the night in the water, are factors that have contributed to her surviving so far. So we are warming her up, very slowly, and we are keeping her in a medical coma while we monitor her brain for swelling and bleeding. We should know more tomorrow.'

Any moment I expect to get it, to understand that this is really happening, but that moment doesn't seem to come and it all feels like make-believe.

'I mean it's bad, but she'll be OK, right? I mean she *will* be OK?' Leo asks, with a sharp edge of anger. The doctor hesitates, maybe worried about answering honestly, upsetting this kid who is six feet tall and properly built. Leo can be scary sometimes.

'We don't know . . . ' she says slowly. 'It's a miracle that she survived any time at all in the water, that the blow to her head didn't kill her outright. She's a fighter, she has to be, that's why she's here now. She's getting the best possible care.'

'Can we see her?' Rose asks. 'Please, I want to see her.'

The doctor looks at Max, who nods his permission.

She scans each of our faces, and I hope she might say no. But she doesn't.

'OK, one at a time, three minutes each. No more.'

'We should talk to her, right?' Rose asks as Max holds the door open for her. 'Because that might wake her up. On TV they say the people in comas can hear you talking to them.'

'Well, this is a medically induced coma.'

'A what?' Rose frowns.

'We've sedated her and intubated her to give her body a chance to heal and recover from everything she's been through. Talking to her won't wake her up, but there's every chance she might hear you so . . . why not.' The doctor smiles briefly. Squaring her shoulders Rose goes into the room, softly closing the door behind her.

'We need to make some calls, will you kids be OK?' Jackie asks kindly. Her mascara has run into the creases around her eyes, making tracks down her face. I nod.

'Will you be?' I ask her.

'Honestly, Red.' Her eyes fill with tears as she tries to smile for my sake. 'I don't know.'

As we wait outside Mr Smith finally moves himself from the spot he's taken up by the lift and crosses over to the window that looks into Nai's room. Peering through the gaps in the blind, the afternoon sun slashes bars of shadow across his face. I still can't bring myself to look at Nai, so I look at him instead. His face is familiar, a safe place.

'Does she look bad?' I say.

'You know I never lie to my students, Red. Right?' he says.

I nod.

'She looks bad.' He nods in the direction of Naomi. 'I think . . . I think Rose needs you.'

When I finally make myself look through the window I see Rose, her fists clenched to her face, eyes wide; her body visibly shaking as she stares at the figure in the bed. Before I know it I'm in the room, grabbing her wrist, pulling her towards the door.

'No, no, no,' she fights against me, snatching her hand away. 'No. We can't leave her here, alone. I'm not leaving her alone. Look at her, Red. She can't be alone.'

'Rose, come on,' I say. 'We aren't helping her if we freak out.'

'Look at her!' Rose demands.

I look. I see her face swollen, purple and grey. And now I can't stop looking because this face is so different from the one I know so well. It's hard to believe she is the same person. There's a dressing that encircles her head, and every trace of her long dark hair is gone. Another bandage is bound diagonally across her face, traces of red seeping through. Bruises blacken and discolour her skin wherever it is visible, one eye swollen shut, the other concealed under the bandage, her dark sparkling eyes seem blotted out forever. I see the machines, the thick uncomfortable tube that comes from her mouth, twisting the soft smile I remember into a frozen scream.

Wires seem to be growing out of her body like she is half-machine, and I get it. I get why Rose wants to stand there and scream her head off. It's terrifying.

'Come on,' I say, pulling her out of the room. 'We need to get our shit together. We need to be strong.'

I tug Rose and close the door behind us, hugging her tightly.

'How is she?' Leo asks. We don't need to answer.

'When I find out who did this to her . . . ' Leo clenches his fists at his side.

'What if she did it to herself?' Ashira, Nai's sister seems to have come out of nowhere.

'Ash!' Rose lets go of me and flings her arms around Nai's older half-sister, who stands stock still, letting Rose sob into her sweatshirt for a few seconds. I watch Ash, she is so still, so composed. On the outside, anyway.

'You don't think . . . I mean she wouldn't have tried to hurt herself,' I say. 'Nai was happy, really happy. Bouncing off walls happy before she went missing. This isn't like before, when she used to run from all the bullying. That all changed when the band got together, and she had us. No one picked on her any more. It makes no sense.'

'No.' Ash turns her face away from Rose, and it takes me by surprise how much more she looks like Nai than I realised, the same long straight nose and cheekbones, the jet-black hair with a ruby-red sheen that shines like a mirror. Unlike Nai, Ash doesn't wear make-up, she doesn't straighten her hair, it's just the way it is. While Naomi would be finding ever more crazy outfits to wear, Ash always wore the same thing, more or less: combats, T-shirt, baseball cap, no matter what the weather. I always liked that about her, that she just didn't give a toss about the world outside her head. But now her sister is in intensive care and she's been forced out into this world with us. It looks like it hurts her. 'No, I guess it doesn't make sense. Nothing makes sense. I need to find Dad and Jackie, do you know there they went?'

'To call people,' I say, taking a step towards her. 'Ash are you OK?' She takes a step back.

'I'm . . . ' Ash shrugs. 'See you later.'

'This is so fucked up,' Leo speaks quietly. 'What happened to her, it's fucked up. This never should have happened, man. If it was just Nai, pulling one of her stunts it never would have ended like this. Something happened to her, I bet you. She wouldn't have tried to top herself.'

'Is that what people are saying?' I look to Mr Smith to make things clear, to separate the truth from the lies. But he's looking just as lost as us. 'Are they saying she meant to kill herself?'

'I don't know.' He shrugs. 'I wish I did. I haven't spoken to the police, only Nai's parents, but I suppose it has to be a possibility that she tried to . . . '

'No.' I shake my head. 'That's bullshit.'

'Nai was scared of water,' Rose says. 'She'd have her period every swimming lesson to get out of it. If she was that messed up, we'd have known about it. We'd have saved her.'

Her voice catches, and she folds herself into Leo's arms.

'I thought finding her would make things better,' I say. 'But I don't know what to do.' Mr Smith puts his hand on my shoulder and I lean into it.

'I don't know what to do,' I repeat, searching out his gaze and holding it. I want him to tell me it's going to be

OK. If he says it is, then I'll believe it.

'Look, this has been hard on you all, really hard. I think maybe I should take you home now. I think we need to give Naomi's family sometime to adjust to what's happened, give them some space and let your parents take care of you.'

'I'll walk,' Leo says at once.

'Me too.' I look at Rose, who cocks her head as she turns to Mr Smith.

'Will *you* be OK, sir?'

'Me? Of course I will.' His tired smile is reassuring. 'Look, like the doctor said, Naomi is a fighter, everything will turn out all right, you'll see.'

As we leave he is still there. Looking through the blinds into her room.

The thing about Mr Smith is that he's more than just a good teacher, he's the only adult in my life who never let me down. It's the same for a lot of the kids at Thames Comprehensive. He never lies to us, he never bullshits us, he treats us like people, not cattle. He's the sort of teacher you can talk to about anything, and he'll really listen and try to help. He helped me, back when things started going wrong at home. He made me see it's OK to be who I am, that I am not my parents. He's a good man, a kind one.

'Her parents aren't back,' I say. 'We can't leave her until they are.'

'You go,' he says. 'I'll hang around a bit longer until they get back.'

Rose nods and offers me her hand. She hooks her other arm through Leo's and guides us to the lift.

'This is fucked up,' Rose says as the lift doors slide shut. 'So we should get fucked up, too.'

One year ago . . .

'Heads up!' Mr Smith had to shout to make himself heard over the class, our first day back at school after the summer, and most of the kids had a lot to talk about. Who was seeing who, who'd done what to who, who was doing who.

Rose – she was a stranger to me then, this kind of mythical stunning girl that I could only look at from a distance – was holding court in the corner, sitting on her desk. At least half the class were turned to look at her and not Smith, riveted by her stories that she illustrated with wild hand gestures.

The only ones who weren't were me, sitting in the back corner, arms crossed, slouched low in my chair, Naomi Demir, dressed like an Anime girl in full false-lashed make-up, tapping her pen impatiently against the desk, and Leo, who was on his phone.

'LISTEN!' Smith shouted and the room quietened a little. 'I don't want to stick you all in detention, but I will if you don't take your seats right now. Got it?'

There had been moans, eye rolling, sighs. Rose just

laughed and stayed sitting on her desk, crossing her legs, and swinging her boots so they knocked against the metal table leg, bang, bang, bang.

But Mr Smith was smart. He didn't try and control her in the way another teacher would. He just ignored her and that deflated her just enough to let the rest of the class settle down around her. I remember liking that, I remember thinking: see, if you ignore the person you like for long enough eventually they will fall in love with you.

What a loser I was back then.

Smith told us he was putting us into bands and that our assignment was to write and perform three tracks together. He started calling out the names and I sat at the back filling up slowly with total existential angst. You see, back then no one talked to me, and that was how I liked it.

No one bullied me. A year ago I wasn't the short, toned ginger drummer in a band, I was a short, skinny – too skinny – kid and no one really noticed I existed. I didn't really care, I wanted to hide inside my own body, make myself as invisible as I could. It was safer that way. I didn't want to be in a group. I didn't want to participate. I fucking hated participating. And I knew that I was absolutely on the very bottom of everyone else's list of who they wanted to participate with. It was a nightmare, the rest of the class being gradually divided up in groups of three and four and sent off to find a place to discuss what kind of music they were going to write, and start jamming.

'Red, Naomi, Leo and . . . Rose.' Mr Smith nodded at each of us in turn and I remember closing my eyes for a long moment and wishing that this was a dream, a long convoluted dream that would end up with me just a few seconds away from undoing the buttons on Rose's shirt and then I'd wake up before anything good happened, like normal.

'Er, fuck no,' Leo more or less shouted. The tone of his voice snapped my eyes open.

'What's your problem, Leo?' Mr Smith wasn't angry, or sarcastic. Leo stood by the window, phone in hand.

'I'm not fucking doing anything with those losers. Fuck that, this is bullshit.'

'How is it bullshit?' Mr Smith had said.

'I don't even want to be here.' Leo strode between the desks right up to Smith. He's just as tall as him and he got right in his face, looking him right in the eye. If there was a fight, I don't know who would have won. 'I don't give a fuck about school.'

'Then leave,' Smith told him, squaring his shoulders. 'Walk off. Go truant. Your mum will be visited by the police *again*, and you'll probably be excluded for good this time. They'll try and send you to the educational behavioural unit, as a last attempt to get you back on track, but you'll ditch that bullshit too, and before you know it you'll be following your brother inside. Do that. That sounds like a great life plan.'

The whole of the class was quiet at last, glued to the anger that flowed through Leo like a current, so strong you could almost see it halo around him, threatening to strike any time. We'd all seen it in action, we'd seen him marched away by the pigs one time after decking a teacher. But Smith stood his ground, he didn't flinch.

'You think I hate you, but I don't. I've heard you play, Leo, and you are better than anyone I've ever taught.

You're a natural, you have a gift. Don't throw that away, because you're worth more than you think you are. You're worth more than this attitude.'

'I don't need you to tell me that,' Leo growled. 'I know who I am.'

'Good,' Mr Smith nodded. 'So are you leaving?'

Leo didn't move for a second, and then he stalked to door and yanked it open. Turning around, he looked at Rose, Nai and Me.

'You coming then, or what?' he said.

Honestly? I was too shit scared not to go.

We followed him down the hall to one of the rehearsal rooms, and Naomi, who had never once spoken to me in three years of school, leaned in close and said, 'Jesus Christ, when he inevitably instigates a school shooting, we will be the first to go.'

And that's when I knew I liked her.

That first session we jammed some AC/DC.

'What we gonna do?' Leo asked, looking at us. 'What do we all know?'

He looked right at me, and I nearly shat myself. 'What do *you* know?'

It sounded like he thought I might not know anything. For a second I didn't.

'Some AC/DC?' I offered, because I didn't know what they would know how to play and everyone knew that. '"You Shook Me All Night Long?"'

He scowled at Nai, who didn't talk, instead picking the riff out on her bass, as a yes. Rose shrugged. 'Not really my thing, but I'll give it a shot.'

'All right, how about this?' Leo kicked in with the riff, dirty and loud, full of fuck you, and I loved it.

'Nice,' Rose said nodding, and I noticed how she was careful not to seem too impressed. I looked at Nai, grateful she wasn't the chatty type, and marked the beat as she lay down the bass line, nodding as she counted us in.

'Three, four . . . '

And yeah, it was beautiful that first time. Like your first roller coaster ride, or first kiss; it was perfect, stomach-flipping excellence, just like I always wanted it be when I was drumming along to tracks at home. Me and Nai, we had never spoken a word to each other and now I was right there with her, underpinning Leo's guitar until it started to sound like the track we all knew, even if we didn't know we knew it.

Head down, hair covering her face Rose joined in on the chorus, and we all looked at her, caught out by the first sound of her voice, deep and throaty, raw liked she smoked twenty a day, which she probably did. It grabbed me, punched me hard in the heart. I hadn't known it was possible to fancy her more, but it was.

She didn't know the verses so she started to make it up as she went along, laughing and singing at the same time. Lifting her head up, she took the mic off the stand and grinned at Naomi.

'She was an Anime girl,
Sometimes wore a tail,
Didn't take no shit from no second-class male.'

Nai grinned at her, and she turned to Leo.

'He was tall and hot,
Knew just what he got,
Could have been a rock star if he stopped smoking pot.'

Oh God, I really wanted her to make a verse up about

me, and I really didn't at the same time. When she looked at me it took all the strength I had to keep playing.

'Give it up for Red.

Bit strange in the head,

Wanders round like a zombie, risen from the dead . . . '

OK, so she didn't call me tall or hot, but she hadn't mentioned me being short and ginger either, so as far as I was concerned it was basically a love letter.

Led by Leo we tore it up, every bit of that fury he felt pouring into his guitar, cutting the air around him into ribbons of rhythm, and I fell in, crashing my way into the heart of the track, catching and pulling Nai with me on the way. Rose wailed over the top, so hard, so raw, so good, that when the song came to an end, without exchanging a word we started over again, this time even better and when we'd finished, sweating and exhausted, I looked up and the rehearsal room door was open and there were about twenty kids standing there looking at us. They cheered and whooped and clapped.

'Fuck off!' Leo told them, then he turned to me and smiled. 'Mate, this is going to be good.'

For the first time in my life I felt like someone.

4

With the hospital far behind us, early evening stretching its arms over the city, wc walk down to the park, the
same park we played in when we were little, although not
together, of course. Kids on their way home from school
have been and gone, and it's empty. We sit under the slide,
and we don't talk. It's good, our silence, it's good we can
come here and not need to say anything, just knowing we
want to be together. That's what the last year has done
for all of us; it's given each of us a reason, when we didn't
really have one before. Our reason is each other.

Apart we were chaotic, spinning and lost, waiting for
this part of our lives to be done with so we could really live, so we could be free. And then there was Mirror,
Mirror, named by Rose because she said that together we
were the fucking fairest of them all.

And with Mirror, Mirror there was us; together and
stronger. Or at least we thought we were, but there must
have been a weak link, something that meant Naomi
could be separated out, almost lost to us without us even
noticing her falling away. What we can't talk about, what

we've never talked about is what it could have been, what could have happened to lead up to this moment.

She's our best mate, and none of us know why she ran in the first place, or why she might have . . . there's no reason I can think of that would make her jump off a bridge into the black water she was so scared of.

So we sit and don't talk, avoiding home. We all have our reasons why. Mine is probably on her third vodka coke by now, Dad is probably tonsils deep in his latest shag.

Leo is the first to break the silence.

'Fuck it, let's do something,' he says.

'We *are* doing something.' Rose leans her head back against the painted metal, etched with names and swearwords, so you could see all of her throat. 'We're wasting our youth in a park. Like proper teenagers.'

'That's not what I mean,' Leo said. 'Something good? Pills and a club. We should get fucked up like Rose said.'

'I'm skint,' Rose yawned. 'Have you got pills on you? Let's just get wasted here.'

'On a Monday?'

Did I just say that out loud? At least I made her laugh.

'Jesus, Red, you fucking dork,' she says, smiling more with every word. 'What would Naomi want us to do? She's in there fighting for her fucking life and we're out here, like . . . losers. What would she tell us to do?'

'Nai would like a movie, or a book club, or some shit,' Leo says wrinkling his nose. 'Or some really dark anime, she loves that crap.'

'Let's do that.' I jump on the chance to do something that won't involve ingesting narcotics or a hangover, and drag them back to mine for a *Black Butler* marathon. Because it's not like I wouldn't ever go near that stuff, it's just that I've seen what pills and drink does to people. I don't want that to happen to me.

Besides, *Black Butler* is one of mine and Nai's favourite, full of Victorian Gothic, Japanese darkness and a ton of cross-dressing. Secretly, we had plotted to cosplay the characters at the next Comic Con, but we'd never told Leo and Rose, because although they wouldn't think any less of us, they would never, ever, stop teasing us about it. We'd designed costumes, I'd even bought a wig in Camden, and then . . . well, the world changed.

My bed. My room.

I painted it black in the summer when Nai was gone. When Mum saw it she rolled her eyes and said, 'I give up.'

And I replied, 'You did that a long time ago.'

I like it black, it feels safe and closed in. But the best thing about it is my kit that takes up half the room, it's the only thing I have that I really care about. It took me two years to save up for it, and Mum only agreed to it because she thought I'd have changed my mind by the time I had enough cash. But I didn't. I walked dogs and washed cars and stacked shelves until I had enough, and then they couldn't say no, so now it sits there in the corner, and I love that it's there. Just ready and waiting to make enough noise to wake up the neighbourhood. When I get to take off the silencing pads anyway.

Right now Leo and Rose are sitting on my bed, Leo's eyes half closed and sleepy, not really into it, Rose with her arm around my neck, her cheek on my shoulder, her warm breath on my neck. She smells of lemon and smoke, which is weird because despite what I thought when I first heard her sing, Rose doesn't smoke. Turns out she's too precious about her voice.

When I asked them over, I forgot for a second that Mum has really gone into overdrive crazy these last few months. I can't blame her for hurting, Dad doesn't even try to hide his crap from her any more. But I can blame her for blaming me. I try to see her so little at the moment that I almost blocked out the fact that she lives at home, too. But as soon as she saw Leo and Rose she did that awful thing she does where she puts on this fake front, grins like a psycho clown, offers us drinks and snacks and 'should she put a pizza in or make us some popcorn?'. FFS. Hair put up in a bun, apron on like she's some TV chef, only she wobbles and waves her hand around too much and laughs too loud while Gracie sits there, eating chicken nuggets and watching *Scooby Doo* on a loop. I know that as soon as we've gone, she'll collapse into a chair and down another drink. Velma will unmask the villain and Gracie will keep on chewing.

Rose's hand, nails bitten short, her plump fingers covered in silver rings, steals into mine. I feel warm and sleepy, flanked on either side by two of my best friends, noticing Leo notice Rose's hand in mine, registered by the disapproving twitch of his mouth.

There's a knock at the door. Dad appears, or his head anyway. He never normally comes in here, which means he wants something.

'You OK in here, kids?' he says. 'I heard about Naomi, how is she doing?'

'They don't really know yet,' I reply. 'It's kind of amazing she is alive.'

'Of course . . . ' Dad lingers in the doorway. 'What did they say happened to her?'

'I don't really want to talk about it right now,' I say to him. 'It's probably on the news.'

'Right . . . well, don't get up to anything I wouldn't!'

Oh God, Dad, shut up.

'These two couldn't handle me, Mr Saunders,' Rose grins at my dad, and he blushes and I find my hand released from hers. 'I need a real man.'

'Well, call it a night after this cartoon, yeah?' He comes into the room a little bit more. He looks at Rose's legs.

'We've got one more to watch,' I say, getting up off the bed and going to the door, more or less shoving him out onto the landing.

'I'm off out, so I'll see you in the morning.'

'Out?' I stare at him. 'You only just got in and it's gone ten.'

'Who are you, my mum?' He laughs at Rose, looking over my shoulder. 'You know what this job's like, half of it is socialising. I don't have a choice.'

'I had no idea being a councillor was so exciting,' I say.

'It's work,' he repeats and as we look at each other we both know he is lying. I feel like I should care about my dad's girlfriends and my mum's drinking, that my family that was once so normal and respectable is imploding from the inside out, keeping up appearances all the while. But I don't care, I don't give a shit about any of them except Gracie.

A few minutes later and Rose is resting her head on my shoulder.

A minute after that she snores, and Leo and I burst out laughing.

'Shut the fuck up,' she mutters, before going back to sleep.

Rose and Red, streak 108 days

Rose
Thanks for tonight pal, after everything that happened today it was fun.

Red
So fun you went to sleep!

Rose
Yaaaysssss, it looked that way, but inside I was 100% ninja pro skills.

Red
What you doing now?

Rose
Listening to my dad and the cow fuck. It's disgusting.

Video link. Tap <u>here</u> to view: Two Pigs having sex

Red
One good thing about my dad going basically awol, no sex noises. Quite a lot of Mum barfing noises though.

Rose
ewhwhwhwhwhhghghghghghghghghgh

Red
You OK? Today was a head fuck, seeing Nai that way. I still can't really get my head round it.

Rose
Go again, tomoz after school?

Red
Yeah, so you OK?

Rose
I'm fucked up on my dad's whiskey, so yeah.

Red
Don't mess around.

Rose
I don't mess around, I'm serious.

Red
Well don't choke on your own vomit, K?

Rose
KK

Red
Rose, about tomorrow . . .

Rose
. . .

Rose
. . .

Rose
. . .

5

Heart racing, acid in my throat, sweat prickling the base of my neck. 3 a.m.

Sit up, my skin prickles and I know I had a bad dream, even though I don't remember it. There is a taste in my mouth like dirty river water. Drag myself out of bed and stumble into my T-shirt and boxers. Opening my door, I listen for the sound of someone up; Mum is often up at this time, or at least not in bed. I'll find her passed out, sitting at the kitchen table, or lying face down on the sofa, a pool of drool beneath her gaping mouth. The last thing I need now is her, half-cut and angry looking for someone to take it out on.

It's quiet and I need a drink, so I risk it.

Dad is in the kitchen, he's been smoking and there's booze in the air too. He doesn't drink like Mum does. Mum drinks likes she breathes, she exists on vodka, her once soft body thin and wiry now, her face reddened and full of shadows. Dad isn't that bad, but he does like a drink too; takes the edge off, he says. Where did he go until three in the morning where he can drink and smoke?

'OK mate?' he says, looking like I've caught him out.

'I need a drink.' My bare feet are silent on the lino as I go to the tap, and let the water run off my fingers until it's really cold.

I hear him shift his weight behind me. He coughs and wheezes; smoking isn't good for him.

'So, Naomi, they think she might have tried to kill herself?'

'They don't know anything.' I rub my eyes. 'Dad, it's three in the morning, you really want to talk about this now?'

'I know, I can't sleep. I might call Jackie and Max in the morning, I got to know her a bit, when I was helping her with her Duke of Edinburgh stuff. I feel like I should say something, see if there is anything I can do.'

'What could you possibly do? You work for the local council, not the Prime Minister.'

'It's just good to show people you care,' he says.

'In that case could you show Mum you care?' I tell him. 'She might slow down on the vodka a bit.'

'Don't talk to me that way,' Dad warns me, but it's half-hearted. He knows I'm right. It's kind of pathetic really.

I don't know how he expects me to react, but ignoring it makes his shoulders slump as he sits back in his chair. There used to be a time when I wanted to be him, when I thought he was the strongest, coolest dad in the world. These days he just makes me cringe inside. A couple of miles away my friend is in a coma with big chunks of her head missing, and it smells like Mum might have thrown up in the hallway. And Dad . . . well, I'm guessing his latest bit on the side likes a fag now and then. Me, I just want to go back to my room. I just want to hide and sleep and forget it all for a couple more hours.

But I can't. Because it's not just me. It's Gracie too. So I take a breath and I try to remember that time when I believed that Mum was the kindest person in the world, and Dad was the bravest, and I try again.

'Dad . . . Mum's drinking. It's getting really bad.' He turns slightly in his chair to avoid looking at me. 'You're not around much to see it, you don't have to deal with it–'

'Who do you think is going to be cleaning that mess up out there?' he snaps at me, as if I should be grateful.

'So?' It hurts to have to find the words to say this to him, I mean physically hurts, like the insides of my chest are bruised, black and blue. 'Don't you think it's serious, like before . . . '

There was a time just after Gracie was born that Mum drank a lot, the first time that I remember, though now I think there must have been times before that. Dad was here, almost all the time, then. Trying to cope with Gracie, trying to get Mum better, he kept telling me how good I was, how brave and strong. And how grateful he was that I didn't make a fuss and just got on with things. It was around then I started to put on weight, not because I was hungry, just because I needed something to fill up the spaces that she left behind. It was then I started hoarding food under my bed and while Dad was busy with Mum or Gracie, I'd try to fill up the pain inside with food. I'd eat so much I couldn't help but fall asleep. At ten years old it was the best of way of escaping I knew. Later, when I turned thirteen, the opposite became true. Not eating was the way I tried to control my life. But at ten years old I was always hungry, always trying to feel full, and never succeeding.

'She's under a lot of stress, you know what she's like,' Dad says. He might as well not say anything.

'If you were home more, were with her more,' I try again. 'Maybe she wouldn't get so down. Maybe she wouldn't feel so alone.'

He shifts uncomfortably, half turning away from me, and I can't help but see him for who he is now. Not the giant, not the god, not the man I looked up to for most of my life as the biggest, smartest and strongest man I know, but a spoilt kid who's bored of his toys and wants something new. And in that second I hate him.

'Just move in with your latest slut, then.' I pick up my glass and pad out of the kitchen, treading carefully around the acrid spots on the hall tiles.

'Get back here right now,' Dad hisses at me, and this time he really sounds angry, but I don't turn around, I don't give a toss what he thinks of me any more. I can't remember the last time he did anything worth giving a shit about.

Back in my room, I close the door softly behind me, and stare out of my window, waiting for the sun to come up. There's something about this time of day that's comforting. Everything dark, everything quiet. Rows of houses with dark windows make me think of all those dreams out there, filling up the final hours of night sky. Different people in their different houses, where none of this is happening to them. I don't know why but somehow that makes me feel better, like if all of this is small enough to hurt just me, then it can't really be that bad.

Sometimes my head is so full of dark, it's like a fog. It stops me seeing the good things, feeling good things. Everything hurts from the outside in. But it's only me, and only now. And maybe one day it will be someone else. Someone I don't know or care about; someone else who looks out of their window waiting for the dawn while I fill the sky with dreams.

I have to sleep. If I don't sleep, tomorrow my head will pound, and my eyes will swim with light and colours. I've got to sleep.

I'll lay down, close my eyes and think of good things. Gracie playing air guitar while I practise. Rose laughing so hard I can feel her whole body vibrate as she leans against me. The way Leo stands like a gladiator when he plays guitar. When Naomi used to raise one eyebrow and say something stupid like it was deadly serious and make us all laugh until it hurt. I want to think about her like that, not with her head caved in.

A few hours later I wake up gasping, and this time I remember. Dark, thick, freezing water filling my nose and mouth, invading my lungs and something, something cold and cruel puling me down, deep down under the water, until I know there is no way I will see the surface again.

Mirror, Mirror – Band news!

Morning guys, I hope you are all coming to our benefit gig.
We've been practising and we are red hot, with four new
songs just for you. The gig is raising funds for our band mate
Naomi Demir, so get your hands on some cash!

Joining us on bass for the concert is musician Leckraj
Chamane! We asked Leckraj what he was most looking
forward to about playing a gig with Mirror, Mirror and he said,
the thousands of fans screaming my name! (Not really.)

Click here to see the video we made for 'You're In With Me.'

Click here to see Rose Carter show you how she warms up
her voice.

Click here for the latest rehearsal footage.

Click here for the Mirror, Mirror gallery.

6

No point in trying to sleep again so I stay awake, getting lost in the screen on my chromebook until it's time to get up.

874 views on our Tumblr this month, that is a fuck ton. Probably about 400 of those are from Rose, checking out the comments on her video, but even so. For four sixteen-year-old kids, it's pretty good. 1385 followers on Twitter and I've applied for a blue tick, I really want a blue tick. A blue tick means we're real.

Our last band video that we put on our YouTube channel was us in the park, it was awesome. It was for our track, 'Roundabout'. Nai and I wrote it about a couple of kids who liked each other, but could never get it together. So yeah, the park. I brought a speaker for my phone and we mimed along, singing and playing. We looked like pricks, there were loads of kids watching and at least half of them thought we were wankers. But I knew it would turn out good in the end. Leo found it the hardest. He hates all that crap, all he wants to do is play, but Rose talked him round, got him a little drunk, a little high, until he stopped worrying so much about looking like a tough guy and stood on top of the slide with his guitar, giving it all that. Rose was lying down on the see-saw, miming to the words like 1980s Madonna, so sexy it was unreal. And Naomi, she went round and round slowly on the round-about and never cracked a smile. I filmed most of it on Nai's phone in its *Legend of Zelda: Tri Force* case, filming the whole track on each band member so I could cut it together later, until it was my turn to drum on the bench. And then Rose took over filming. I had shades on, finger-less leather gloves. It's had 924 views. I feel pretty good about that. 2300 likes on our Facebook page. 760 follow-ers on Instagram. And I am getting us on Spotify, one of these days.

Because you see, I like the me in that world, the one you see on social media. That me looks like a person who knows what they are doing, what they want, where they are going. That me is on-point. That me always looks good, always looks relaxed, and when I've got the sticks in my hand every single little bit of me works like it is supposed to, every muscle, every reflex, every heart-beat, every brain cell. The reflection of me, that lives behind the shiny screen, is the one who gets the likes, and the hearts, and the direct messages. Sideways smiles from girls who think maybe, actually, even though they have never thought it before, they *could* like me that way, because although I'm short and skinny, man, can I play those drums. That kid is pretty sexy.

But it took me a long time to think that way about this me. The real life, no-filter me.

This me, the me made of blood, bone, nerves and syn-apses is the me that I never used to be into. Back when

I was hiding in those folds of fat as a little kid, my body felt like an inescapable prison, because that's the me that my heart beats in; a fleshy bloody prison that I hated as much as I needed it.

And then something happened that made me stop eating.

I saw myself one day, in the mirrors in the changing rooms at school. Like a weird angle that showed me my reflection in way I didn't recognise, and I saw a stranger. A person I hated, and loathed, and pitied.

And over the next year or so I worked really hard on becoming invisible, whittling away that person to almost nothing, not throwing up but hardly eating. Bingeing was for a baby, a little kid out of control. Not eating was for the new me, the one that had total control, and I was sure they'd notice, and they did. But it was only to tell me how much better I looked. Even when my hip bones looked like they might cut through my skin, even when I felt cold on a blazing hot day. I blew myself up like a balloon because of them, I turned myself into a skeleton because of them and nothing changed. Except me.

The band, Leo, Nai and Rose, they were the ones who saved me, because they saw me, not the way I was, but the way I could be. And when they saw that version, I saw it too. I realised that if I didn't live my life for me then very soon I'd get to a place I couldn't get back from. I didn't want to be the next member of my family to fuck up, that wasn't going to be me.

So slowly, slowly, over that year behind the drums, playing and hanging out with the people I began to realise were my mates, I was too busy letting go of control to think about what I was eating. It was terrifying; I was scared but

I was excited too, because I had friends, and music, and dancing, and laughing, and going out all night, hopping from club to club, bar to bar, and howling at the moon.

Doesn't sound like a fitness regime, does it, but it was. The more I played, the fitter and stronger I got. I stopped thinking about eating, so I ate when I wanted and it seemed to be about as much as I needed. And the more I let myself be me on the inside, the more it matched me on the outside.

It wasn't a health kick, it was a happiness kick, it was realising that no matter how much I *wanted* it, I didn't *need* my mum and dad to take care of me. I could take care of myself. I do take care of myself, and Gracie. I'm better at this shit than they ever were.

Christ, I am so self-obsessed, I bore myself.

I used to be too fat, I used to be too thin. Now I'm fit as a butcher's dog. Get over it, Red, there are more important things going on right now.

I just want to see Nai again.

Leo's waiting for me on the corner.

Leo and some of his mates, mates he had before the band and still hangs around with now and then, which is cool because they don't mind me and I don't mind them.

It's when there are girls around that I turn into a fuck-wit. How do I walk again? What do I say that isn't a string of shit? Am I funny? Am I a loser? All these thoughts chasing each other at maximum speed, racing round and round my head. I even have to tell myself to walk when I'm around girls I fancy. I have to say, Those are your feet, dumb-ass, they go one in front of the other.

And then I thought, shit, I remember when Leo and

those guys used to scare the crap out of me, especially when Leo's brother Aaron was still at school. I used to wonder if him and his mates had weapons in their backpacks, and how they chewed gum like someone who would definitely win a fight and probably had already murdered a few nobodies and dumped them in the river. It doesn't help that just shy of his nineteenth birthday, Aaron went inside for stabbing some bloke in the chicken shop, and hurting him pretty bad.

But Leo isn't Aaron. And now I walk to school with them, and you know what? They are pretty much just like me. Only taller. But fucking everyone is taller than me.

'Mate,' Leo says, as I approach.

'Mate.' I nod, and we all nod at each other in turn as I fall into step with them, short and skinny, as if – I like to imagine – I'm David Bowie with a fuck-load of bouncers. The sun is warm on the back of my neck, even the car fumes in the air smell kind of good today, the constant sound of traffic, brakes squealing, engines revving, cyclists swearing, radios turned up loud, my favourite city background noise.

'Top three guitarists?' Leo asks me.

'Well, Hendrix, obviously, then May, then Slash.'

'Ah shit.' Leo shakes his head at me. 'Hendrix is a given. But fucking May? Fucking Slash?'

'Yes, fucking May and Slash, fucking Brian May is the fucking best guitarist there has ever been.'

'You are wrong in the head, mate. You'll be saying fucking Phil Collins is the best drummer next . . . '

'Well . . . Where were you last night?' I ask him.

'Round yours, moron.'

'No, I mean after, online. Me and Rose were chatting for a bit.'

'Oh. I had to talk to my mum.'

'Shit.'

'Yeah.' Leo pauses, He's the kind of bloke that shows everything he's thinking on his face, and what he's thinking isn't good. 'Just when you thought it couldn't be any more fucked up . . . '

'What?'

'Aaron's coming out.' He doesn't say any more but he doesn't have to.

'Shit.'

We walk on in silence, letting the noise of the city do all the talking. Before Aaron went inside Leo hung out with him a lot, looked up to him, followed his lead wherever it took him, and it took him to some pretty scary places. Because Aaron really didn't care what he fucked up, that's what made him so scary. I guess once, a long time ago, he must have been just a boy but when he was pretty young he fell in with some older kids on that estate, and they got him into skunk, and that pretty much blew up his head. Some people can get into it, and it never really affects them that much, and some, some like Aaron, it does something to their brain. They get in so deep, they can't ever see the world like they used to again. They're broken. So he got dragged down, and for a while he took Leo with him.

That version of Leo, the version I first played with a year ago was angry and dark. He was frightening, at least that's what I thought. Always on the outside edge of dangerous things: the gangs that Aaron ran with, the drugs he dealt, the favours he did for a little cash here and there. Things that Leo knew could suck you in so fast and so deep, you don't know you're drowning until it's too late. Aaron going away had been the best thing that had ever happened to Leo. For the first time in his life he got to find out who he was, without his big bro telling him. If Aaron had been around there's no way he would have stayed in Mirror, Mirror, playing air guitar on a slide. No way.

Aaron out, means Aaron calling the shots again. Or at least trying to.

'So . . . what did your mum say?' The best response I can come up with is a shit one.

'She said she don't want him back in the flat, but he's her son. She says I'm not to hang around with him, not to let my school work suffer like it did before. Not to let him get me into trouble, like he's all bad and I'm the fucking golden boy.'

'So are you OK about it?' I'm careful not to look at him.

'Yeah, he's my bruv, course I am,' Leo says, but there is a split second delay that makes me wonder.

'Hey!' Rose arrives behind us at full pelt, wearing shades, hair in a mess.

'Hungover from your dad's whiskey?' I ask her.

'I can't help it if I've got mature tastes.' She grins, 'I needed something. I still can't believe it, you know. When Nai was missing, it was like I could pretend she was OK. But now . . . fucking hell.'

'I've been thinking about Nai all night,' Leo says. 'It don't make sense that she'd do that to herself, right? Remember at the end of last term? She changed, stopped wearing all that anime make-up and clothes and shit. She looked . . . sunny. The day before she disappeared she looked sunny, right? I'm not making that up, am I?'

'No, you're right,' I agree. 'End of last year she was on a permanent high, writing really good songs all the time, more than we could record. There was nothing, nothing at all that would make her want to . . . you know.'

'So,' Rose says. 'The answer is that something bad happened, something really fucking bad happened to her while she was missing. That's the only thing that makes sense, right? Something so dark, she couldn't live with it.'

We don't realise that we've all come to a stop as we try to imagine what that could be.

'Hi!' The voice sounds so much like Naomi's that we all start. It's Ashira. Leo's mates walk on.

We exchange looks; did she hear us talking?

'Hey, Ash.' Rose's smile is uncomfortable. Lips pressed together, not quite sure what to say.

'Look, this is awkward, but Jackie thought you guys might like to come over after seeing Nai tonight. Have dinner? There's nothing she can really do at the hospital, she needs something to take her mind off it all.' Somehow Ash finds a shadow of a smile to end her sentence. It looks like it costs her. 'I think it's a stupid idea, but that's Jackie for you, she thinks everything can be solved with a decent meal. And I think you make her feel better. Like everything will be OK again, you know?'

'Course,' I say, a little uncertainly, looking first at Leo and then Rose, who both nod.

'I know it's going to be weird . . . and fucking awful,' she sighs, her chin dropping, her dark eyes downcast. 'Jackie says the house is too quiet. And I don't have mates round. Or mates. No one knows what to say to me.'

'Shit, sorry, Ash.' Rose goes to touch her, her hand falling back to her side before she reaches her. Ash never gives the impression that she wants to be touched.

'Not your fault.' Ashira shrugs, raising her gaze to

meet mine, and for a moment I think that maybe there is something else she wants to say, but only to me. 'I never really was into people all that much, anyway.'

'We've been pretty crap.' Leo shakes his head. 'We should have been there for you. I don't know, we all lost it a bit.'

'Well, the concert that you're organising, I mean that's good. Something to focus on.' Ash forces a smile. 'And I got my ways of dealing with it. Anyway, Jackie'd love to see you, overfeed you. If you can stand it.'

'Sure,' I say. 'I miss Jackie's cooking.'

'What about you?' Finally Rose crosses that invisible line around Ash and picks up her hand, in that way she does, always breaking down borders, never scared of what might be waiting for her.

'I'm fine.' Ash gently tugs her hand free. 'Dad was there all night with her, he came back this morning and she's stable, so . . . See you at the hospital, probably.'

The three of us watch as Ash walks off, head bent once again, hair swept behind her by the velocity of her need to get somewhere where no one can see her cry.

'I never thought about going round there,' Rose said as the school bell sounds, and we realise we are the last left outside. 'Or checking in with Ash.'

'None of us did.' Leo drops his arm around her shoulder and she turns in towards him, resting her forehead on his chest just for a second. He drops a kiss on the top of her head, and lets her go as if nothing happened, and in a way nothing did, except for me to be able to kiss the top of Rose's head I'd need to grow a foot, and seeing the way she leans towards him kind of pulls at the centre of my chest.

'Hey, guys! A word.'

Mr Smith jogs across the concrete towards us.

'Going to the hospital later?'

'Yeah,' Rose says. 'Of course, sir, are you?'

'No, I don't think so. But keep me updated, will you, Rose?'

'Sure.' Rose smiles.

'The thing is, I forgot that before all this happened I had the local radio guys coming over to tape your rehearsal as a promo for the concert. And now I need to talk to Naomi's mum and dad, maybe we should postpone.'

'No.' Rose puts her hand on his arm, like she's comforting him. 'No, we were just talking to Ash and she said they were into it. We shouldn't postpone.'

'So you'll do the interviews, then?' he asks.

'I guess so,' I say. Leo nods.

'Right, well, get to class. Blame me if you're late, OK?'

'Yes, sir.' Rose smiles, tilting her head to one side. 'And you blame me if you're late, K?'

'And Rose, don't forget to come and see me later about choir,' he calls as he walks across the yard. Rose's flirt bombs slide off him like water off a duck's back, but Rose is still beaming.

'Why do you do that?' Leo asks her as we walk into the building. 'And choir?'

'They need a shit-hot soloist, apparently, for some competition.' Rose's laugh glitters as she drifts in close to Leo, lowering her lashes. 'Anyway, I can't help my natural charms, men just can't resist me.'

'You can't resist men more like,' Leo snaps back, sidestepping Rose, leaving her hanging. He stalks off to registration.

'What's got into him?' Rose looks at me, as we stop in the corridor. The jangle and chatter of kids getting to class gradually falls away to distant doors closing and silence, a sure sign that we are officially late.

What's got into him is you, I think but I don't say.

'Aaron's getting out.'

'Fuck.' Rose frowns, shrugging her bag off her shoulder, so that it drops onto the lino with a clatter that echoes off the walls. 'Aaron is a dickhead, and Leo thinks the sun shines outs of his arse.'

'I know.' I run my palm over the shaved back of my head. 'I'm worried about him, but what do we say? What do we do? He worships Aaron.'

'It'll be OK.' Rose picks up her bag again. 'We're not fucking losing anyone else. Not on my watch.'

I smile at her, and in my head I see myself as one of those cartoon characters with pounding love hearts bouncing out of their eyeballs.

'What?' Rose looks at me, cocking her head, as we begin to walk towards class at last. 'What?'

'Nothing.' I love how she lives every moment right down to the tips of her fingers, how she tests and challenges literally everything, spoiling for a fight every five minutes.

'Right, well, I can't hang around waiting for you to get your shit together. Later, loser!' She gives me the finger as she strides down the corridor and she's nearly at the end when she turns around and shouts at the top of her voice.

'I love you, Red!'

'I know,' I say. When I finally get into my form room I'm grinning from ear to ear.

Chat History

Rose 1 m ago 109 days streak

Leo 1 hour ago 43 days streak

Kasha 6 hours ago 6 day streak

Parminder 3 day streak

Luca 4 days ago

Sam 5 days ago

Naomi 27 July (Naomi is Offline)

7

Fuck this.

I thought I'd feel something, when she came back. Happy or sad or *something*. Instead the three of just sit next to her bed saying nothing, and feeling . . . well, nothing. We're sitting in a vacuum.

'You're here.' Jackie smiled when she saw us, so at least there's that, knowing we make her feel a bit better. 'She needs people her own age around her, instead of her stuffy old mum boring her rigid.' She talked as if Nai was sitting up in bed, rolling her eyes and making sarcastic comments like she always used to. 'It's all right, Nai, love, your friends are here now, OK?'

She pressed her palm to my cheek, and I smiled for her.

'You stay with her and I'll go home and cook for you. I'm looking forward to it, it's something to do. Max will be here with her when we're eating and then we'll swap again. I don't want her to be on her own any more, you see, she was on her own in that water and . . . ' Her voice strains to breaking point.

'It's fine, Mrs Demir,' Leo says, serious and solemn, putting his arm around her shoulder, sheltering her with his height and width. 'We've got her now, yeah? You go and cook, you're the best cook there is, but don't tell my ma I said that.'

Jackie nods, and kisses him on the cheek before taking a ragged breath and kissing Nai on the one bit of smooth brown skin on her face that's left.

'Back later, poppet, don't wear yourself out chatting,' she whispers.

'She looks better, I think,' Rose says once Jackie has gone. 'Don't you think she looks better? Less . . . cold.'

Her skin tone was better, that was true, if you concentrated on that one uninjured patch and the closed eye it surrounded, it almost looked like she was just sleeping very deeply. If you didn't look anywhere else.

'What shall we do? Shall we tell her what's been going on?' Leo asked, his hands deep in his pockets. 'Are we supposed to talk to her, or what? This feels weird.'

He paces to the door, leaning against it, as if he'd really like to be on the other side.

'What we going to say?' Rose snaps. 'That Parminder is still a cow and school is still fucking lame-as?'

For a moment all we can hear are the machines and our own breathing.

'Music,' I say, nodding at Rose's phone. 'Open up Toonifie. She made her playlists public, let's find one for her.'

'Yeah, music, good idea.' Rose busies herself with her phone, opening the app we all use to stream our favourite songs. 'I'll search her playlists . . . she gave them all such dumb-ass names, can you remember any?'

'"No Apologies", Sum 41,' I say. 'She had that on repeat before the summer. Her playlist was called "FU A-Hole."'

Rose searches, and I wait for the music to start, but instead she just frowns, staring at the phone. 'That's weird . . . '

'What?'

'Open your apps, search that playlist. NaySayo1 is her username.'

I do as she says, and I see it: there are two playlists that come up under that title. One is Nai's, created in July last year. And there's another one created in August, same title, same songs on the list, different username. I pass it to Leo, who shrugs and hands it back.

'So who the fuck is DarkMoon?' Rose asked. 'Look. If you search Nai's username, fucking DarkMoon has cloned all of her playlists. All of them. What does that mean?' We stare at the phone as if somehow we might be able to figure it out, just by looking.

'Nothing, it means nothing.' Leo shakes his head. 'It'll be some fuckwit from school, who did it after she went missing. Probably wanted to be more interesting or some shit. People are cunts, don't forget that.'

'If I find out who that is, I swear to God . . . ' Rose growled at her phone.

'Just play the music, yeah,' Leo says and soon the small, quiet room is filled with angry guitars, and it's so much better than the sound of machines, or us not talking.

Curious, I scroll through DarkMoon's playlists. There are more than just the ones they've ripped off Nai. And then I see it. There are playlists made up of our songs, stuff that only about eleven people in the whole world make playlists from. Yeah, Leo is right, someone from school probably, a fan of the band definitely. Fucking weirdo.

Looking up from my phone, I see that Rose and Leo are glued to theirs; Rose standing facing out of the window, Leo sitting on the one visitor chair, his long legs splayed out at odd angles.

Slipping my phone into my pocket I make myself look at Nai.

We're used to our friendships being at least 50 per cent online, so used to it sometimes I think we forget that there's a beating heart on the other end of that avatar.

I can see from the stubble at her temple that parts of her long poker-straight black hair have been shaved away, the bruising that creeps out from under the dressing has begun to yellow and spread. Her face is painful to look at, and it's hard to see that girl that I hung out with every day, so smashed in. Not as hard as it is to be her, I guess. What does she know about this room she's in, what does she dream behind those closed eyes?

Focusing on the one eye I can see I try to imagine what could possibly have happened between the last time I saw her – eight weeks ago, when she'd wiped off all her anime make-up, and was wearing a yellow summer dress, legs bare and brown – and now. I try and try, but there is nothing I can find that connects the dots from that girl, laughing and dancing with her shoes kicked off in the park, to this one here, with her face bruised and bloody.

Someone has arranged her arms neatly, so they lie by her sides over the sheets. Bruises flower up and down them too, though less severe than the ones on her face, and, I suppose, inside her head. I trace the pattern of them on her right arm with my eyes, right down to her wrist, and find myself leaning in closer. Has anyone else noticed that these marks look like fingerprints, purple, oval, clenched and claw-like? Like someone has grabbed her wrist, tight enough to crush the bones inside?

The thought of someone hurting her that way sends ice through my veins. I'm trembling.

Glancing back at the window, I see Dr Whitecoat outside talking to the nurses, expression intent and serious. She doesn't look like the kind of person to have missed something that mattered.

I mean they must have looked, right? They aren't going to miss something that obvious, and they aren't going to want me to ask them about it, are they? Like I can tell them how to do their job. But on the other hand, Nai was out cold when they found her, and has been ever since. She couldn't tell them if her wrist was hurting. I find my hand reaching out to take hers, but I stop myself.

This was the thing with me and Nai, we hung out a *lot*.

That was why, after she disappeared, the police asked us if they could look at our phones and laptops and trolled right through them to see if there were any clues to where she had gone. I told them, if I knew anything, I'd fucking tell them, but they said it was better to look, so we let them. There was nothing there to say we knew where Nai had gone, because we didn't know.

The police thought I had to know everything about her, because that's what people said, her family, her friends. Even my mum. They said if anyone knew where Nai was, it would be me. Because we liked the same things, we made each other laugh. We finished each other's sentences. They thought there was something going on between me and Nai. Because we'd written most of

Mirror, Mirror's songs together, and a lot of them were love songs.

But we were never writing those songs about each other.

Nai never asked me who I was thinking about when I came up with those lyrics, and I never asked her. It was understood that we were both into someone who wasn't available. One of the things we liked about each other was that we didn't need to know each other's secrets. We just needed to know each other. If anything she was the only girl I was ever around that I didn't think about what it would be like to kiss. That just isn't us.

Now, as I sit here and want to take her hand, I hesitate. Once I would have held her hand and not cared what anyone said, because me and Nai knew what we were. Now, though, I don't know who else has held her, or hurt her. Now she is a stranger, and it's only now that she is back that I really, really miss her.

Very carefully, in case it could hurt her, I lace my fingers through hers. Her skin is warm, I can feel the steady beat of her pulse against my wrist. Glancing at Leo and Rose, I see they are still lost in their screens, so gently, very gently I lift her hand to my mouth, and whisper into her skin, 'Come back, Nai, OK? Come back, I need you.'

And that's when I see it. Just a glimpse at first, like a crescent moon. It hadn't been visible before but suddenly there it was, fresh and new. Stark and bold.

'Fuck,' I say out loud, and Rose and Leo look at me.

'What?' Rose comes over.

'A tattoo,' I tell them. 'While she was gone, Naomi got a tattoo.'

8

This is the thing about tattoos. I have three of them that no one but me knows about. Not even Rose and Leo. Not even Nai. I guess there will come a moment when it comes out and there will be more shouting and disappointment, but it hasn't yet, which is one of the upsides of your parents basically ignoring you.

I'm too young to have them legally, but the first one I had was a stick and poke tattoo, which I did myself with a needle and a pot of ink. I watched this video on YouTube and did it to myself, on the sole of my foot, under the arch. It hurt like a mother-fucker, and it's really shit.

It's supposed to be the infinity symbol, but it looks more like a pissed number eight. I don't even know why I did it, except it was something to do and I liked the pain. On that day I was hurting already, like my whole body was a bruise, inside and out. I wanted to feel something else apart from the stone-heavy pain in my chest.

I got my second tattoo on the same day that I had half my head shaved. I didn't know I was going to do it, except that I had this idea of what I looked like in my head and while my body was changing to the way I wanted it, my 'look' wasn't.

Then I woke up one morning and thought, what about that is right or fair? My body's been through so much, and no one, no one cared. But if I get a piercing, or cut my hair it's world war three. Fuck that, I thought. If there is one thing I should be allowed to control in my life it's what I look like.

When my hair was gone, I stared at my reflection and I felt . . . well, I felt like we'd only just met. I didn't want to go home yet. I wanted a bit of time to just be me, to put off getting the grief I knew was coming, for not being the nice middle-class clean-cut kid that my parents want me to be. So I stopped outside this tattoo place and looked at the designs. I had money saved from working Saturdays in the supermarket, enough to get a pretty good one. And I thought what the hell, I look about eleven, they are bound to throw me out.

Maybe it was the new haircut. But they didn't ask me for ID and they didn't throw me out. This massive dude with a long grey beard that came down to his waist just gave me book after book of designs and waited. And I saw this Hammerhead Shark, made up of tribal symbols, and I said to the bloke, what does this mean?

'It's a symbol of strength, the protector, the warrior,' he said. 'The kind of person who'd do anything for the people they love.'

'I want that one,' I said, a blush creeping over my face as I realised there really was only one place I could get it and not have a chance of it being spotted. 'On my butt.'

He looked at me for a long moment, and I am pretty sure he was wondering what about this shaven-headed ginger git looked even a little like a warrior protector, but he shrugged and said, 'It'll hurt there.'

'I can take it,' I'd replied.

'It's your skin, mate.'

He wasn't lying. It fucking, fucking hurt. I felt the gun vibrating like it was in my bones, my skin screaming, nerves twisting and jangling with every pinprick, stretching out for what seemed like hours, until eventually I kind of rolled into the pain and it became part of every breath I took. When he finally stopped and put the needle down, I peeled myself off the table, and went to the mirror. The colours of the shark came alive as I looked at them, blues and greens flexing and flowing on my skin and muscle, and this sensation of warmth and peace spread through me, and I felt good about myself. I felt relaxed about who I was and comfortable in my colourful, ink-stained skin. And that's when I knew I had done the right thing, because showing your true colours is always the right thing. It has to be.

Sure, it hurt for ages, days after, but I didn't care. I liked it. I liked the pain, and I liked my shark, even when I couldn't see it, because I knew it was there and it meant that no one really knew me, not even the people I am closest to, and I liked that.

The last one, I got under my arm, by my heart. Just after Nai had gone and the pain was so bad, I needed something to cancel it out. The ache of the last tattoo was only just fading and I realised that I missed the distraction of it, so I went back again and the guy with the beard inked me good. It's a wave breaking on rocks, water moving, reforming, changing, gathering strength. I'm a wave, I thought: even when I'm breaking I'm strong.

I remember wanting to tell Nai about it, because I thought that was a good lyric, but she wasn't there to tell. She was in that place where *this* happened to her.

This tattoo.

And that's what freaks me out.

Naomi would never have a tattoo. She hated them.

We used to watch *Tattoo Fixers* together and all she would do is harp on about what kind of prick gets pissed and then gets a prick tattooed on them, and how gross they would look when your skin was old and saggy. She said they were about vanity and lack of identity.

The girl I hung out with the day before she vanished in her bright yellow dress and bare feet would never have had a tattoo. Not in a million years.

'Fuck.' Rose kneels next to me and peers at the strange pattern, inked in dark blue.

'Shit,' Leo says, standing behind us. It's a semi-circle, quite small, no bigger than a fifty pence piece, filled with a finely lined abstract pattern that seems to make no sense. Curves, right angles, dots and dashes, layers and layers of meaningless detail that make it look almost solid, until you really start to look at it, and then when you really do, you see faces, animals, depths and shadows. Blink and it all disappears.

'Whoever did this, it took skill to do it with this much detail in such a small area. It's all carefully defined, no bleeding ink. This wasn't something she did to herself, or had done in a squat somewhere. This is professional. We need to tell the police,' I say.

'How the fuck do you know so much about tattoos all of a sudden?' Leo says. 'And fuck telling the pigs! What difference does it make?'

'Because she didn't have it when she left and now she does. It happened while she was missing. Maybe they can trace where it was done? Find out who she was with, how she paid for it . . . ' I look at Rose. 'We have to, right?'

She nods and Leo shakes his head.

'Why are you so touchy about it?' Rose asks him, and he drops his gaze.

'I'm not touchy about it, it's just . . . it was bad for me after she ran away or have you forgotten? I don't want them around me again, especially not now.'

He isn't lying. When the police know you live on Leo's estate, they pretty much assume you are guilty right from the get go. There are plenty of good people that live there, people like Leo and his mum, but it's not them that people hear about, it's the criminals, the drug dealers and gangs. The minute they found out that Naomi was friends with a boy who lived there, a boy whose older brother was inside for aggravated assault, the police were all over Leo, right up in his business. They spent much longer with him than the rest of us; even though they took all our phones and laptops to look at, it was Leo's they kept for the longest. They asked him about everything, from the porn on his browser to the assault charges his brother went away for. It hit him hard, made him angry, and the little bit of trust he had left in them was gone.

We can't blame him for wanting to be as far away from anyone in a uniform as possible.

'I guess we could just not get the police involved,' I say, wavering.

'We have to.' Rose steps in, shrugging at Leo. 'This is evidence, isn't it?'

'You're missing the point,' Leo says. 'Runaway kid gets

tattoo, big wow. It don't mean nothing, Rose.'

Rose looks at me and I shrug, he's right.

'The thing is we know this is fucking weird, but they won't think so. They won't give a toss. We need to find out where she got it, because they won't care.'

'Well, we'll tell Jackie and Max, because they know Nai, they know she wouldn't ever do this,' Rose says, defensive. She hates being wrong.

On that we all agree.

'I need air,' Leo says, shaking his head. 'This place . . . '

When he leaves his head is down, his hands shoved deep in his pockets.

'How did we not see it?' Jackie holds her daughter's wrist, staring at the tattoo, Max standing behind, a deep valley forming between his brows. Ash stays by the window, the afternoon sun lighting up the fiery reds of her hair, her face perfectly blank as she watches. I watch her, wondering what is going on behind those dark eyes. 'You can tell it's new, the skin is still raised under the ink. It's even a little bit pink still. Why didn't you see it?' She looks up at the doctor.

'When she came in, there was a lot activity designed to save her life,' Dr Whitecoat, or Dr Patterson, it says on her name badge, speaks. 'It wasn't top priority. Besides we had no idea what tattoos she might or might not have, there is a mention of it in the notes . . . '

She rifles through the folder she is holding, and Jackie turns back to her daughter.

'I thought I couldn't touch her,' Jackie looked at me, 'I thought I might hurt her if I moved her. I didn't even pick up her hand. If you hadn't, Red, we would never have known.'

It seems like a strange thing to say, but I suppose everything seems strange to her now, especially since her daughter had been returned to her looking like a stranger, wearing a stranger's mark.

'Max, do you think we should tell the police? Because Naomi hated tattoos, thought they were tramp stamps, she always said. Our girl wouldn't do this . . . '

'I dunno.' Max's hand rubs Jackie's shoulders. 'The Nai we thought we knew wouldn't but kids do stuff you don't expect all the time, love. I'll call them, I'll let them know, OK?'

'This means something,' Jackie half mutters to herself, and I see Ash's expression shift, just a little bit. Ash thinks the same, I know she does.

Max is right. My parents don't know anything about me, nothing that matters. Maybe Nai just got fucked off and fucked off. Maybe she got drunk and stoned and tattooed and maybe she hated herself so much it seemed like a good idea to throw herself off a bridge, or maybe she just fell.

Except.

'What about the bruises, though?' I look at the doctor. 'The ones around her wrist?'

'She was probably injured in the water,' Dr Patterson glances at the door, keen to be somewhere else. 'Knocked unconscious, battered around—'

'Not here . . . ' I take Naomi's arm and carefully lift it. 'These look like finger marks, like someone gripped her arm really hard.'

Nai's mum covers her mouth with both hands, stifling a cry.

'I'm not sure you are helping your friend's mum very

much,' the doctor says as she takes Nai's hand carefully from mine.

'It's impossible to tell what caused these bruises. Naomi is bruised all over.' She stands straight, taking control of everyone in the room. 'Naomi is in a fragile state. We still don't know the outcome of her injuries. This is going to take time, and she needs peace and quiet and rest. I suggest you all go home now. Come back tomorrow, perhaps we will know some more then.'

I look at Ash and find her staring right at me, eyes glittering with all the anger she is shutting in. And I know how she feels. These people that don't know Nai, they are ready to think the worst of her. Like she's nothing; trash that brought it all on her herself. They don't know the sweet, funny, talented girl we do. They aren't seeing her at all.

'I want to stay with her,' Jackie tells the doctor, her tone lower. A warning.

'You can, of course,' Dr Patterson says. 'But she doesn't know you are here. She is heavily sedated. And you all need a break, some rest. Come back refreshed.'

'Refreshed?' Rose laughs, shaking her head at me.

'We should go.' Max puts his arm around Jackie. 'Come on, kids, we're still on for dinner, right?'

Leo is waiting for us outside.

'Well?' he said. 'What did they say?'

'They don't think it means anything,' Rose says. 'They think she is just a crazy mixed-up kid who ran away, got a tattoo and probably tried to top herself. It's like they don't want to even look into it, it's too complicated. It doesn't change what they think happened.'

'But they're wrong,' I say, talking to myself. 'I know they are.'

9

Going back to Naomi's house felt like a sort of home-coming, if an imperfect one, knowing that she wouldn't be there. The truth was, all of us felt more at home around Nai's place than we did with our own families. Jackie and Max were always pleased to see us, happy to feed us, let us hang out and stay over whenever we needed to. Nai's house was a safe space, but even so it couldn't protect her from the bullies that used to make her life a misery at school. Before us, before she had the band to insulate her, she'd run and run again. Jackie and Max tried to help, the school tried to help, but bullies don't quit easily. There'd be days, Nai used to tell me, when she couldn't stand the thought of school and she'd have to disappear for a little while, just to get her strength back, but she always came back eventually. I asked her why she never moved schools, and she said it was because then they would've won.

'As scared as I was, I wasn't going to let them win, ' she said.

And she smiled at me.

'Because look at me now, I rule the school, dude.'

Nai's mum is the best cook out of all of our mums, though you'd never say that to Leo's mum if you wanted to see seventeen. The three of them, Ash and Naomi and Jackie, always cooked together, it was just what they did. I don't know how to explain it exactly, but it was so full of love, that tiny kitchen. Full of steam, and smells and tastes and love. Jackie would tell us the story of her life over and over again, each time a little bit different, and never boring. Max was Turkish, widowed young for over a year and struggling alone with toddler Ashira when he'd met Jackie one day on the bus into Soho where he worked at a tailor's. Jackie was loud, and tall – taller than him – skinny and blonde and never stopped talking. Every day they sat together on the bus, every day Jackie talked for England and Max would listen, smile and laugh. Every day for a week, Max dropped Ashira off at her aunt's on his way to work. On the Friday Max asked Jackie out. They were married three months later.

'There was no point in waiting, you see,' Jackie would tell us, over and over again. 'Because when you know, you know.'

And I'd try to remember my parents ever telling me with the same kind of love and happiness about how they met, and I realised that they never did. In my house, everything was proper and respectable, traditional, cold and miserable. In Nai's house love was a constant, like the water in the tap. In mine, you had to look hard to see it, and you had to be six years old to feel it, or to imagine that you did, anyway.

Before all this happened, I'd sit there around the table while Leo and Rose goofed off about this or that, and watch Nai and her mum. I'd watch the way Nai's eyes would meet Jackie's when they talked, or passed a plate, or anything. I'd see this understanding and *care* between them and it was a bit like being that kid you see in movies with their nose pressed up against the sweetshop glass, full of longing. It's embarrassing, to be my age and still have this thing where all I want is a hug off my mum, not that I'd ever tell anyone that.

Anyway, there was a big part of me that was looking forward to being there again, in that little love-filled kitchen. I thought it would be OK, right up until we got to the steps that led to the front door of her modern terraced council house, halfway between my home and Leo's estate. It was a neat little house, respectable, but nothing like the glamour and swagger of Rose's place, or even the roses-round-the-door veneer of my middle-class bullshit semi-detached. It was when we were standing right outside and I looked up at her window and saw the light wasn't on in her bedroom that it hit me so hard.

That broken, battered girl in the hospital, and my friend Naomi were the same person. There was no escaping it any more.

We get out of the car, and no one says anything.

Jackie and Max walk ahead, arms around each other, her head resting on his shoulder, fingers almost digging into his back with desperation. Ash walks a little behind them, slow small steps. My hand reaches out for Rose's, the need to be anchored to someone that loves me engulfing me in a second. But she doesn't see it, she just keeps walking and I close my empty fingers, one by one.

'I don't know if I can do it,' Leo says it first, keeping his voice low. 'This is doing my head in.'

'We can't not go in,' I say. 'They invited us, they want to see us, they need us.'

'I know what you mean,' Rose speaks to Leo, not to me and her voice is soft and gentle. 'But Red's right, we've got to go. For Nai.'

I watch as Rose puts her hand on Leo's bicep, and I see how he leans into her, just a little, as if there was an invisible force between them pulling them closer. Just a little, but enough for my gut to contract.

Ash is sitting on the bottom of the stairs as we push open the front door. All the expressions on her face seem to slash downwards, like the gravity of her pain is pulling her slowly to the ground.

'You coping?' I ask her as Rose and Leo follow the smell of Turkish spices into the kitchen.

'No,' she says, keeping her eyes on me. 'I'm mad as hell. You?'

'The same.' I nod, glancing in the direction of the kitchen. I don't want anyone else to hear what I'm about to say. 'I'm starting to think something bad happened to Nai, something really bad. Something she never saw coming.'

Ash stood up, so that we were just a few millimetres apart, her mouth right next to my ear.

'I think you're right,' she whispers, before turning on her heel and heading into the kitchen.

'Oh kids, what a day.' Jackie opens her arms to us the moment we enter the small square kitchen, dark pine cupboards on every wall, a tiny round table in the middle. Her eyes fill with tears as we take turns to be hugged by her, engulfed by the sweet perfume she likes to wear, the taste of salty tears still on her cheek when I kiss it. I hug her back, as tightly as I can, wrapping my arms around her. It's been a long time since anyone hugged me. I feel dumb for admitting it, but sometimes you need a hug and I like the way she grabs my face between her hands and kisses my forehead.

'Oh it's good to see you, I miss you being here and the noise and the chatting, and telling Naomi to turn it down!' Jackie's smile looks like the kind of smile that takes work to maintain, as she tells us where to sit, pours us tumblers of coke, offering dish after dish of home-cooked food: shish kebab on skewers, marinated chicken, warm pitta, fragrant rice. When I look at it I'm suddenly starving. Not only for good food, but also for the memories that come with it, all of them good ones. As we eat, Jackie walks continuously around the table, touching her hands to our shoulders or cheeks. Max doesn't talk much, but he smiles, tears in his eyes as he looks from face to face. Ash sits with us, eating nothing, saying nothing. Head down, her hair a midnight curtain shielding her from view, like the moment we just had in the hallway never happened. I want to talk about it to her more, but I've no idea how. It seems like you don't ever approach her, you just wait for her to call on you.

Finally the food is almost gone, and gradually we stop eating and talking. The table falls silent and all the things we haven't talked about since getting back from the hospital hang over us like shadows.

Leo coughs and pushes his chair back, but before he can get up, Jackie speaks again.

'What Max said before, about us not really knowing

Nai, it seems impossible to me that I didn't know every little thing about her, but she did change in those last few weeks. She stopped wearing all that make-up and the wigs. She started to look . . . normal. And she seemed so happy, so loving. But you all knew her, probably better than me. Why do *you* think she ran away? Do *you* think she was unhappy enough to . . . to . . . '

I close my eyes for a moment, searching for something useful to say.

'If we'd known anything, we'd have said,' Rose says before I even come close. 'If Nai was planning this, she didn't tell anyone. Not even Red.'

I make myself look Jackie in the eye.

'Nai hated tattoos,' I say. 'She loved being in the band, and she tried hard at school. She wouldn't have left because she was unhappy, she wasn't unhappy. Something else happened. I don't know what, but I know that something happened to her. And when she wakes up she'll tell us.'

'Except . . . ' Ash's voice is sharp and hard. 'Except we don't know if she is going to wake up, and if she does, she might be brain damaged, so we might never know. It could be a secret her head always keeps.'

'We've got to keep hoping for the best, Ash,' Jackie says. 'We've got to keep thinking positive love, and—'

'As if thinking positive is going to fix the big dent in her head, yeah right,' Ash almost shouts, slamming her chair back so hard it sways, topples over and clatters on the tiles. We hear her feet on the stairs.

Max reaches for Jackie's hand and brings it to his cheek, she turns her face from us, and in an instant I feel like an intruder looking in at their pain like it's a sideshow at the fair.

'We should get going,' Leo says, maybe picking up the same vibe. 'I've got to get back, family stuff.'

'But we'll be at the hospital again tomorrow, right after school,' I say.

'Yeah, well, as soon as we can get there,' Rose adds, and I glance at her, but she doesn't meet my eye.

'And the concert is going ahead, just like we planned,' I say. 'So many people want to come and support Naomi and you guys.'

'Thank you, Red.' Jackie smiles at me. 'Will you kids do something for me now?'

'Yeah, course,' I say.

'Go look in her room, see if you can find some photos, posters maybe. Something you think she'll like to brighten her room up. I know that doctor says she doesn't know what's going on around her, and maybe that's true at the moment, but I do believe she will wake up, and when she does I want her to see her stuff, so she knows she is safe. Go and choose a few bits, maybe take them into the hospital for her tomorrow?'

'Sure,' Leo says and we nod, although I'm pretty sure all of us wish the ground would swallow us up and we could be anywhere else in the world than trying to choose things that our comatose friend can't see.

Naomi's room was always neat. Small, with barely any room for anything more than her single bed and a wardrobe, anime posters on the wall, a selection of brightly coloured wigs hanging off a hook her dad put up for her over her bed. On her bedside table is a shit-load of make-up, more than I've ever seen almost anywhere else, the colours so vivid and so like Nai used to be, that it's as though she is there, somewhere in all that jumble of mess and false eyelashes, and if we knew how, we could put her back together again.

The three of us sit on her bed, Rose in the middle, our thighs touching.

Rose opens her school bag and pulls out a bottle of wine, twisting the cap off, taking a deep long draught straight from the neck.

'When the fuck did you score booze?' I ask her.

'I've got contacts,' she smirks and passes me the bottle. I pass it to Leo.

'Fuck's sake, Red, you can be such an arse,' she says, voice sharp, edged with anger. But that's Rose, the girl who hides everything she really feels behind blades and thorns. Complicated and difficult as the bulletproof plates that make her armour strong.

'I don't like booze,' I say, looking her in the eyes. 'It turns people into wankers.'

'Poor Red, I forgot your gin-soaked mum for a second there.' Rose grabs the bottle back off of Leo before he's had any. 'A swig isn't going to get you drunk, you know, just one, for Naomi.'

'Rose,' Leo takes the bottle out of her hands. 'We get you're upset, but don't be a dick, OK? Red doesn't drink. Leave it.'

He takes a long, long drink from the bottle, much more than he normally would, and I know why. The more he drinks, the less there is for Rose. A bit like when I pour half a bottle of Mum's vodka down the sink, and fill it up with water. This is Leo's way of protecting her, dumb though it is.

Rose watches him nearly drain the bottle. For a minute,

I think she might totally lose her shit, but she doesn't. The sadness and anger sort of fades from her face, and she looks different without it. Almost ugly, almost beautiful. I don't really know which, and it doesn't matter, because either way I can't stop looking at her. I keep looking until it hurts.

'Right, let's get this over with, I guess.' Rose wipes her mouth with the back of her hand. 'These anime posters?'

I nod, looking around the room, as she begins to peel them off the wall over the bed. 'And her custom-made Lego mini-figure of Link from *Zelda.*'

'Yeah.' Leo picks it up and looks at it, before putting it in his pocket. We all used to tease Nai about her geekery, and she really did not give a fuck what we thought.

'Her phone dock,' I say, picking up the charger and speaker. 'Where's her phone, it'd have all her playlists on it, we could set it up to play all the time for her.'

'We can't find her phone, remember?' Ash appears in the doorway. At once we stop touching everything, feeling like we've been caught breaking and entering. 'We looked for it, the police looked everywhere for it when she went missing. But it was turned off on the night she left and no one knows where it went.'

'Oh yeah, I forgot for a sec,' I say. Now I remember thinking at the time that Nai leaving without her phone was weird. The girl I know would rather go without her right arm than her phone.

'There's an old iPod Nano somewhere that should fit that dock. Look in her bedside drawers.' I kneel on the carpet, pulling the drawer open. Even though I know the police went through them, took everything out and put it back again, it still feels wrong. Intrusive. If anyone, even my friends, looked through my stuff, I'd be wishing myself dead pretty quickly. It'd be like someone sliced the top of my brain off and got a look at all my secret thoughts. Would they still like me if they knew everything about me, everything I think, everything I want? I'm not sure they would.

'Here.' I find a slim black iPod, the apple logo turned into a skull with a sharpie, and hand it to Leo. It's then that I notice the notebook. Crammed with other bits of paper that look like lyrics. I pick up the book and open it, my finger tracing the patterns made by her handwriting. This was everything she wrote after we started to write songs on our own. Some charts too, like she'd been putting them to music.

'Songs,' I say holding the book up to Ash. 'You looked at these?'

Ash shakes her head. 'You can keep them if you want. Maybe you can do something with them. Finish one of them. That might be something she'd actually give a shit about, if she's got enough brain left to give a shit about anything.'

'She's got a lot of stuff,' Leo says picking up a pot of plectrums, all the colours, a rainbow of plastic. Naomi collected them from the gigs we went to, went down the front after the set, stayed after everyone had left, and picked up set notes, plectrums, water bottles. I asked her why once. Because she never wanted to get them signed or anything, or put them on eBay. They were just bits of rubbish the second she took them out of the venue.

'This is where life happens,' she'd told me. 'In the stuff that gets left behind.'

'Nai, that doesn't mean anything,' I'd said.

'But it's a great lyric, right?' She'd grinned at me, I can see her now. The way the light would fizz in her eyes, full of laughter even when she was being serious. And the way she'd glow when she was having ideas, when we were writing together, as if the way she thought set sparks off in the air around her.

That afternoon, we'd sat on this single bed, with her acoustic guitar and wrote one of our best ever songs.

Naomi was the only person I knew who still wrote stuff down with a pen and paper; she was always making notes, scribbling ideas on anything she could find, and she'd shove them in this box she had, to look at later.

'Mate, why are you so analogue?' I'd ask her.

'Because no one has ever hacked a piece of paper,' she told me. 'That's why I keep all my deepest darkest secrets either up here,' she tapped her forehead, 'or written down in the olden-days way.'

And now it made sense to me more than ever. Somewhere in this room there were little pieces of her, little excerpts and extracts of the girl that she had been, her fingerprints and DNA, caught up in the neat loops and swirls of her handwriting.

That girl can't be gone, she has to still be somewhere inside her bruised and damaged head.

10

Rose and Leo are already outside, but not me. I go to the bathroom, and let the cold tap run, cupping the water in my hands, sluicing it over the shaved sides of my head, feeling it trickle down between my shoulder blades.

When I come out I see Ash sitting at her desk, where she has three computer monitors arranged around her like a fence, and a laptop open. This is her thing, tech. She's the kind of girl who codes for a laugh. The kind of girl who scares the shit out of me. This could be my chance to try and talk to her again, to find out how she feels about Nai, if she really thinks the way I do. How though, how do you open a conversation with someone who is so very closed?

Shrugging, I go in with my best shot.

'What you doing?' I ask her and she starts, swearing under her breath. My best shot is shit.

'Fuck, Red. Man!'

'Sorry, I just wondered what you were doing?'

'Come in and close the door,' she snaps, and I obey her because it seems like there isn't an option not to. Once the door is shut she nods at her central screen. It's the City of Westminster traffic camera CCTV,' she says, turning her laptop to face me.

'Like on YouTube or something?' I ask. I mean Ash is pretty weird. Maybe watching CCTV is how she relaxes.

'From the night before Nai was found, right up until the moment the tugboat picked her up. They data-dump it in a cloud, which seriously everyone should know by now is a fucking terrible idea.'

'Wait . . . what?' I take a step closer to her, peering over her shoulder at the image.

'Well, the police theory is that she ran away, got mixed up in *something* and somehow jumped, right?' Ash thinks I'm asking about the evidence, not the highly illegal activity she is engaged in in her bedroom.

'Well, if she jumped, it had to be pretty near to where she was found, and not too long before either, because anywhere else and she would have drowned, any longer in the water and she would have frozen to death. So I thought I'd look for her. I don't think they've even thought of looking for her here.'

'Ash . . . ' I almost don't want to know. 'Did you hack the Borough of Westminster?'

'Only the CCTV storage part.' Ash grins at me. 'And only this bit. Though if you fancy re-setting your parents' council rent down to zero now's the time to let me know.'

'We own our house.'

'Fancy,' Ash mocks me absent-mindedly.

'Shit,' I say watching her work.

'I know.' She returns her attention back to the screen. I see something different in her as she clocks from screen to screen. It's not happiness exactly but she looks comfortable, at ease. It might be the first time I've ever seen her this way. 'I do rule at this. The thing is,' she goes on. 'I've been over this footage – hours of it – several times now, and Naomi isn't there. Not in the six hours before she is found. And there's no sign of her anywhere within the radius of where she could have survived a fall from. She isn't there. So that means—'

'The theory is wrong.' I sit down next to her, perching on the end of her bed.

'Yes.' Ash's dark eyes search mine. 'Can I trust you?'

'Yes,' I say. 'I think so.'

'I looked at the CCTV footage of the last time she was seen, too. Walking down towards Vauxhall tube at three o'clock in the morning. She walks under the railway bridge and we don't see her again until she turns up almost dead eight weeks later.'

'It's crazy,' I say. 'But we know all of this.'

'The only answer is that she got into a car,' Ash says. 'That's the only thing that makes sense.'

'But the police vetted all the cars that came in and out of the tunnel both ways. There were only ten, and one of them was a cop car. Between then and the morning rush hour, every single driver was in the clear,' I remind her.

'That has to be wrong.' Ash looks back at the image of her sister that she has frozen on one of her screens. Nai in a summer dress and trainers, nothing else on her, walking completely calmly, totally alone into the dark of the tunnel under the railway. 'That has to be wrong because there can't be any other explanation. One of those drivers is lying.'

'Or she used an access tunnel, one of the doors

under the bridge had been vandalised and wasn't locked, remember? Or she was on the wrong side of the road for the CCTV, in the blind spots, or shadows. There could be a million other reasons why they didn't see her again after that image. This is the police, Ash. I mean they are wankers, but I kind of think they are good at this investigation shit.'

'Oh, do you?' Ash looks up at me. 'Except they didn't notice the tattoo on her wrist, did they? Or the bruises that look like fingerprints.'

'I'm probably wrong,' I say. 'I'm probably seeing shit that isn't really there.'

'But what if you're not?' Ash leans close enough for me to be able to taste her breath, spicy and sweet. 'What if you're not, Red? What if you and me are right about this and no one is listening to us?'

'I don't see what we can do. We're school kids!'

'There's loads we can do. All I needed was to find a place to start to look, and you were the one that found it. The tattoo. If we can find who did it, and when, that's a big lead. Did you take a photo?'

'No.' I shrug, feeling like a dumb-ass for not thinking of it. 'It didn't seem like a good time.'

'Fuck.' Ash slams her desk, and I stand up.

'I'll get one tomorrow, when I visit.'

'No, that's a waste of hours. I'll go now.' Ash really is angry with me for not photographing the tattoo.

'They won't let you in. She said no more visitors before tomorrow.'

'I'll find a way in,' she says, 'It's my thing.'

'You'll get into trouble, hacking is a serious crime . . . '

'I looked,' she says, pulling on a hoodie over her jeans

and zipping it up. 'I didn't hack. Hacking is stealing, or lying, or scamming. I just went to see if there was a way in, and there was. And I looked. That's all.'

'What if you get into trouble, what about your dad and Jackie? It would kill them!'

'Don't you think I don't know that,' Ash says sharply. 'I bloody know that. But I also need to know what happened to my sister. I need to find out in case . . .'

'In case of what?' I ask her.

'In case she doesn't make it, and whoever did this to her gets away with it.'

Ashira
Red, I'm serious. Don't talk to anyone about this.

Red
Course not. But Ash is it worth it? If you get caught, get into trouble. It would be bad, man. Your parents . . .

Ashira
I got to know. It's the only thing I can do. I've got to find out.

Red
KK. I'll help you if I can.

Ashira
And you won't talk?

Red
Didn't I say that?

Ashira
Sure, ok. I'll trust you. Fuck with me and I'll be in all of your internet accounts in less than five minutes.

Red
Threat not needed, but ok!

Ashira
Wait to hear from me. And only message on this forum, it's encrypted.

Red
Understood. Over and out.

11

'Finally,' Rose says as I exit Nai's front door. 'What were you up to?'

'Ash wanted to talk,' I say, rubbing the back of my neck. It feels wrong to have a secret from these two, but it feels to wrong to talk about Ash, too.

'How is she doing?' Leo asks. I shrug. I'm glad when neither of them ask me more.

As we walk down to the river, the heat of the September evening gradually warms my skin and the sunlight leaps off the water with flashes and sparkles. As I look at the city, unwinding along the riverbank, like every high rise and tower block has been there a thousand years, I smile. I love this place. It's hard not to be happy when you see all the life, and all the possibilities out there, clamouring with ideas. Pushing everything Ash said to me to the back of mind, I break into a run and hang over the railings that separate me from the muddy shore below, my feet dangling in the air, a breeze that's travelled all the way from the sea cutting across my face. Leo and Rose join me a few seconds later, Leo climbing up and sitting on the railing, and for a little while we just look at this place we live in. I haven't travelled very much, but I don't need to know that London is the best place in the world, and looking at it like this, I feel like part of its army, invincible.

Back there with Ash, her theories and ideas seemed so real. But now, in the sunlight, with my friends at my side . . . ? Ash is pretty intense, what if this is all in our heads? It would be easier just to let the adults deal with it, to trust them. That would be so much easier. After all, that's what they are for, right?

The only problem is that adults like reasons, neat little answers that fit inside a box they can slap a label on. What happened to Nai isn't neat, it doesn't have a reason that makes any sense, and it doesn't fit in a box, but they don't want to admit that. Maybe they are afraid to.

'I don't want to go home yet,' I say.

'We don't have to,' Rose replies. 'All I've got to go home to is my dad and the insipid stepmother, and they'll want us to do something together. Like watch a movie or play fucking Scrabble. As if spending time with her will make me any less disgusted that she is young enough to be my big sister.'

Without any need for further discussion we peel ourselves away from the riverbank and head towards the shop at the end of the road.

'I just know that Mum will just be stressing about Aaron when I get home,' Leo says. 'Soon as I walk in the door, I'll be getting lectures up to here.' He taps the top of his head.

'Thing is though. . . ' I look at Rose and she raises her brows quizzically. I know she's wondering what I'm going to say, and the truth is so am I. I say it anyway. 'I can kind of see why your mum is worried, mate. You got into a lot of trouble round Aaron. And since he's been out of the picture, like hardly any. So . . . '

'Fuck off, Red,' Leo says, not angry but blunt, shutting me down. 'I'm not a little kid. I'm my own man. I make my own choices. Aaron is my brother, he's not Al fucking Capone. Everybody needs to calm down. I'll get some more booze.'

'Just leave it,' Rose says to me as we stand outside the Spar waiting for him. 'It's not worth it.'

'But do you want him to end up like he was before?' I say. 'Aaron knifed a bloke, put him in hospital. What if Leo got dragged into that shit?'

'Leo's right, he is his own person. And he's not the same kid he was a year ago. We should trust him.'

'I trusted Nai,' I say in a low voice.

'Yeah, but Nai isn't Leo. Leo had it tough all his life, Red. I fake my poor-little-rich-girl routine, but we know that my life is pretty cushy, even though my dad is a twat. And you, you have a home to go to and food in the fridge even though your mum is, like a textbook drunk. But Leo. Leo has never had that, and he knows exactly what's coming, and when the time comes he'll decide what to do about it, and you and me with our nice houses, and full bellies, and bills paid, don't really get to tell him what that is.'

I study her face, like I've never met her before, even though I know every sweep and plane of every feature. She always surprises me, always amazes, she's deep when you think she's shallow, kind when you think she's cruel. And more than any of those things she is brave, one of the bravest people I know.

'Bad things have happened to you,' I say very quietly. 'You know more about being strong than anyone I know.'

Rose says nothing, turning her face away from me.

'Yeah well, I'm all good, so . . . '

'And my life . . . ' I struggle to find the words. 'It's not exactly textbook.'

'It could be.' Rose still doesn't look at me. 'Hey, what do you think of Maz Harrison. He's cute, right?'

'Tina Harrison's older brother?' I look at her. 'He's like twenty-five.'

'And?' Rose gives me a 'so what' look.

'Well you are disgusted by your not-that-old stepmother, hypocrite,' I remind her.

'That's totally different. Anyway, he likes me.'

'How do you know?'

'Because he messaged me on Facebook.'

'On Facebook! That's how you can tell he's old, he uses Facebook.'

Rose giggles. 'Yeah, right? I haven't looked at that account since I was like, thirteen. It's deadly.'

'So, he's a twat then.'

'But he is really cute,' Rose says. 'And if you can connect with someone spiritually, romantically like a meeting of true minds, why does age matter?'

'Because it's gross,' I say.

Leo comes out of the shop walking past us, bottles clinking in his plastic bag and the subject is dropped.

'Come on then,' he says and we follow him, leaving the subject of Maz Harrison behind us. Or at least I hope we do.

Leo and Rose pass the bottle of vodka between them as we watch the river change colour from grey to pink to something like purple, as the sun is finally swallowed whole by the ragged-toothed skyline.

We don't talk. Leo looks at the water as he drinks, steadily without pleasure, like it's a task he's got to get through. Rose is messaging someone, I don't know who, but I see how the corner of her mouth twitches with a smile every time another notification pops up on her home screen, how her expression softens. There's a boy on the other end of the notifications, which is nothing new, just another one in a long line of fools that she will have dumped before the week is out. I wonder if it's Maz, and hope not. Maz is all about his flashy car, and not much else.

'Park?' Leo says, twisting the lid off the second bottle.

'What about Seren?' Rose says out of nowhere, as we take the short walk to the park. Seren is this girl with blue eyes, and long legs and a very high voice that makes it sound like she's been sucking on helium. 'She fancies you, bad.'

'What about her?' Leo says, glancing at Rose.

'Girlfriend material, Leo,' Rose says like it was obvious, like we've been talking about this all along. 'Come on, you are the hottest boy in the school and you don't have a girlfriend, why not? You telling me all those muscles aren't for us girls?'

Why Rose is choosing to do this now, I don't know, but I do know that out of all the girls he wants to tease him about seeing someone serious, Rose is the very last on the list. He rises to her challenge, and her eyes flash.

'Why have one, when you can have them all?' Leo says, rolling his shoulders and puffing out his chest. 'Girlfriends just give you grief, Rose, they just pull you down. Telling you what to do, what to say. I don't need that, not when I can just get a little action and be on my way.'

Rose laughs at him, as we tumble into the park, empty now and dark.

'That's right, you are the big man, aren't you?' she says, jumping onto the roundabout and sailing away and back again. 'OK, so who did you last fuck? Out of all of the girls that have given it up for you, who was the last?'

'I'm not telling you that,' Leo says.

'Because you can't.' Rose grins at him as she rolls past. 'Because you've never fucked anyone.'

I sigh, she's hard to understand this girl, who'd bait and torture someone she cares about so much. Someone she was, just a little while ago, talking about with such love and respect.

'Fuck off, yes I have,' Leo says and Rose comes round again.

'Leo, Leo, it's OK, it's nothing to be ashamed of, being a virgin. Is it, Red? Red's a virgin too. You two could be in a club. Or maybe you two should get together, you'd make a sweet couple, the oddest gayest couple there's ever been, but I dunno, you kind of suit each other.'

I shrug, nothing she says can bother me, and anyway it's true. There's no point in denying it, I don't look like the kind of person who has ever had any kind of meaningful sexual contact, because I never have.

'Why do you care anyway?' Leo asks her. 'What's it to you?'

Rose stops at the roundabout and looks at Leo for a long time, and Leo looks right back at her, right into her eyes, like he was going to kiss her or something. And I know that any second this friendship between them could turn into something else, something I'm not part of. I feel this ripping in my gut, and it hurts and I have to do something.

'Annabelle Clements,' I say.

Leo's mouth opens as he gives me this WTF look. 'Not cool, Red.'

'Annabelle Clements, you had sex with Annabelle Clements. I'm just saying. Nothing to be ashamed of, she's fit.'

I shrug, talking like this about Annabelle doesn't make me feel good, but at least it will shut them both up.

Rose recoils as if she's been slapped, and at once I regret every word.

'Whatever. I don't care.' Turning away from Leo, Rose nicks the almost empty bottle from his hand, draining it.

'Got anything on you?' She looks at Leo, after pills or weed or both. Leo shakes his head. 'Nah, skint.'

'Ugh,' Rose tosses her head back in frustration. 'This is so lame, getting pissed in a fucking park, and we can't even get pissed properly. I want to get wrecked, man, I want to get out of my head.'

She rounds on me, winding her arm around my neck, and pulling me in close, somewhere between a headlock and hug.

'Go get some more, Red.'

'I can't,' I say, wondering where to look as she pulls my face close to hers. 'They know me in there, they know I'm underage.'

She pushes me away in disgust. 'Then go home and nick some of your alco mum's.'

I probably deserve that after bringing up Annabelle, but still it stings.

'No.' I shake my head and she walks away from us, the empty bottle hanging from her hand. She tips her head back until she's looking up at the sky and she just sort of . . . roars.

She just fucking *roars*.

This banshee howl of fury and sadness and all the things that I know she can never say out loud, the things I know that no one else in the world knows, are there, a chorus of fury and sadness and loss.

Rose stands there looking at the sky and she ROARS.

And after a second, I go and stand next to her and I roar too, except my roar is more like a howl, and then Leo joins in and his is a long raspy shout and we stand there, and we scream at the last of the daylight bleeding away into the night.

So none of us notice the squad car pulling up, until two cops get out, one bloke, one woman.

The bloke cop says, 'Hadn't you kids better be getting home?'

Rose says, 'What the fuck is it to you?'

And he says, 'You better watch your mouth, young lady.'

And she says, 'Fuck the patriarchy!'

And he says, 'Right, that's it, you're coming with me.'

And Rose runs away, *she runs away*.

It's the funniest thing I have ever seen in my life, Rose running, cackling her head off like a crazy person, while the cop chases her and she dodges him, and doubles back and runs in circles and he skids and puffs after her, Leo and me, and the other woman copper standing there, her open mouthed, us two trying not to laugh and failing.

'He is never going to live this down,' the woman says, grinning at us. 'I'll make sure of that.'

But then Rose slips, falling onto her arse, and she just sits there and laughs as he helps her to her feet, and escorts her towards the car, punching the air in victory.

'Officer.' Leo has to make an effort to smile politely, as the cop opens the passenger door of the car. 'Look, she's an idiot, but she's having a rough time. Our friend, she was the girl that was missing, the one that turned up in the river?'

'Funny that,' the cop says as he opens the door, putting his hand on the top of Rose's head as he pushes her in. 'I hear that a lot recently.'

'You can't just take her away, she's a minor,' I say, not knowing if that's true, but thinking it worth a go.

'No I'm not! I'm a major!' Rose shouts from the back of the car. 'Come on, you lot, are you getting in? Taxi's here!'

We try to, but they won't let us.

'Go home,' the woman copper tells us. 'She'll be all right, I'll keep an eye on her, and once he's calmed down he'll let her go home with her dad. I know you kids. You're in that band aren't you? My son really rates you.'

'But—' Leo puts his hand on the door.

'Son.' The woman, she was nice, kind. 'I know you, too, and I know your brother. So take it from me when I say the best thing you can do is go home. I'll take care of her.'

She reaches into her pocket and hands me a card: P.C. Sandra Wiggins.

'What your pal needs to do now is calm down, and we can all get home quickly.'

I tuck the card in my pocket, shaking my head at Rose as she bangs on the window of the squad car, gesturing for me to take a photo.

I don't even hesitate, taking my phone and taking a snap.

I mean, why the hell not?

Nine hours ago . . .

We were all sitting in a row on the edge of the stage, in the main hall, feeling like a row of pricks. Well, maybe not Leckraj, because he doesn't talk much. He sat on the end and took out his packed lunch, setting it out neatly on the dusty stage.

Mr Smith was there with Miss Greenstreet, our drama teacher, standing close enough together that their elbows touched, heads bent towards each other, in close conversation. I studied them for signs of unresolved sexual tension, or more interestingly, resolved sexual tension.

We know Mr Smith is single, because when we ask him about it he always says he'll invite us to the wedding when he meets the right woman. Miss Greenstreet isn't quite as obvious though, she's not the sort of teacher to be drawn into gossip like Mr Smith is. I like her a lot, I like the way her yellow hair is longer at the front than at the back, and if you are very close to her you see that there's a hole in her nose from a piercing. I like to think she puts it back in on the weekends. Could she and Mr Smith be having sex?

'No, though I think she wouldn't mind,' Rose whispered.

'But she's not his type, not girly enough.'

I turned to look at her, freaked out that she's mind-reading now.

'Seriously, dude, it was written all over your face.' Rose grinned. 'But you don't have to worry, your crush on Miss G is safe for now.'

'I do not have a crush on her!' I hissed back.

'Settle down, guys,' Mr Smith says.

Rose touches the back of her hand to my cheek, snatching it away as if it had been burnt by the heat of my blush. 'Oh no, you totally don't. Nope. Uh-uh.'

'Don't what?' Leo grinned.

'Have a crush on Miss Greenstreet,' Rose said, loud enough for everyone to hear.

'Oh man, you so have the hots for Miss G,' Leo laughed, shaking his head.

'Kill me,' I said burying my face in my hands, trying not to notice Miss G pretending not to have heard.

'It's OK,' Leckraj offered me a segment of his tangerine. 'I have a crush on her, too.'

'Right.' Lily from the radio station clapped her hands together to get our attention. 'I'm all set, levels are set, so we'll record it as live, so just be natural, funny, don't swear, OK?'

We all mumbled in agreement, and Lily counted us in.

'I'm here with Mirror, Mirror a band from Thames Comprehensive that are fast gaining an army of fans. Hi, guys!'

She nodded at us, waggling her eyebrows furiously to try and get us to say something.

'Hi . . . ' we all chorus back.

'So, Red.' For some reason Lily picked me first, shoving

her microphone under my face. I stared at it, all those rock star fantasies of endless media interviews in which I am fascinating, witty and devastatingly attractive coming back to haunt me in an instant. 'Tell us why you are holding a benefit concert for your band member and classmate Naomi Demir.'

I stared at the microphone, and then back at Lily, who bobbed her head, encouragingly.

'Um . . . ' Nothing. Seconds pass and I've got nothing.

'It means the world to us.' Rose grabbed the mic and pulled it towards her, giving me some serious side-eye. 'When we planned it, Naomi was still missing. We wanted to shout out her name as loud as we could, and hoped she'd hear it and come home, because she isn't just our friend, she's our family, and when she went it nearly broke us. She's back now, and whatever it is that has happened to her, she's going to need a lot of support to get better. And this concert is for all kids like her, like us, out there who sometimes feel like there's no one to talk to. This concert says if no one is listening, shout until they do. Everyone deserves a voice.'

'Great, thank you, Rose.' Lily smiled, clearly impressed. 'And what about you, Leo? Do you agree with Rose?'

'Fuck yeah,' Leo said and Lily snaps the recorder off.

'Shit, sorry,' Leo said, as Rose dissolved into giggles.

'No swearing,' Leckraj reminded him helpfully, before taking a bite of his sandwich.

'Guys,' Mr Smith tried hard not to laugh, 'settle down. This is important. For the concert and for you all, this is a big deal. And no swearing on the radio.'

'Fuck, sorry,' Leo said and Rose lost it again.

'Sorry,' Rose said, taking a deep breath.

'That's OK.' Lily took a deep breath, and lifted the mic. 'We can cut out the F word, so Leo, pretend I've just asked you the same question and answer it again.' He nods as she presses record.

'Yeah,' he says. 'A lot of people care about Naomi,' he said. 'Probably a lot more than she realised. She's back now, and she's gonna need to know that more than ever, and I guess that we wanted to do something big for her, and any other kid out there . . . maybe, I don't know.' He drops his head bashfully, and Rose rubbed his shoulder.

'And Leckraj?' Lily brought the microphone to Leckraj, who paused – his sandwich halfway to his mouth – and blinked.

'What does it feel like to be replacing the beloved band member?'

Leckraj put his sandwich back in his Tupperware box and resealed the lid.

'I'm not replacing her,' Leckraj said, thoughtfully. 'I'm honouring her. She's the best bassist I've ever met in real life, and when she's out of that coma, I'm going to ask her on a date. She will turn down me down, probably, because she is way out of my league, but why live your life in fear, right?'

Leo, Rose and I all turned to look at Leckraj, and finally I figured out what to say. 'Dude,' I said. 'You are *so* in the band.'

Leo
That girl be crazy

Red
What do we do, do we go down there?

Leo
No . . . she's fine her dad's a lawyer, Red

Red
We shouldn't have let them take her

Leo
No way I was going down there, I wouldn't have got out again, Rose was cool, she knew what she was doing, even off her face

Red
What was she doing?

Leo
Thinking about what a cool story she'd have to tell at school tomorrow. Check out her Insta

Click here to view

'Everything's beautiful, even jail when you are falling in love!'
87 reactions   **Nineteen comments**

Red
How the fuck did she take a selfie at the police station?

Leo
I dunno, but she's lovin' it. Chill. Rose can handle herself

Red
She says the same about you

Leo
She's right. I'm fucked though, head bangin. Gotta close my eyes. Don't freak out, K

Red
KK

Red
Falling in love with who?

Leo

Leo is offline

12

Who is Rose falling in love with?

I sit on my bed, hiding my phone under the pillow. My body is wiped out, strong and healthy as it is now, the fat years and the thin years still hang around like ghosts, like I permanently used up 10 per cent of me while I was trying to shape my body to mask my hurt, or show it, I'm not sure which. But sometimes as fit as I am, it just crashes and burns, and today is one of those days.

My brain keeps fizzing away; the tattoo, Ash and her mission that somehow I'm now part of . . . and something else. There's something else just out of reach that seems to hides every time I try to think about what it is. Like I've forgotten something important, but whatever it is I can't seem to catch hold of it.

Next door, Mum is passed out fully dressed on the bed, a glass of vodka and tonic tilted in her hand. I thought about moving the glass when I saw her there, but I didn't. I want her to be woken up some time in the night by the shock of the cold liquid on her thighs, or even the sound of breaking glass. Maybe then she'll get an idea of what a state she is.

Dad must be out again, if he was ever in.

Across the hall, Gracie is asleep beneath her fairy lights. I hope she had a decent tea and a nice afternoon with Mum after school. Usually she does, usually she gets the jolly, tipsy Mum, affectionate and fun. It's not until later that the anger sets in, after Gracie is in bed. I creep across the landing and check on Gracie, her face is so soft like her soul, and I remember what it was like to be seven years old, at that point in your life when you have no idea that sometimes the world hates you for no good reason at all.

Now, as tired as I am, I'm fully awake.

I try messaging Leo again but he's checked out.

I keep thinking about the way he looked at Rose before the police turned up. And the way she looked at him and the pain it made me feel. If those two get together then everything will change, first we were four mates, and then we were three, but if those two get together, it will be them and me tagging along. And maybe it makes me a prick, but I just don't want that. Us four was the best thing I've ever had in my life. I don't want to go back to that skinny ginger nobody that never meant anything to anyone. I don't want to be invisible again. God, sometimes I make myself sick.

Reaching for my bag, I pull out Naomi's notebooks. Stuffed full of random bits of paper, ideas she's had and scribbled down on anything she can find, a ripped-up sandwich packet, a tissue, the corner of an exercise book. Anyone else would put them in a note on their phone but not Nai. I guess that makes sense when your big sister could take a peek at all your online stuff any time she liked.

I shake the loose bits out of the notebook, and push

them aside. I turn to the finished lyrics written inside, and the more I read, the more I feel like I'm peeping in through a window, watching something that isn't meant for me. Each one is filled with heat and lust, which is so not like Nai. When we wrote together we wrote about being free, being yourself. Not fitting in, not giving a fuck. Sometimes we wrote about wanting people who would never want us back, but we never wrote stuff like this. These songs are for someone, these songs aren't about wishing and wanting. They are about doing.

Soft
Desire
Kiss
Stroke
Touch
Mouth
Hard
Tip
Parted

Words leap out at me from the pages, words that tell me something we all should have seen as clear as day, but none of us did.

Naomi was with someone just before she vanished.

Naomi was in love, but more than that, she was having a fully charged, maximum-graphic, certificate-18 sexual affair. That's what these songs are about. She was in love, she was obsessed. Sitting up I scan the songs over and over again, looking for a clue about who they might be addressed to.

When I think back to those last days of term, yes, it all makes sense.

Twelve weeks ago . . .

It was warm, and we were so done with school already.

Mocks were finished and there didn't really seem any point to the last few weeks, everyone was tired and slow, drifting along waiting for the final bell that would set us free for the summer.

We were rehearsing some new songs in the music room that had we had kind of taken over, so that no one else ever really tried to use it. At least that was the plan. Rose, Leo and I were already there, but Nai was late, so I started taking Rose through the lyrics, Leo picking out the tunes I'd written out for him on a chord chart.

As Nai came into the rehearsal she took off the fire-red manga wig she'd been wearing that day and shook out her long brown hair, which fell in honey coloured ripples.

'Too hot to look hot?' Rose asked her and she shrugged, sitting on the floor. Naomi was smiling, I remember that she wasn't smiling at us, she was smiling to herself. Like she wasn't really in the room, but somewhere else in another moment that meant something just to her. I'll ask her later, I thought. But I never did.

As we talked through our set list for the next gig, the year-twelve prom, she took out this massive packet of baby wipes, and began to take off her make-up. I looked at Rose who raised an eyebrow, and Leo who was so focused on the music that he didn't even really notice at first.

The thing was, I'd got so used to it, the dead-white foundation that wiped out any trace of her own features, turning her face into a canvas. The big anime eyes, drawn on with pencils, accentuated with huge false lashes. The sweeping eyebrows that had nothing to do with the shape of her own. The tiny rosebud mouth painted on top of her real lips. It was so much a part of Naomi, that I'd stopped looking for her own face underneath. I suppose that girl had become invisible.

We kept on talking about the set list, which songs should go on it, and which should go where, and she kept on cleaning stuff off her face, finishing the whole pack of wipes. By the time we were ready to play, her face was clear and plain, her coffee-coloured skin glowing and fresh, cheeks a little pink, lips a deeper shade. And yes, she looked really pretty. For a second I even felt shy of her.

'Shit,' Leo said, appreciatively. 'You look good, girl.'

'You do!' Rose said. 'Let me put make-up on you!'

'Fuck off!' Nai laughed. 'I just took it all off. I'm over that now, you know. I'm more into just being natural, I think.'

'Since when?' Rose asked her.

'Since just now.' Nai grinned.

She took a pair of scissors from her pencil case and cut off the laces that held on this kind of corset thing she always wore, unzipped her funny frilly skirt, so that she was wearing just a black vest and leggings, and you could see the shape of her, soft and rounded, gentle and vulnerable.

'Right,' I said. It had taken me a moment to remember this girl was my best friend, one I'd hung out with a million times and never thought about *that* way, and what a shallow prick I was. I shook the thought right out of my head. Nai was Nai, she was more than a girl, she was my mate.

When we played, we were good but Nai was better than ever. Instead of standing at the back, head down, she made eye contact with us all, laughing and moving around. Like the sun had just come out over her head or something.

'So I'm cutting school for the afternoon,' she told us as we packed up.

'What? You bunking off?' Rose gasped. 'You never do that! Why?'

'Because it's a bullshit waste of my time,' Naomi said. 'I've got some cash so I'm going to go and find some stuff for my new look.'

'Wait, I'll come with . . . ' But Naomi had left before Rose could tell her she'd come too.

'She looks good like that,' Leo said, after she'd gone. 'She's going to get some attention.'

'Prettier than me?' Sometimes Rose is like that, she asks questions that no one over the age of five should ask. But in particular Rose shouldn't have asked Leo in the way she does, drawing him in, breaking him down and then pushing him away again. He fell for it every time though, and I couldn't exactly blame him, because so did I.

'You're not pretty,' Leo said, making Rose gasp and her eyes widen. 'You're beautiful.'

She preened for a moment, as Leo slung his guitar on his back, just before adding, 'For a crazy girl.'

'Arsehole!' Rose called after him as he left.

'He's a fucking arsehole, right?' She cocked her head to look at me. 'Wanna cut school and come and lay in the sun with me?'

And with the thought of long grass, and Rose with her hair full of daisies, and her eyes full of laughter, I'd forgotten everything Nai had said and done even before I said yes.

This is Where Life Happens
By Naomi and Red

Walking like a zombie,
Sitting like a fool,
Wanting like a lost boy
Trying to be cool.

When you smile that's where Life happens
When you touch me that's where . . .
When you kiss me that's here . . .
When I'm with you I'm there.
When I'm with you I know,
This is where Life happens.

Eating like a robot,
Sleeping like a lion,
Drooling like a hungry dog,
Wish you were mine.

When you smile that's where Life happens,
When you touch me that's where . . .
When you kiss me that's here . . .
When I'm with you I'm there.
When I'm with you I know,
This is where Life happens.

This is where Life Happens.

Repeat to fade.

Click link to see video

13

We are waiting for her at the school gate, when Rose makes her appearance, climbing out of Amanda's Audi looking like a fucking movie star. Floor-length leopard print fake-fur coat, hair crazy, shades on, lips intense pink.

Leo and me stand there watching her, and I just know that my expression is the same as his, jaw dropped, eyes wide, head slowly shaking side to side in a perfect mixture of what-the-fuck and God-I-love-her. Her dad doesn't get out, doesn't even shout goodbye; he pulls away as Rose slams the car door. She doesn't bother looking over her shoulder as she marches towards us arms outstretched.

'My people, my people!' she cries, flinging her arms around us both, kissing us in turn, first Leo and then me. I feel the sticky imprint of her hot-pink lipstick on my cheek.

'What the hell?' Leo says, laughing and grimacing at the same time.

'You get taken to jail and you're back at school the next day like nothing happened?' I ask her as she hooks her arms through ours and marches us through the year-eleven entrance, head held high like she's had the best time.

'Who knows?' she asks, beaming at everyone we pass. 'Does everyone know?'

'We didn't tell anyone,' I say. 'We didn't have to, it was all over your profiles.'

'Cool, right?' Rose chuckles. 'Redster? This is amazing! This is the most rock 'n' roll thing we've ever done. What we have to do next is write a song about jail.'

'Mate, an hour at a police station, ain't real jail.' Leo crosses his arms, determined to be unimpressed. After all, he's seen the inside of a police cell once or twice.

'Whatever.' Rose shrugs. 'It doesn't matter how long it *was*, it matters what it *looks* like, right? It was a piece of cake actually. I cried, the nice woman talked the fat one down.'

'Did your dad go mad?' I ask her and she laughs.

'Dad doesn't even know it happened.'

'But how? You need an adult to get you out. Was it Amanda?'

Rose just laughs at me.

'I have my ways.'

'Fuck's sake, what ways, Rose?' Leo shakes his head.

'I'm not saying.' She grins and I want to kill her. 'Let's just say older men have their uses.'

Leo turns his face away from her, hiding whatever it is she has made him feel.

'Fuck, Rose, you could have messaged!' I say. After reading Nai's lyrics I could really have done with talking to her, even if I wasn't sure I should tell anyone else about them. But the first thing she'd done was put a fuck-load of selfies on Instagram and call who, Maz Harrison?

'Where's the drama in that?' Rose's grin snaps on and off.

'Your dad is going to find out that some creep sprang you from jail,' I warn her.

'Nope. He won't, and he isn't that interested in me.' For a second Rose looked disappointed. 'I told him I had a hangover this morning, just to see what he'd do, and he said that in a few weeks we'll be taking our GCSEs and that I'm a bright girl, and if I stop fucking around I will have a bright future. But that if I am determined to ruin my own life there isn't much he can do about it, he needs to focus on Amanda. Really she's all he cares about, it's like keeping Amanda happy is a full-time job. Me, I'm just an inconvenience, a great big fat hairy gooseberry in their eternal honeymoon.'

'Well at least he was at home,' I say. 'Dad wasn't there when I got up this morning. I don't even know if he came home.'

'Ugh, who needs fathers, right? Actually, it's better this way,' Rose says, wiping the lipstick mark off my cheek with her thumb. 'Life would be much more boring if he did care. And I don't need him to care about me, anyway, there's a new daddy in town!'

'Rank,' Leo groans.

'What does that even mean?' I ask her as the bell sounds.

'What do you think it means?'

God, Rose is infuriating.

'Rehearsal at lunch,' Leo calls to us, breaking into a jog to get to class, clearly keen to get away from Rose's drama and taunts about older men.

'Yes, boss!' Rose salutes him, before turning to me. 'He thinks I'm a dick, doesn't he?'

'You are a dick,' I say. 'And, anyway, since when have you cared what anyone thinks about you, and what the fuck do you mean a new daddy, because that sounds as creepy as hell.'

'I'm just messing around,' Rose says. 'And I do care, I care what you two think of me, and Nai. And maybe Leckraj a bit.' With the corridor clear she takes off her glasses, behind them the thick black eye make-up that she usually wears is gone, just her pale blue eyes, rimmed with red, lids swollen from crying. 'It's the rest of those fuckers I don't give a shit about.'

I pull her into a hug, getting lost in the sweet scented cloud of her hair.

'Leo doesn't think you are a dick,' I reassure her. 'I totally do, though.'

She thumps me pretty hard in the ribs but at least she is laughing as I watch her fall into class, her sunglasses firmly back in place.

Rose takes her place on the teacher's desk, sitting right in front of Mrs Hardyman and waits until the whole class is looking at her.

'You'll *never* guess what happened to me last night . . . '

'Red?' Mr Smith leans out of his classroom and beckons to me, standing alone in the corridor.

'I'm late for registration, sir,' I say, tearing my eyes off Rose as Mrs Hardyman closes the door with a notable slam.

'I'll give you a note, I just wanted a quick word on how things were going with Naomi? Must be hard on you all seeing her like that, but you most of all, I guess. You two were really close, weren't you? I mean you are, of course . . . '

'Yes,' I say as I walk into his classroom, and he closes the door behind us. 'I used to think we were but I don't know what happened, it doesn't make sense to me. She never said anything to me or the others that made us think this could happen. I feel like I let her down somehow.'

'Don't be so hard on yourself. Everyone has something they don't talk about with anyone,' Mr Smith says. His voice is low, kind. 'I know I do, I bet you do, too. Doesn't mean you weren't, *aren't*, important to her.'

'S'pose,' I say. I could go now, but I don't want to. I like it here, it's quiet and still. 'What's your secret, sir?'

He laughs and shakes his head. 'I guess I walked into that one. I like urban exploring, there you go. That's my secret. Getting into derelict and old buildings you're not supposed to be in and having a look around. Not strictly always legal, but a lot of fun.'

'If you say so.'

He laughs again. 'Keep that to yourself, OK? I don't want to get into trouble.'

I don't really see how you can get into trouble over that but I nod anyway.

'How's Naomi's family doing? I thought about going round there, but I don't want to intrude.'

'I don't think you would be, sir,' I tell him. 'I think Mrs Demir likes it, people round, lots of support and stuff. Takes her mind off things. I think she'd appreciate it.'

I watch as he carefully rearranges the papers on his desk.

'Anything else you'd like to talk about?'

I shake my head, so close to telling him everything that's circling round and round in my mind. But I don't. I don't even know why, really, except that if I say all the things I'm thinking out loud, he'll think I'm having some sort of breakdown and make me go to Inclusion and talk to a counsellor about feelings and shit. A girl killed herself a few years ago, and ever since then all you've got to do is look a bit sad and they send you off to therapy, and therapy has never helped my mum. But if I'd turn to anyone, it would be to him.

'Red—' He hesitates for a moment. 'Your exams are coming up, and . . . look, I don't want to put you on the spot, but I think you are coping with a lot. I saw your mum the other day in the supermarket and . . . '

Oh God, please tell me he didn't. I want to turn inside out from shame.

'She was pissed,' I say, every word feels stone heavy.

'Looked that way; you hadn't told me she was drinking a lot again. Are things very bad at home?'

If I say yes, what then? Social services again, and this time anything I tell them will only makes things worse. It's hard, I want to pour it all out, every little thing that makes up the cracked mosaic of life at home. If anyone would understand, it would be him. But I can't. Me, I might come out of it OK, but what about Gracie? What if she got taken into care or something? I can't risk that.

'No, no they aren't as bad as they look. I mean Mum isn't great but Dad's around and he's getting her help. And she wants to stop, so you know, it's all under control. Please don't talk about it with anyone, sir. You know Dad's one of the school governors, he'd be sick as a pig if it got out.'

I find the idea briefly appealing, but if I'm honest, I don't want the truth about our mess of a home life getting out any more than he would.

Mr Smith nods as he looks into my eyes and I drop my gaze, not wanting to be caught in a lie.

'I just want to know that you can come to me for help, if you need it,' he says. 'You're a talented kid, you've got a bright future ahead of you. And sometimes we all need someone to be on our side, right? Well, I've got your back.'

I nod, 'Thanks, sir.'

'Here. ' He scribbles out a note for me, and I take it and go to the door.

'Red?' Turning back I look at him. 'Remember, my door is open, any time.'

And weirdly, as I head for registration I do feel kind of better.

Neither Leo nor Rose are at the hospital when I get there.

There's a message from Leo.

Soz, shit I've got to deal wiv at home.

But nothing from Rose. So I'm on my own, following the now familiar route through a maze of corridors to get to Naomi's side. There's no one in her room, no nurses around or any sign of her family. It seems dumb to just stand outside, so after a moment I open the door and go in.

'Hey,' I sit down next to her, 'what's up? Same old, here. How's your head? Still caved in? Hey, Mr Smith asked about you today. I think the whole school is making you a get well card, and choir is recording a song for you, which is probably enough to make you want to stay in a coma, to be honest.'

Naomi doesn't answer, of course. I don't know why but I keep expecting her to.

Three days in and the bruising I can see has faded, her face looks a little more like the one I knew before she vanished.

'And my mum's been spotted pissed and in charge of a trolley. Wake up, Nai,' I whisper into her ear, desperate to hear the sound of her voice, that low sardonic growl when she tells me to get my shit together. 'Wake up and tell us what the fuck is going on.'

'She couldn't today, even if she wanted to.' Dr Patterson walks in. 'You aren't supposed to be here, you know, only family.'

'But Mrs Demir said come any time.'

'Mrs Demir doesn't quite grasp that this is ICU, it's not like she's just broken a leg. She needs quiet.'

'Is she getting better?' I ask.

'I can't tell you,' said Dr Patterson. 'Family only, remember?'

I reach for my bag, and she sighs. 'You can stay for a minute. I'm updating her family when they come in. You'll know more then.'

'Thank you,' I reply. As she leaves I open my phone, searching my recordings.

'Listen,' I say, turning back to face Nai. 'I hope you don't mind, but I took your notebook, the ones with the lyrics you wrote after, well, when you started to write on your own, and I set one of your songs to music last night. I couldn't sleep so I recorded it. What do you think?'

Pressing play, I hold the phone up to her ear.

As the music plays on I think about the words.

'The way you touch me, turns me inside out,
The way you want me,
Makes me scream and shout,
I don't want to take another breath unless you're in my face,
I don't want to fake another death unless you're in my place . . .'

Fake another death. Is that a clue? Was Naomi planning to vanish into thin air all along? I shake my head as the recording finishes; fuck, any of those words could mean anything. It's crazy to try and read stuff into them, other than the obvious fact they have been written by someone who has had a lot of hot sex.

Sighing I go to our Tumblr blog, and see someone has commented with a link to a fan page. A Mirror, Mirror fan page!

'Fuck, Nai, we've got a fan page.' I can't help smiling as I click on the link and there are loads of our song lyrics, set against these beautiful intricate drawings, the words merging into the pictures, and vice versa. 'It's amazing, Nai,' I say. 'Someone has really listened to our stuff, they really get it.' I scroll on and on, and follow the blog. No new posts for a few days but before that there was one almost every day. And then I see the blog owner, user-name Eclipse, and follow a link to her Instagram.

Her avatar is an illustration of a girl, her profile and long loops of hair encircled in a full moon. Only a few posts, no selfies, just some motivational shit, some boring photos of the same exact view and that's it.

Typical, our first super-fan, and she's a loser.

Then I see that the link in her Instagram profile is to Toonifie, so I follow it. Only there her username is different. DarkMoon. This is the person who has cloned all of

Nai's playlists. Wow, that really is a super-fan. Or some-one with a morbid curiosity. Dark things bring out even darker shit in people, that's for sure. In the weeks after Nai disappeared our social media following doubled, and again just after the news broke that she'd been found and was in a coma. People like tragedy. People are weird.

DarkMoon really wants us to notice her.

I wonder if she's hot?

Maybe she might be our first groupie.

Or stalker.

I mean I guess she's a she, but who knows? She could be a forty-five-year-old trucker called Ken.

'Who is this person, do you reckon?' I say to Nai. 'Probably some year seven art student wanker. Still a proper super-fan and we always wanted one of those, right?'

The mechanical sound of her breaths, the beeps on the machine continue, and it feels like my insides are col-lapsing in on themselves.

'I miss you so much Nai,' I whisper. My throat feels thick, and my eyes burn, but I'm not going to cry. Nai would never let me forget it if she caught me crying over her.

My phone suddenly starts pinging with notifications. Twitter? I haven't used that in months. But one after the other, the notifications keeping coming.

@Keris has retweeted your tweet
@BeeCee has retweeted your tweet
@HunNun94 has retweeted your tweet.

What fucking tweet?

Hurriedly, I log into @mirrormirrorband and see I've got 29 RTs and they keep coming. Apparently I've tweeted a photo of Nai's tattoo.

Do you know who did this, or have one like it? Please help us find out what happened to Naomi.

'Fucking Ash,' I say.

'Rude,' Ashira says, standing in the doorway. She gestures for me to follow her, which I do, into the corridor outside Nai's room.

'You hacked my Twitter!' Keeping my voice low, I shove my phone in her face.

'No, I borrowed it to post the photo of the tattoo. Twitter made the most sense as a platform to get it out there, more likely to get re-tweets, more eyes on it, more likely to get a hit. I knew you'd say yes, so I thought I might as well just get it up and running. 4 p.m. is optimal tweet time, you know.'

'You fucking hacked my Twitter,' I say again, getting a pretty stern look from a passing nurse.

'It's the band's Twitter, so at least twenty-five per cent is Nai's, and anyway what kind of a prick doesn't set up a two-step verification. You. You've learnt something, you're welcome.'

'Hello, darling, hello, Red, love.' Jackie and Max come out of the lift, looking crumpled and weary. 'Others not here yet?'

'Not yet,' I say. 'Leo's got something going on at home, but Rose says her dad's dropping her off later.'

'OK then.' Jackie pats me on the arm before going to see Nai.

'I need to tell you something,' I whisper to Ash, pulling her away from the open door of Nai's room. 'I was reading Nai's lyric books last night and I . . .'

'Mr Demir?' A voice behind us interrupts us and Ash puts her fingers to my lips to quiet me, taking me completely by surprise. She nods at her dad, taking my hand and leading me back over to where he is talking to the doctor.

'Dr Patterson?' Max smiles at the doctor, but the doctor doesn't smile at Max.

'Do you want to get your wife,' she says. 'So I can brief you both at once?'

Jackie appears in the doorway, tears already standing in her eyes.

Max takes her hand and holds it tightly as Dr Patterson talks, directing her gaze anywhere but at us.

'So Naomi's last CT scan shows the bleeding on her brain has stopped, which is positive news. However, her brain is still very swollen. We've decided to keep her sedated for another twenty-four hours and reassess the situation then.'

'But she's no worse?' Jackie frowns deeply.

'Slightly improved,' Dr Patterson says. 'It's going to be a long road, Jackie, you can't expect miracles. More importantly, you shouldn't.'

'But she's no worse.' Jackie nods as if that is all she wants to hear.

'She's no worse,' Dr Patterson repeats heavily.

Jackie and Max go in to sit with her and Ash looks at me.

'You know what, it doesn't matter,' I say.

'Tell me,' she says, taking a step closer to me. I remember

her fingers on my lips and take a step back.

'It's just a hunch,' I say, shaking my head. 'I have literally no proof.'

'What the fuck is it?'

'I think . . . ' I sigh. 'I think Nai was seeing someone. Someone really serious before she disappeared. I think maybe it wasn't that she was running away from us. More that she was running towards someone. Someone she thought was more important than anything else. Someone she didn't want to tell us about.'

'I think so too,' Ash says, taking me by surprise for the second time.

'You do?' I glance at her, and she nods.

'It's the only thing that makes sense to me, that something, someone happened to her to change her so completely.'

'So what do we do?' I ask, as she closes that gap between us once again. This time I don't back away.

'We find out who the fuck it is,' she says.

14

I walk up and down the white-tiled floor of Rose's kitchen in my bare feet, my socks and shoes out on the decking of her small walled garden, glad to be out of the hospital, away from Ash and her confusing intensity. On the one hand it's cool to be around her, she's got this sort of buzz that makes me feel like maybe I can do something about Nai. On the other hand , I don't know. There's something about her that puts me on edge.

Here, in Rose's house, it's quiet, it's sunny and tranquil.

She only lives a few streets away from me, but that's London for you. High-rise flats and council estates, iden-tikit semis like mine and then something like Rose's place – fancy houses with drives, and dug-out basements and glass extensions – all crammed together in the same post-code. The rich and poor live side by side, in million-plus mansions like this one, and Leo's two-bed flat a stone's throw away. It's always been that way round here, the rich and the poor don't have to look very hard to see how the other half live.

When I got Rose's text, telling me she needed to talk

to me, I left the hospital quickly, and I could tell Ash was angry with me for bailing on her. In her head, something bad happened to Nai, that was the only explanation, she couldn't believe that her sister might actually have wanted to run away to a new life, might actually have planned it. And I understand why, I guess, but whatever it was that put her in that river, isn't it better to know that she wasn't abducted by a psycho?

Not that we know anything, really.

I sigh and cool my toes on the marble kitchen tiles. Rose's kitchen is so different from my kitchen, which is old and dark, with a massive noisy fridge and a washing machine you can tell is a washing machine. Rose's dad is rich, and her house shows it. You can't see the fridge or the washing machine or the dishwasher in this house. The telly in the living room is the size of a wall. The floor is cold under my hot feet, so I pace, back and forth, in and out of the open doors that lead into the garden, where Rose is sitting under a gazebo practising what she is going to say to camera, and back into the living room to look at my reflection in the giant telly. Repeat.

'Hello, love!' Amanda sees me as she comes down the stairs, shades perched on top of her swishy blonde hair. She dresses like a photo in a lifestyle magazine, coordinated and neat, little bit of make-up, a lot of hairspray. Actually I kind of like her, she seems kind, but I'm not allowed to say that to Rose. Maybe that's what comes from your mum dying when you were a little girl. For her, there will never be a mum as good as hers. For me, every mum seems like a vast improvement on mine.

Amanda's eyes are instantly drawn to my bare feet, and I clench my sweaty toes. 'How's Naomi doing?'

'No change, Amanda,' I say. 'Thanks for asking, though.'

I give her a lame little smile, careful not to make small talk. Rose hates it when she tries to be friends with us all, telling us to call her Amanda, but honestly, I'm grateful I don't have to call her Mrs Carter. It would be too embarrassing, when she is only just over ten years older than me.

'Want anything to eat, Rose?' Amanda calls out to her stepdaughter.

Rose doesn't reply.

'Because I'm going out. Want anything?'

Rose doesn't reply again.

'OK! Have fun!' Amanda never shows that she hates Rose, but somehow you know that she does. It stays in the atmosphere after she leaves a room, along with her expensive perfume.

The minute the heavy front door shuts, Rose shouts from the garden, 'Red, get out here!'

It's warm outside, even for late September, and Rose has set up her mirror, make-up and chair carefully on the outside table to ensure the best light.

'So,' I say. 'Who is the poor sucker you are seeing?'

'What?' Rose screws her nose up. 'Shut up, no one.'

'Well, what did you want to see me about so urgently then? I was with Naomi.'

'Not that Naomi knows,' Rose says.

'Rose, Nai's your friend!'

'I know that, dickhead. She's my friend till death, and I'm going later, aren't I? I just find it really hard to look at her that way. Don't you? Doesn't it make you want to scream to see her face all . . . ' She gestures, but she can't find the right words. 'Anyway, a new vid on the website before the concert is what we need, right now, so, here you go. Slap some lipliner on me, will you?'

'Rose,' I look at her holding out a pencil thing towards me. 'I don't know how to put lipstick on, for fuck's sake.'

'You don't have to, you just have to draw an outline round my lips and then fill it in. You can do that, can't you? It's basic colouring.'

The idea of being that close to her suddenly does my head in. It's stupid, we spend a lot of time hip to hip, side by side, why this makes me feel squirmy and anxious, I'm not sure. But I also know that she is not going to stop until she's got what she wants from me, and I don't have the energy to fight her.

'Fine.' I pull up a chair, pick up the lip pencil. It's not one of her usual colours, but instead a moist soft pink, more like the natural colour of her lips. I lean in, our faces close as I trace the outline of her lips, the rise and fall of the cupid's bow, the glistening fullness of her lower lip, which undulates under the pressure of the pencil tip. And as I draw, my eyes fixed on her mouth, I feel my chest tighten, and this feeling dragging up from my toes, building like bubbles, constantly rising and as they rise all I can think about is what it would be like to kiss her, to feel those lips with my lips and there is such an overwhelming sense of longing that I can't be near her for one single second more without giving myself away.

'Done!' I stand up quickly, walking away, the pencil falling from my suddenly thick fingers, so that it clatters on the table and rolls onto the floor.

'What, have I got bad breath or something?' Rose frowns as I shrug. She picks up her phone, tapping in the code and putting the camera on video mode.

'Are you ready?' I can't look at her just yet, I don't want her to look at me, I need this feeling to fade to something I can handle. 'Shall we get on with this? I told Gracie she could help me practise before bed.'

'Seriously, dude, what just happened?' Rose cocks her head at me. 'Why are you suddenly so salty?'

'I'm fine,' I lie. 'I've just got other things to do than be your make-up artist.'

'No you haven't.' Rose frowns. 'Red . . . ?'

I know that tone, it usually means the beginning of an awkward conversation.

'Rose, just leave it please,' I say. 'Not everything is about you.'

Which normally would be a lie, because more and more each day everything is about her, but not today. Well, not until just now, anyway.

'I know that. Look, I'm worried about you. We never talk about your stuff, and you've clearly got a shit-load of baggage. And you never ever unpack it. Why not?'

Rose closes her make-up mirror, and walks over to me.

'We talk about me all the time, how misunderstood I am, neglected at home . . . .' She is smiling, but under that smile is something serious, a promise she trusts me to keep. 'I know I can say anything to you, Red.' She picks my hand up and holds it to her cheek and in that moment I would like to combust and disappear in a flash of flame and ash, that would be perfect. Instead I just stand there, a lump of flesh and nerve endings.

'Do you know that you can say anything to me?'

'Course I do . . . ' I draw my hand back from her face and wonder if that's really true, could I really say anything to her? To the girl that has laughed in the face of pretty much any sincere declaration of love that has come her way? Not that I blame her for mistrusting the world, the world hasn't exactly given any of us a reason to trust it.

'Isn't there someone that you like?' she asks and I sigh, shoving my hands in my pockets, along with her phone. 'Because if there is, you should go for it, tell her how you feel, whoever she is. You deserve to be happy as well.'

'As well as who?' I ask her.

'I dunno, all the other happy people. Me, I'm happy, and Leckraj, he's seems pretty snazzy beans.' I can't help but smile.

'Well, that's because the love of his life is his guitar,' I say. 'Rose, when are we going to do your poxy video? Amazing though it may seem to you, I actually do have a life outside of being your flunky.'

'OK, OK! I'm just saying I think you are a great catch, and there are other girls that think so too. I know that Milly Harker in year ten constantly makes cow eyes at you and—'

'Rose, just stop it,' I say, more sharply than I mean to. 'Look. I don't want a girlfriend, OK? I'm not into that yet, I'm into the band and Leo and . . . y . . . you . . . ' I stumble over the last word. 'You might be able to fool around with some stranger while Naomi is in a coma, but I'm not like that.'

Rose watches me for a moment, then shrugs and turns back to her table, reorganising her make-up.

'So you are basically saying I'm a heartless self-centred cow,' she says, and I know I've hurt her, which hurts me.

'No, I'm just saying I don't want that right now, I don't think about it.'

'Well, you are about the only sixteen-year-old in the world who doesn't,' she says. 'Come on then, let's get on with the video. I'm ready for my close-up.'

Before I can press play, Rose's phone buzzes into life in my hands. A message from a number she hasn't saved. I read the preview before I know it.

Can't stop thinking about what we did today, when can we do it again?

'Hey!' Rose snatches the phone off me.

'Who is it, Rose?' I ask her. 'Who are you seeing? Is it Maz?'

'Jesus, Red, calm down! I hung out for a bit with this guy from St Pauls, we were just messing around, you know, nothing serious. Obviously he has fallen in love with me.'

The hesitation in her reply was tiny, but all the same it was there. Rose was lying to me, about a boy? Why would she do that? Why would she lie to the person she has told everything to? There's a tiny smile as she replies to the message, her cheeks flushed. She likes this one.

Anger flares in my chest and I go and put on my socks and trainers, cursing the laces.

'What are you doing?'

'I'm going, I told you, I've got to back for Gracie.'

'Red, please!' She stares at me. 'It will take three minutes, please. I'm sorry, OK? I don't know why you are so bothered. He's just someone I met at that drama camp thing Dad made me go to. Obviously he's crazy about me, obviously I've already gone off him. Please don't go feeling angry with me! I can't help it that I'm a sexual siren.'

She's joking, but I don't laugh. If it was some guy from drama camp, I wouldn't care. If it was 'some guy' she'd be reading out his texts and showing us his Snapchat feed so we could all have a laugh.

'I'm not angry,' I say. 'I'm worried.'

'Worried?' she splutters. 'Fuck, Red. You aren't my dad. Now can we please do this video?'

'Fine,' I say, picking her phone up again. 'You've got five minutes, make it good.'

I watch as Rose focuses her gaze on the lens in the back of the phone, talking to it like she was having a gossip with her best girly mate, except, of course, she doesn't have one of those. I watch her laugh, her eyes sparkle, her lips part as she talks her way through her ironic make-up tutorial, and she's funny and clever and looks destined for greatness. I think about how she walked into school this morning, like she owned it. How she took every step like she was conquering the world. And I thought, even as she looked for all the world like not a single person or thing could ever hurt her, how she was the most terrified and lonely person that I knew.

And that if I ever let anything hurt her, knowing what I know, then I couldn't live with myself.

23 June

 Rose
Sometimes I can't get it out of my head, you know what I mean?

 Red
What's up? It's late, you OK?

 Rose
The flashes, they come when I don't expect them. Out of nowhere, and I think I'm having a nightmare, but I'm not. Because it happened

 Red
Everything is all right. I'm here. Want a video of some kittens?

Click here to view

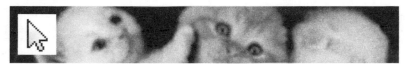

 Rose
You get me

 Red
Someone has to. Want me to come over?

 Rose
No, it will pass in a minute. Just be there OK? Don't go to sleep or log off, send me more videos

 Red
Dog stuck in a sofa

Click <u>here</u> to view

 Red
Sea otters holding hands

Click <u>here</u> to view

 Red
More

 Rose
More. I love you

 Red
I know

15

I get home and Gracie is sitting in the front room watching *The One Show.*

'Red!' she leaps up and into my arms, she smells of ketchup and school. 'Drums?'

'Sure thing,' I say, securing the weight of her in my arms by hefting her onto my hip. 'Where's Mum?'

'In the bath,' Gracie says as I carry her upstairs. 'Daddy came home! He bought pizza!'

'Yeah?' I grin in response to hers. 'Where is he?'

'Don't know. Think he went out again.' She doesn't seem to mind this, as long as he dropped off pizza. It's funny that, how little kids will love their parents no matter how shit they are, because they don't know any different. And then one day, one day that all changes. And that makes me sad. I don't want the day to come when Gracie isn't thrilled by twenty minutes with her dad and a pizza.

'Well, you go into my room and get ready, OK?'

I pause outside the bathroom door.

'Gracie's just going to play drums and then I'll put her to bed,' I call through the door.

There's no reply, but I can hear the movement of water and the tap running and then turning off. So I shrug and join Gracie. There is only one way I can practise at home which is for me to plug my headphones into the stereo and put mute pads on my kit. I sit Gracie on the stool and wire her up, sorting out some dirty hard rock, which is her favourite. I press play and off she goes, bashing the crap out of my kit. I watch her for a while, her eyes closed, this big stupid grin on her face. Really I need to spend more time with her, I need to make sure that she's doing OK; I mean she seems like she's doing fine, but how would she know if she wasn't? How would I?

She bashes and crashes and that moment with Rose comes back at me with a sudden thrill of want, and I feel guilty. Knowing everything she has been through. Everything she has kept secret and how much my friendship matters to her and yet I still want her. So badly that sometimes it hurts, deep in my chest.

'Where's Gracie?' Mum shouts from right outside my door.

'Here,' I say. 'I said I'd put her to bed.'

'Come on.' Mum whips the headphones off Gracie and drags her complaining to her bedroom.

'I wanna play with Red,' Gracie moans.

'I said I'd put her to bed!' I say again, but Mum doesn't answer me. Sometimes it's like I am actually invisible to her, or at least it would be if she didn't make such a concerted effort not to look at me at all. Instead I get the worst of both worlds, Mum both ignoring me and focusing her fury onto me with a red-hot laser beam at exactly the same time.

'Fine,' I say, closing the door hard enough to annoy her.

I sit on my bed and check my phone.

No one is online.

I feel restless and useless, stupid and stuck inside my own skin. Sort of like this painting I saw once on an school trip to a gallery, of a thin pale young man with bright red hair, sprawled on his bed, maybe even dead, and I feel vaguely like that. Like I'm a poet or an artist, destined to always be doomed in love. The feelings I had earlier around Rose, they knocked me off balance. Scared and excited me. But there are two very important reasons why I need to get over it.

I am just not Rose's type and there is no getting around that.

And even if I was, I know her. I know her in a way that no one else does, in a way that matters more than anything else. Which seems crazy, but it's true because, you see, I know the truth about Rose.

Apart from her, and the ones that did it, I am the only one that knows that when she was fourteen years old something terrible happened to her. Something that changed her forever.

Eight months ago . . .

She was still, suddenly. Like the light had gone out in her eyes, and she switched off, lost in some other moment from the one we were in. We'd been laughing, talking and watching stupid movies in her bedroom. Our friendship was fairly new, we were still circling each other, trying to figure the other one out, suss out what we meant to each other.

I can't even remember the movie we were watching, some crappy generic high school movie where the nerdy girl gets a makeover just in time for her first kiss.

'What's up?' I asked, and when she didn't reply I touched her wrist with the tip of my fingers. 'Earth to Rose?'

Rose blinked and shook her head, and I sat back on my heels as I noticed the tear that rolled down her cheek.

'Shit, what?' I was caught between wanting to reach out to her, hug her, and wanting to head for the door. But I promised myself that I'd never be the sort of person who looks away when someone is in pain, I'd never pretend that everything is fine when it isn't. So I made myself stay. 'Rose you can talk to me, you can say anything to me.'

She seemed to look at me for a very long time, so long I wanted to look away, but I didn't. I waited.

'If I tell you something, something I've never told anyone, will you swear, *swear* to keep it a secret?'

'Yes,' I said at once, and I meant it. Pledging my loyalty to her was that easy, whatever she would say next, it didn't matter as much to me as letting her know that I was her friend.

'That girl, with her prom dress and shiny eyes, and first kiss . . . ' She nods at the TV where the actress is freeze-framed in a moment of dreamy-eyed romance. 'That's not real, you know. You grow up surrounded by princesses, and pink things, and happy endings and romance, but that's not real. The world is brutal, and cold. That's what they should be teaching little girls, not this shit.'

'Yeah, I know.' Unease crept up my spine. This wasn't about a fight with her dad, something else was coming, I knew it.

'When I was fourteen, I went out with Martin Heaver. I liked him, because he was one of those boys that everyone knew. Showy, popular. Walked with a swagger and girls seemed to fancy him, even though he was clearly a class A fuckwit.' When she spoke she kept her eyes focused on the TV screen, that girl, lips parted ready for that perfect kiss.

'We went on a few dates, and it was nice. Cinema, romantic walks, he took me out for pizza. He was sweet and funny and I felt . . . totally happy, actually. The happiest I have ever been in my life, I think, which makes it sort of worse. I thought we were in love, everything seemed special. Shiny and golden, like it was covered in glitter. He was the first boy I kissed. It was perfect, at least that's what I thought. What a fuckwit. Now I can't think about it without wanting to be sick.'

'Rose . . .' I moved forward on my knees, sitting between her and the screen, making her look at me. 'Tell me.'

Her eyes met mine for a moment, and then she looked away again. That's when I realised she didn't want me to look at her, in that moment she didn't even want me to see her. So I switched off the TV and went over to the window, looking out at the street below, quiet and still.

'We'd been seeing each other for about two weeks.' She spoke again, voice flat and full of shadow. 'He kept telling me how into me he was, how serious. How he wanted to show me how much he cared. I thought he meant buy me a present or some shit. Jesus.'

Across the road a light comes on in a living room, and I watched two little kids chase each other round and round a coffee table. I could see her, sitting behind me, reflected like a ghost in the window, see-through. Like she wasn't really there, and in that moment she wasn't. She was somewhere much worse.

'He took me to a party; it was an older boy's party, back from uni, there was booze and weed. I drank a bit, smoked a bit, it was my first time but I wanted to impress him. And I thought he'd take care of me. We sneaked off to a bedroom and we were kissing and he wanted us to have sex. But I said no, I wasn't ready. Like they tell you to, don't be pressured into sex they say, don't they? Don't they, Red?'

'Yes,' I said. By then I knew what was coming next, I knew what she was going to tell me, but still I had to let her say the words out loud, because she had chosen me to listen to them.

'I told him I wanted it to be him.' She was looking at me now, I could feel her eyes on my back, so I tore my eyes off the happy family across the street and turned around. She held my gaze. 'But not then, that's what I said. Not in some stranger's bedroom, on a pile of coats when anyone might walk in. I had this idea about rose petals and candles. We went back to the party, we drank some more, smoked some more and he took a pill, and gave me one. He said, "This will bliss you out."'

Rose hesitated, her eyes dropping for a moment, and I crossed the room to her, I didn't mean to. I meant to stay where I was, scared of crowding her out, but when I looked at her sitting there, she looked so young, like a little kid. Like the little kids we all still are when nobody's looking. And I knew she needed someone to hold her hand.

'I trusted him,' she whispered, her hand clenching mine so tightly that her knuckles stood out, white and stark. 'After that I don't remember a lot, flashes sometimes. Faces in mine, lights going off. Pain. Laughter.'

'Oh Rose, I don't know what to say—' If she heard me she didn't acknowledge it, she just kept talking.

'I woke up, and I was cold. And I was sore,' she said. 'I was cold because I was naked, and I was sore because . . . because I'd been raped. I don't know who by, or how many. I don't know who was there, who watched, or if they took photos. And I didn't know what to do, so I got up, and I found my clothes and put them on. And I went home. Dad had been out all night; he didn't even notice that I hadn't been home. I had a bath. I thought, well, that happened, now I just need to get over it and move on. I thought I could do that. I couldn't even really remember what happened, after all. I thought it would be OK. I thought it would be like breaking up with someone, or doing something embarrassing or stupid. I really thought that's what it would be like.'

'Didn't you tell anyone?' I asked, and she shook her head. 'There was no one to tell, that's what it felt like. It was before the band, before I had you, Leo and Nai, and there just wasn't anyone I could talk to about it. Not Dad. Not fucking Amanda. Mum was gone. Everything was different, everywhere I looked and I got scared. People looked different, they looked meaner, they sounded louder. Every noise, like shouts in the corridor or a kettle boiling, made me jump. Suddenly I was frightened all the time, waiting for something terrible to happen. And Martin, I saw him at school and he walked right past me, like we'd never even met. I'd see him at break, hanging out with his mates, and sometimes they'd look over at me and I got it in my head they were talking about me, and I realised . . . I realised I didn't know which of them had . . . '

Rose stopped speaking, and her body shook and retched. She bent over, her head between her knees. My hand on her back, I waited until she could breathe again, talk again.

'I didn't say anything to anyone, I couldn't bear to. I thought, if I just close it in it will go away. Martin left at the end of that year, and his friends. So every day I'd just put on a bit more armour, you know? Layer after layer, until I felt safe again. That's what I decided to do, I decided to be this person, the person I am now. But the thing is . . . sometimes I feel so frightened. It's like everything is fine, good even, like tonight with you and then suddenly out of nowhere comes this feeling of . . . of dread. And I want to scream and run away and hide, but there's nothing to hide from, no place to hide. Because all the scary shit is inside my head. I just want it to go away. Why won't it go away, Red?'

'I don't know,' I said, 'I don't know.'

We stayed there, in her room, not talking, hardly moving until the lights that had switched on in the houses across the road were turned off again, and Rose's dad knocked on her door and said, 'Time to go home, Red!'

'I can stay,' I offered at once. 'Sleep on the floor.'

'No, you go.' Rose finally let go of my hand. 'I'm glad it's you I told, Red. You're the first real friend I've ever had since Mum died.'

After that night, if I had ever questioned anything that Rose said or did before, I never did again. Because I know now that everything she does and says makes sense to me in a way that maybe doesn't make sense to anyone else. People think she's confident, full of herself, an attention seeker who always wants to be in the spotlight, always wants people to look at her and hear her.

But the truth is Rose wants to be in the light, because she is afraid of the dark.

She wants people to look at her, because she is afraid to be alone.

She wants people to like her, because sometimes inside, she really hates herself.

And that is why I can never ever fall in love with Rose.

And why that look on her face when she lied to me about that text message today makes me feel so afraid for her. Rose can't take being hurt again.

Ashira
I'm going to find you today

Red
OK, why?

Ashira
I'll tell you when I see you

Red
Everything all right?

Ashira
Will probably be lunchtime.
Be somewhere obvious

Red
Can't you take control of a
satellite and track me from
space?

Ashira
Oh, I hadn't thought of that.
Good plan

Red
You're joking aren't you?

Red
Aren't you?

16

Leo is angry. I can see him across the concrete of the playground, leaning against a wall, arms crossed, face compressed like a clenched fist. And he's alone, which is rare for Leo, normally at break and lunch he's surrounded by people who just want to hang out with him, because being near him makes you feel kind of relevant. If he's managed to shake them off then that means they've been scared off by something he said or did, like back in the day when Leo was mostly known for being scary as fuck.

We were supposed to start rehearsing five minutes ago, Naomi's concert is only a few days away now, but only Leckraj and I turned up, Mr Smith arriving just after us with a box of donuts and a multipack of coke.

'Where is everyone?' he asked me. 'I thought I'd just drop these off as a treat, to keep you going. Concert's nearly here, after all.'

'I don't know . . . ' I look at Leckraj, who shrugs.

'I'll go and find them,' I say. 'I'll tell them you're waiting.'

'No, don't.' Mr Smith looked exasperated. 'I've got a lunchtime meeting, I can't wait, but Red, tell me you've got this. I've put a lot into getting the concert up and running for you. I let you lot get on with the music side of things because I trust you. You're not going to let me down now, are you?'

'No, sir. No, course not.' He put the box of donuts in my hand.

'You'd better not,' he said. 'I'm counting on you.'

'What the fuck is wrong with everyone?' I said, the moment he left the room.

'Don't they see every time we don't stick together, everything slides just a little closer to the edge?'

'I'm here,' Leckraj says putting his hand up, like he's in class.

'Yes,' I said. 'Well, don't go anywhere, I'm going to see if I can find them.'

'Red!' he called as I got to the door.

'What?'

'Can I have a donut?'

'What's up?' I ask Leo as I approach. He sees me and his head drops like a little kid that's been caught out. 'Leo, we get thirty minutes max at lunchtime to rehearse and that's mostly all gone now, the concert is almost here, Smith is freaking out and Leckraj isn't ready! What happened to you?'

'Nothing.' Leo shrugs, and the way that he spits out that one word reminds me that what seems like a lifetime ago he used to be this big scary kid in my year that I'd never dream of speaking to, let alone as frankly as I just did.

'Don't tell me that,' I say. 'It's me, Leo. It's your mate,

Red. Tell me what the fuck is going on. Why didn't you come to the hospital last night?'

'I went, but it was late. I couldn't get into her ward. So I stood outside for a bit. It was better than going home.'

'Wait, what?' He's not angry, he's sad. Leo is hiding away from his entourage because he is sad. 'Dude, what happened?'

'Aaron came home last night, earlier than we thought. It was a fucking shower of shit. Mum got upset, he got angry.' His face is clenched tight shut. 'It was bad, but like I say, when I got to the hospital, I couldn't get in. I didn't want to go home. Fuck.'

'Right.' I reach for something to say, a way to identify, but can't find any because this part, where your violent brother gets out of jail, is the part where what I know and understand about life, and what Leo knows and understands about life, part ways. We are both sixteen, we both like the same music, we both like the same films, we can chat bullshit about almost anything all day long, and go quiet when a girl we fancy walks past, but I have never lived what he has lived through with Aaron.

'So . . . '

'So Mum freaked out, like I knew she would. Got all up in his face, telling him that while he lived under her roof he lived by her rules and shit.' Leo shakes his head. 'I tried to tell her, just leave it. Just let him be, but she was all like, he's not coming back here and dragging you into his bad ways.'

He bowed his head, rubbing his hands over his face.

'Aaron lost it. Broke up the place. Smashed up her stuff, told her she'd better not talk back to him if she didn't want to . . . '

'Fuck,' I say. It does sort of make band practice sound unimportant.

'Mum was in his face the second he walked in the door,' Leo added.

'So it's your mum's fault, then?' I say, thinking of Leo's mum and the way she pretends to be strict but how she can't stop smiling while she watches him play, and how she'll make him his favourite tea when she knows he's feeling down.

'No!' Leo's eyes flash. 'I'm saying, she's got to see that it's got to be different now he's back. She's got to get her head round that, or it's going to be shit for all of us.'

'I think she's just trying to look out for you . . . '

'I know what she's doing!' Leo springs off the wall and begins to walk away. 'But she shouldn't, I can take care of myself. Look, I'm sorry, Red, I'm not really into rehearsing today.'

'Leo, wait.' I grab his arm. As he jerks away a phone springs out of an unzipped pocket, and skitters across the tarmac, but he doesn't notice as he stalks on back towards school.

'What the fuck?' I pick it up, a shitty little Nokia. The screen is cracked but it's still working. I know Leo, I know he loves his iPhone and all his tech, so what's he doing with this sim-only piece of shit? People only have phones like this if they have smashed up their good phone and can't afford to replace it, or if they are up to no good.

A burner phone, that's what they call them on TV. A phone you can do a dodgy deal with, or have an affair via and no one will be able to tie it to you. The only reason I can think that Leo would have this would be to do with Aaron, but Aaron's only been out five minutes and this looks knackered. I unlock it, and click through the menus: no texts, no call records. I go to the contacts list, ten numbers, that's all, but one jumps right out at me because it ends in 887.

Taking my phone out I click on a number and compare the two. They are the same.

So why does Leo have Naomi's number in a burner phone?

I am the first out of class on purpose, scrambling from behind my desk on the first metallic note of the bell, taking up position by the gate that I know she always leaves by.

For a minute all is quiet and still.

Then the building erupts with a crawling swarm of life desperate to be out of there. Kids tumble past, shouting, talking, singing, fighting. A few of them I know, a few of them I don't and not one of them is Rose.

Ashira walks past, her head down, earphones in, expression carefully neutral. And then at the last minute she shoots me a look, jerking her head to behind this old garden shed the caretaker keeps his stuff in.

'So what's this about?' I ask as she pulls her earbuds out.

'Nothing from Twitter,' she says. '238 retweets, and nada. It's nothing that anyone has seen.'

'Fuck, so what now?'

'Well you've got tattoos, right?'

'How the fuck do you . . . ' Shit, I remember taking a photo of them soon after they were done. Ash has been in my cloud, too.

'After she vanished, I just had to check out whether or not you guys knew anything, for myself.' She says it as casually if she's been checking out my Instagram.

'Ash, that's so fucked up. You get that, don't you? Just because you can do this shit, doesn't mean you should. You could hurt people, real people. You could get into real trouble. You understand that, don't you?'

Ash just blinks at me and I see that she really doesn't understand that. Either that or she doesn't really care.

'I like your tattoos,' she says, breaking eye contact. 'They look good on you.'

'I . . . well . . . thanks, I guess.' This girl, she is constantly wrong-footing me.

'Anyway, Twitter is too random, we need to focus our energy on experts, and then it hit me – we can go to the place you got yours, it's a start. Maybe they recognise the style, maybe they will have a lead. What do you think?'

She smiles, and it's an almost sweet, hopeful smile, and a kind of off-kilter artificial intelligence fixed grin at exactly the same time.

'Fine,' I say. 'Sure, whatever you think, you probably already know their address, so—'

'But I need you to come with me,' Ash says.

'Why?'

'Because I don't like people.'

'No kidding,' I say.

'I mean you're OK.' She shrugs.

'Same.' I shrug back. 'Ash . . . ' I hesitate. 'Have you thought any more about the chance that she might just have run away with a boy?'

'Yes,' Ash says.

'And?'

'And if she was in love with someone who presumably loved her back so much she wrote songs about him, where is he now? She's in a fucking coma, where is her Romeo? If it had just been a boy, a nice kind boy who loved her, he'd have brought her home. But he didn't. Whoever it was kept her away from her family. And now? Where is he now?'

I think about Naomi's number in Leo's burner phone. Could there be any way that he was that secret love? Nothing about that seems possible. But nothing seems impossible any more either. Keeping it tucked in my pocket I say nothing to Ash. I need to ask him about this myself.

'You're right,' I say.

'So you'll come with me to the tattoo place, we can go now?'

'We could, it's just . . . ' I look over her shoulder, searching the crowds.

'I thought you were with me on this,' she says, insistent, standing a little bit closer to me than I'm comfortable with. 'I need you.'

I find the way she looks at me kind of scary, like she thinks I can solve this for her, but I'm the last person that can. Still I want to try.

'We'll cut class after break tomorrow, go then, yeah?'

Ash nods, grudgingly. 'Are you coming to the hospital today?'

'Later probably, I've got this thing . . . '

Ash doesn't bother to hear the end of my sentence, she speeds away, ear buds in before I've even finished speaking.

What I can't tell her is that I'm standing here like a total prick, waiting for Rose because I haven't seen her all day. And I miss her.

*

Rose is almost past me, disguised in the crowd, when I see her.

'Oi, dork!' I call out and she stops, her shoulders dropping. Was she trying to sneak past me?

'Oh, hey.' Rose half waves, her hand at her waist.

'Walking back?' This is not a question I normally ask her. Normally we just walk back.

'Yeah, I guess.'

'Where were you at lunch? The concert is only a few days away you know, and suddenly half the band's gone awol. It's important. It's for Nai, and Mr Smith has got a lot invested in this. I don't want to let him down.'

'I know.' Rose stops for a moment. 'I know it's for Nai. It's not like I don't care, Red.'

'Sorry.' Suddenly I feel completely exhausted, utterly tired. 'I just want it to be good. For all of us.'

'I know, sorry.' Rose doesn't look or sound sorry, she looks like she wants to be alone, which is so unlike Rose, it's scary. 'But really I know what I'm doing, I don't need as much rehearsing as you guys. It's you and Leo that need to bring little wossisname up to speed.'

'Leckraj,' I say, feeling like at the very least the kid deserves his name.

'Yeah, him.' Rose fidgets, like she has somewhere to be.

'So where were you?'

'Around,' she says. It's warm now, and her fur coat is slung over her shoulder, her shades low down on her nose. A sharp spike of anger pushes its way through my chest and I do my best to ignore it. Stay calm, don't spook her.

'With that guy, the one that texted you? Was it Maz?'

'Jesus, Red, chill. I mean we are friends and everything

but I don't have to share my daily itinerary with you. You know, sometimes you are a bit much.'

Her words are so unexpected they take me by surprise, turning me inside out in an instant. She's never spoken to me that way before, and it hurts, it really hurts. Stupid fucking tears sting my eyes, and I don't want her to see that so I don't reply, I just slow down as she walks on, leaving me behind, blinking until the moment's passed, and I'm just left feeling gutted. The other kids around me pretend they haven't noticed, dropping their eyes and nudging each other as they pass us by. I stop just before the bridge, looking down into the dark water and remembering that dream.

'Fuck, sorry.' Rose has come back. She speaks with a smile and a laugh and an it's-only-me-dicking-around expression on her face.

'It's fine,' I say, uncertain, shy of her.

'Well come on, then.' She walks a few steps and looks back at me. I don't know why I'm not moving, not walking, not following her, like I always do and then the words come out of my mouth.

'What did you mean?' I ask, even though I don't want to.

'What do you mean, what did I mean?' Rose sighs, she knows what I mean.

'That I'm too much sometimes?'

Rose flings her head back, her shoulder bunching in exasperation.

'I didn't mean anything, I just . . . I just want something that's private, OK? Something I don't have to share with you and Leo.'

'Fine,' I say. 'Except . . . '

'What?' She takes a step towards me.

'Well, just tell me about this guy, not everything. Just something.'

'Why, pervert?' Rose starts walking again, and I try with all my might to just stand still and let her go, marching off to disappear amongst the buses and cars, but I can't. I even run a little to keep up with her.

I hate myself sometimes.

'Because I don't want you to get into something you can't handle,' I say. 'It's one thing getting drunk in the park, it's another ending up in the back of a squad car. Or disappearing from school with fuck knows who.'

'Ugh, Red, it's called being a teenager,' Rose sighs.

'It's not, though, is it?' I say. 'Who else has been down the nick this week? Or spliffed up in the stationery cupboard, or wherever? Look, you've been through some really heavy shit, Rose and—'

She shoots me this steel-trap look that clamps my mouth shut.

'Oh poor damaged little me, can't cope with my life and now I'm going off the rails, if only I had a knight in shining armour to save me! Is that what you're thinking?' She shakes her head. 'Except that's not what you are, Red, you aren't a knight in shining armour, you are just a loser, riding on mine and Leo's coat tails. You think you know me, but you don't. You don't know me at all and honestly, I'm getting kind of bored of this bullshit act of yours. How dare you tell me how to live my life when you don't have the first clue how to live yours?'

It is like I am looking at a stranger, there is nothing in her expression that I recognise, and something new, something I have never seen before, not even on that first day that we were thrown together and told to form a band whether we liked it or not.

Contempt.

For the first time ever, Rose is looking down on me. What's happened to her? Why now?

'Rose,' I take a step towards her, 'I don't want to fall out with you over this, you've got to see that I'm just worried about you. I care about you.'

'I know.' Rose's expression softens but only a little. 'It's just before you worry about me, Red, maybe you should look in the mirror, you know? You got your own issues, babe.'

We walk on again, but it's different, like all the ease and comfort between us has turned into friction and difficulty. We don't fall into step like we usually do. I'm afraid to look at the water as we walk over the bridge, afraid in case somehow the river calls me to it, like in my nightmare.

Waterloo Road turns into urban side streets and then finally suburban avenues, and last of all the corner of Albion Street, my street. I pause on the corner for us to say the long protracted goodbyes that we normally do, but instead Rose just gives me a half-hearted smile.

'See you tomorrow!' She shrugs.

'Rehearsal at lunchtime, OK?' I call after her, feeling kind of pathetic when she doesn't reply.

I tell myself as I walk down my road to my front door, that none of this means anything, it's just one of those things, just a little blip in our friendship. Or maybe it's more than that, maybe it's the ripples from what happened to Naomi widening out in slowly disintegrating rings, still strong enough to shake and tilt everything that makes the four of us what we are, or what we were anyway. I tell myself that tomorrow everything will be back to normal again, but as I reach the front door, somehow I know that won't be true.

Standing here, in front of the chipped green-painted door with my key hovering over the lock, I know only one thing, and that is I don't want to go in. Dad's car isn't parked on the road, again. Heart radio is playing too loud in the front room, and somewhere inside Gracie will be building her own little bubble to keep it all out. I know what I should do, I should go in and see my little sister and hang out with her and give her some normality, but what if I am not it, not normal?

If I go in now, Mum will still be sober, maybe she will be able to look at me, maybe she'll look at me like she used to when I was Gracie's age, with this soft smile and big eyes like everything I did and said was a wonder. Or maybe the second she catches sight of me her expression will sour, her eyes will cloud over and whatever it is in the world that is too hard to face sober today, it will be my fault. And the truth is, it really hurts. It hurts me when she looks at me that way, because I miss her. So badly.

So I don't open the door. Instead I stash my school bag in the thick hedge that runs between ours and next door, taking the tenner that is supposed to last me the week and stuff it in my pocket with my oyster card and I turn around and run.

![Instagram] Photo of Camden High Street.

0 likes.   Posted Just Now

17

No idea where I'm going, or what I'm really doing, just that I want to be somewhere where I am not me, so I run as fast as I can, for as long as I can until my lungs burn and sweat pours into my eyes. When I look around I see I'm standing outside Vauxhall tube station, and I know exactly what I want to do.

I take the tube to Euston, until I'm thrown by the escalator into a station that's packed full of zombie humans, staring dumbly at the same departures board, waiting for the signal to move. I march through them, dodging in and out of the static crowds until I come out onto Eversholt Street.

And start heading for Camden Town.

I've been to Camden a lot in the last year with the guys. There was a time, a couple of years ago, when it seemed like somewhere important and exotic, where freedom and music existed just out of my reach, and getting there would be like finally getting somewhere. But the first time I came with Leo, Rose and Naomi I remember how scared I felt, like something terrible would happen to us, we'd get lost, or kidnapped, or drugged and wake up robbed and broken on a boat in the middle of the channel . . . but then we went and it was *nothing* like I imagined.

It was a tourist trap, full of stalls that sold tie-dyed tat and novelty hats, and theme pubs and people wandering around searching out some bit of identikit originality to take back to their boring little lives. People just like me.

And when I understood that I felt somehow powerful, somehow adult and in the know, and then nothing about Camden, from its litter-strewn streets to its packed pubs, scared me any more, and going there alone, that's the best of all.

Because nobody looks at the short ginger kid with a half-shaved head, nose ring and quadruple-pierced ear in Camden. Here that barely scratches the surface of weird. Here I can just breathe out and be me and no one gives a shit who that is.

I weave in and out of a mass of strangers, and I love that no one here knows who I am, and that no one in the world knows where I am. The air smells of beer and cigarettes, and is filled with the noise of traffic and shouts of laughter. I find my way to a basement bar called the Gin Bath, a place that works hard to look as grimy and dingy as it does. When I was standing outside Vauxhall tube that's when I realised their open mic is tonight, and it suddenly made sense. Now, normally-socially-awkward, sticks-out-like-a-sore-thumb me, doesn't even hesitate to walk in, because here I am no one, here I am invisible, and here I am allowed to be me.

It's almost as if I've inhaled a kind of drunkenness on my way here, cloaked myself in a sort of illusion of cool.

The guy on the door doesn't stop me, and when I order a Coke at the bar, the barman hardly gives me a second glance.

It's early still, not even six; when I check my phone there's no signal, no one can touch me here.

Gradually the bar fills up with people, a few musicians and all of their friends, until the sheer mass of people pushes me and my flat warm coke away from the bar, and into a corner near the stage. I lean against a grey and grimy-looking wall, fold my arms waiting for the first act. It's a girl with a guitar, because it's almost always a girl with a guitar, and sure enough she is followed by another girl with a guitar. They are talented, they can all sing and play, and it's kind of peaceful to listen to the sound of their voices entwined with the strings of the guitar, but it does nothing to my insides, it hasn't got a fraction of the guts and power that Rose has when she rips a tune out of one of our songs. But in a way it doesn't matter, not as much as it matters just being here, watching the audience made up of boyfriends and mates cheering and stamping their feet.

When the lights come up and music plays through the PA, I don't want to move, I want the half a centimetre of Coke in the bottom of my glass to last forever and the rest of my life that is waiting for me when it's done to disappear.

'I was watching you.'

I jump when one of the girl singers talks to me suddenly; I was so lost in being invisible that I almost forgot people could see if they looked. She was on in the middle of the bill, Danni Heaven, long straight dark hair to her waist, and pale, almost white, skin, a wreath of tattoos around her hips. Older than me, by a few years I think, and taller too.

Sometimes I really wonder when that growth spurt everyone else has already had will kick in for me.

'Bit creepy,' I say, with a lopsided smile. After all, here I am not sidekick Red, I am witty and brave, the kind of person who headlines their own life.

'Yeah, sorry, it did come over that way, didn't it?' She laughs, she thinks I'm funny. She touches her hair, and then her neck, and I follow the trail her fingertips leave. Is this really beautiful girl flirting with *me*? That can't be possible.

'I just noticed that you've been on your own all evening.' She speaks in smiles. 'And I've been with all my mates looking at you and feeling kind of envious. It takes some guts not to need to be with other people.'

'Maybe I just don't have any friends.' I smile, and fuck, *I* am flirting with this girl, me, suddenly I am a legend. If she turns on her heel and flounces off now it won't matter, and that's what excites me, the thrill of being able to push my luck and see how far it holds.

'I bet you've got loads of friends,' she says. 'I bet you are really popular. I love your look.' Her hand brushes against mine, she takes a step closer, her perfume is sweet, like vanilla. 'Listen, we're going on to a club? Want to come?'

'I can't,' I say, and then for some reason I sabotage my own chances in the very next breath. 'I've got school tomorrow.'

Red, you are a fucking coward.

'Fuck, you're at school?' Her eyes widen, her mouth making a big round 'O'. 'Oh my God, how old are you?'

'Sixteen.' I shrug. 'Sorry.'

'Fuck, and so cute, too.' She shakes her head, but she is still smiling and then she grabs my phone out of my hand.

'Here, let's have a selfie.' I stare dumbfounded at an image of myself with this girl's arm around my shoulder, as the flash goes off, burning the image on the back of my eyeballs. 'Well then, I'd better let you get home to bed as it's a school night, but here's a little something to remember me by.'

The next thing I know her mouth is pressed against mine, just for a second, maybe three, and I feel the sticky glue of her lip gloss and the sweet wine-scented taste of her breath, as she pulls away, tipping her head to one side to look at me once more.

'Come see me in a couple of years,' she says. It's as her hand slips off of mine that I see the tattoo on the inside of her wrist. Almost exactly like Naomi's but this time a triangle.

'Wait.' I catch her hand, and she smiles at me.

'Changed your mind, jail bait?'

'I just wondered where you got this cool tattoo?' The fingers of her other arm cover her wrist at once, and she frowns, drawing away from me.

'It isn't cool, it was a mistake, a big one.'

'But where did you get it? The thing is my friend, she has one a lot like it and so I . . . '

Her eyes widen, and she looks around, before putting her face very close to mine. This time there is nothing sexy about it, she is suddenly angry . . . and frightened.

'Tell your friend to run,' she hisses. 'Tell her to get far away as quickly as she can and hope they get bored looking for her. Tell her to run.'

She pushes her way through the crowd before I can ask her what she means, what she's talking about.

Run from what?

The house is dark when I get home. Creeping in through the door, I struggle to contain the energy that's fizzing and popping in every muscle.

One half of me is buzzed and wired, strong and invincible, and I can see a time, a few years from now, when everything will feel good, and in the right place and I will be where I should be, and who I should be. Like a dream, or a glimpse of the future, just for a second, but it doesn't matter, because a second is enough for me to feel . . . hopeful again. I hadn't even realised I'd stopped feeling that way, until feeling that way came back. And the other half of me is like, seriously, what the fuck?

What are the chances I'd meet someone with a tattoo like Nai's? What was she talking about when she said 'run'? Questions cram my headspace, each shouting for an answer, doing my head in. I shake them away. It's just me seeing connections to Naomi's tattoo where there are none. Me, spinning tales out of nothing. And I probably freaked her out, got too intense. After all, I do that. At least according to Rose I do.

I've got to get a grip, set up my own reality check, otherwise I'm going to totally lose it.

As I climb upstairs, Gracie's door is open, and she is curled up asleep on top of her bed covers, still wearing her school uniform. There is no one in my parents' room, which means Mum passed out early somewhere downstairs, and Dad isn't here again. I left her all alone while I was out disconnecting myself from this life, making a space just for me in the world. I'd left her to fend for herself, and I don't even know if she's eaten tonight.

Me, I'm close to getting out of here, a couple more years and I'm gone. But Gracie, she isn't anywhere near close, all she has is me. How am I going to fix things for her?

Opening my laptop I Google Danni Heaven, but all of her social media accounts are set to private, which is pretty unusual for a singer trying to build a platform.

I didn't imagine one thing though – she was upset, really upset, when I noticed that tattoo.

There has to be something that links all of this together. Something that links Danni to Naomi, and the only thing I think of right now is music. What if Danni has a crazy fan that attacked her and . . . tattooed her? I mean that sounds mad, but everything sounds mad right now. Maybe that's what happened to Naomi too, except we don't have any crazy fans, and most of the fans we do have are in my year, and I've got their phone number. Except DarkMoon.

I go back to DarkMoons's Toonifie playlist, wondering if somehow there might be a link here, maybe she/he has Danni's stuff on her playlist too. I skip through the ones that duplicate Naomi's list and look for newer ones. I can't find any Danni Heaven, although, unlike Mirror, Mirror, Danni is a Toonifie artist. Then I see something that makes my blood thicken and slow in my veins.

There's a Mirror, Mirror song here: 'Find Me, Before I'm Lost.'

Like all songs on Toonifie, the lyrics are right there,

under the track, and it annoys me more that the song this prick has ripped off is the one I put a tune to and sang for Naomi in hospital . . .

Except that's impossible. Because I took that song, those words from the notebook I found in Naomi's bedroom. The only two people in the whole world that know this song exists are Nai and me.

DarkMoon must be her boyfriend, then. That's it. That makes sense. This must be the person she ran away with. Maybe if I can find out who he is, I can find out what happened to her and where she's been, why she never got in touch.

Clicking on the song, I bring my phone to my ear, and hear an acoustic guitar. A melody that is incredibly similar to the one that I came up with for these lyrics unwinds in my ear. The guitar sounds a little faint even with the volume turned right up, the quality is kind of amateur, probably done on a phone. And then the vocal comes in and my heart rate increases. It's a soft, sweet, sad girl's voice, rising and falling, soaring and yearning, weaving in and out of the guitar, creating a poem of sound.

I know that voice, because it belongs to someone I love. I know every note and intonation.

It's Naomi. I'm certain of it.

This list was created on 22 August. When Naomi was missing. And then at last I get it.

DarkMoon isn't Naomi's boyfriend. It's Naomi.

Why the fake name?

Why not get in touch with us? Why not at least tell us where she is?

Unless . . . I reread the title of the song again.

'Find Me, Before I'm Lost.'

Naomi's fake internet ID makes no sense.

Unless she was trapped, and she knew she was being watched all the time. Unless she was doing all she could to get our attention, without attracting any.

Unless she was scared.

Reaching for my phone, I call Ash.

'What?' she answers on the first ring.

'This is going to do your head in,' I say.

Rose Carter Instagram
Posted at 11.03

'Sometimes you just have to let go of what everyone else expects of you and be who you want to be, do what you want to do, because real love is too much of a great thing to missed.' **64 likes**

Kasha: Drunk?

Sarah: Lolz. What's his name?

Leo: Does anything you ever say make sense?

Ben: Slut

Ava: Is that the hot AF guy from St Paul's with the shoulders? I ship that!

Holly: You look so pretty, babe. Who is your new Boo?

Jade: Love that look!

Ben: I've fucked that

Leo: Shut the fuck up, Ben, or I'll shut you up

Celeste: Dude, that hair is awesome. Product?

Beth: Rose, you think you are all that, but seriously, get over yourself, will you?

Ben: You are getting fat

Leo: Ben Akerman (tagged) you better stay out of my way tomorrow

Ben; What, is this post about you then, loser? No, didn't think so. Have some pride, dickhead

Leo: I'll see you tomorrow

Red: Rose (tagged) I've sent you a DM, did you see it?

18

Didn't sleep. Couldn't really, not with everything going on, like a big loud carnival band that keeps getting nearer and nearer and louder and louder.

I argued with Ash all night.

'We have to tell the police,' I said.

'Why?' she replied. 'All they will see is a teenage runaway who uploaded some songs to a music site. Big deal. No, that's not what we do. Not until I've had a look at DarkMoon. If it was Naomi, if she wanted help, she would have known that I'd look for her, she'll have left other clues.'

'If it was Naomi, and she wanted help, why wouldn't she just have emailed, or texted. Or caught a bus? Why wouldn't she just have come home?'

'This is why we aren't telling the cops,' Ash says. 'Because they are about as dumb as you are. I'll catch up with you at school.'

And then she hung up.

It seems pointless going to school with all this happening, I want to go and see Nai and ask her what happened, that's what I want to do. But I can't.

That's the other thing Ash told me, that Nai is out cold for another forty-eight hours at least, that the doctors took Max and Jackie aside last night and said, 'normally we would have expected a faster recovery, we try not to keep a patient in an induced coma for longer than a few days. The longer she is under, the more likelihood there is of permanent brain damage or no recovery at all. We think you should prepare yourselves for the worst'.

Just like that, that's how she told me, flat and monotone. Like it wasn't really real, and that's how I feel about it now, too.

So I'll get up and go to school, because honestly? I don't know what else to do.

'Did you put on fresh clothes?' I ask Gracie as I come into the kitchen, and find her sitting over a bowl of Coco Pops. She looks down at her crumpled uniform and shrugs.

'Come on, squirt,' I say, taking her hand and leading her back upstairs. 'Let's get you a clean sweatshirt at least.' Luckily there is one, and a fresh polo shirt, so I help her unbutton yesterday's uniform, telling her I'll wait outside while she gets some fresh undies on. She's out of her room very quickly, I'm not sure she bothered, but I don't think that matters when you are seven.

'Where were you last night?' she asks me as I lead her into the bathroom to wash her face and brush her teeth.

'What do you mean, where was I?' I ask vaguely. I'd sort of assumed that no one had noticed I was out. I find one of Dad's old combs at the back of the bathroom shelf, behind half-used bottles of various different moisturisers that Mum buys and gives up on week after week.

It's odd to find it there, dusty still with a little of his hair in it, like a relic. Like I really have forgotten that he lives here.

'I came to find you,' Gracie says. 'Mummy was having a nap, so I had some cereal and came to find you to play drums, but you weren't there. Or anywhere, I looked.'

'Shit.' I say the word out loud as I set to work, trying to make some kind of sense of her thick curly hair, a shade of red lighter than mine, which I think makes her a strawberry blonde.

'Shit,' Gracie agrees, and I stifle a laugh.

'Kid, I'm sorry, I had a bad day and went out, I shouldn't have left you on your own.'

'Well, Mummy was here.' Gracie points to the shelf where a pair of My Little Pony bobbles sit, entwined with yesterday's hair. 'Do those,' she says.

'I'll try,' I say, 'but you know hair-dos aren't really my thing.'

'Are you OK, Red?' she asks me. I scrunch one half of her hair into a bun, twisting it into a fist and then wind the bobble round it to keep it in place.

'Course I am,' I say. 'Why do you ask?'

'Because you look sad, and tired.'

I stop for a moment, and look at my sister, one half of her crazy hair screwed into a ball on the side of her head, the other exploding out of her head like a fireball.

'Of course I do, kid, I'm a teenager, it's in my job description. When I get home from school today I'll teach you how to have an existential crisis.'

'Awesome!' Gracie's eyes widen.

'There,' I say, admiring my handiwork. 'You look like a psycho Princess Leia.'

She stands on her tiptoes to look in the mirror.

'I like it, but I want hair like yours.' Gracie turns, reaching out to touch the shaved sides of my head.

'Mum would have a fit,' I tell her, pulling a face and she giggles.

'Red, can I play on your drums when I get home from school?'

Mum's bedroom door opens and I can see through the crack that the bed has been slept on, not in. No sign of Dad.

'You all ready, love?' Mum smiles at Gracie, warm eyes, soft voice and I know that she feels like shit because she doesn't remember what happened last night. 'Good girl.'

'Red helped me.' Gracie smiles at me proudly.

'Thanks.' Mum doesn't look at me. By now I should be used to the fact that everything she says to me is some kind of dig, but even so, it hurts. Almost as much as it does that the only person who noticed that I didn't come home last night until one in the morning, was Gracie.

'Dad go to work early again?' I ask, holding her gaze as she stands in the doorway, her hair going in all different directions, yesterday's make-up halfway down her face. 'Sometimes I wonder if he's moved out and just not bothered to mention it.'

My reward is to see her face crumple, as much as she fights against it. To see her bloodshot eyes tear up and her mouth compress into a thin unhappy line. I will say this for my mum, at least she refuses to let Gracie see her unhappiness and fury. At least when she is sober.

'Come on you,' she says to Gracie. 'Go and get your shoes on.'

I wait until Gracie is out of sight before I say something.

'She was asleep in her uniform last night.'

'I know,' Mum snaps back at me. 'She wanted to sleep in her uniform, and I thought what's the harm, she's only a little girl after all.'

'Mum, you know that's not true. You can't keep pretending everything is OK, it's not fair on her.'

'And why do you think everything isn't OK?' she asks me, her eyes stretching wider with anger.

'Because before Gracie had even eaten you were passed out on the sofa,' I say. 'Things are not OK, Mum, they're . . .' I can't find a way to finish the sentence.

She pushes the door shut. 'Don't you think that my life is hard enough as it is, trying to keep this house going, while your father runs around with his bit on the side, only coming back to get his washing done. Trying to protect Gracie from all of this vile nonsense . . . ' She gestures at *me*. I am the vile nonsense. 'Without you, *you*, trying to tell me I'm a bad mother? Like it or not, *sweetheart*, I'm the one you've got. And while you live under my roof, you better show me some respect.'

Her forefinger has found its way into my face, an angry jabbing weapon.

For maybe a millisecond I think about reaching out and taking her hand, and saying, Mum, please, I love you and I miss you and I am so worried about you, and what you are doing to yourself, and I'm lonely and I'm scared and I need you. Please, let me help you. Please help me. Because that's what I want to say, that's what was on the end of that sentence I started and couldn't finish. But instead the sparks ignite, and fury takes hold and it's not love I feel for her, but hate.

'I don't think you can call it your roof, when you don't

do a thing around the house except drink Dad's money and neglect your kids,' I say, elbowing past her. 'You look disgusting, you smell like shit. Everyone knows that you drink, everyone on this street, everyone at my school, everyone at Gracie's school, it's no wonder Dad doesn't want to come anywhere near you. I'll take Gracie to school today. For Christ's sake have a shower, and make sure you don't stink from every pore when you pick her up.'

I run down the stairs, grabbing first my rucksack then Gracie's, pulling her out onto the street and then slamming the door behind me. Somehow I know that at the top of the stairs behind a locked bathroom door, Mum is crying.

And I feel like shit, but that is how she makes me feel too.

Leo
Where you at?

Red
On way

Leo
Why late?

Red
Went out last night. Things got interesting

Leo
Went out where? With who? Player

Red
Camden. Met someone. Want to see a pic?

Tap to view

Leo
Fuck! Hot!

Red
Right? But that's not the interesting part. We need to talk

Leo
What happened?

Red
Not on here. In person

Leo
What? Why?

Red
Reasons. You OK?

Leo
Dunno. Aaron back to it already. Shit is going down

Red
How?

Leo
Dunno but he wants me involved

Red
He can't make you

Leo
Maybe he don't have to

Red
I've got something that belongs to you

Leo
What?

19

'Hey, Leo.'

I see him in the lunch queue at the front. Pushing in can get you punched, but I need to talk to him about the phone I found. About DarkMoon. I need to know he isn't hiding anything about Naomi. Ash said not to tell anyone, in case it's nothing, but I need to know. 'Leo, are you coming to rehearsal?'

'Yeah, I'll be there in ten,' Leo says, jerking his head at Kasha; popular, curvy, scary as all hell. 'I'm a little bit busy right now, Red.'

But I don't have time for Leo to set up his next conquest, especially when I know that Kasha isn't the girl he wants to be next to. 'Leo, I need to talk to you. It's important. Seriously.'

'Shit.' Leo turns to Kasha, leaning in closer. 'I'll catch up with you later, baby, yeah?'

Kasha gives him a maybe, maybe not smirk.

'Serious, Red,' Leo looks at me as we walk out of the dining hall, 'I was in there.'

'This is more important.'

'What now?'

I wait until we're outside of the main building, a corner reserved for kids who want to kiss or smoke, or both.

Fishing the Nokia out of my pocket, I hold it out to him.

'Shit.' He shakes his head.

'What's it for? Leo?' I ask him. 'Because it's weird, a kid your age carrying around a burner phone. And why do you have Nai's number on it? Was there something going on between you two? Do you know where she's been all this time?'

'What? Shit, Red, no!' Leo shakes his head. 'I don't even know what you're talking about. You think I've been hiding Nai away and not mentioning it? That's what you think of me?'

The look of hurt on his face catches me off guard, I'd never realised before that what I thought of him meant anything to him. It's a shock to catch a glimpse of Leo being just as insecure as the rest of us.

'No.' My hands fall to my side, and I shrug. 'Truth? I don't know what I think. Everything is so weird and out of whack. I thought I knew Nai, but I had no idea that she was planning to run, or whatever it was that was going on in her life that meant she had to . . . '

I stop myself. I'm still not ready to tell him everything about Nai's song on Toonifie yet. 'And Rose, she's distant and weird, like she's trying to shake me loose . . . '

'Not just you, me too,' Leo says. That look of hurt again, and suddenly I see why the sudden interest in Kasha, he's trying to forget the girl he's secretly in love with. I know that feeling.

'Something is going on with Rose,' I say. 'And you are

carrying a burner phone with Nai's number in it. So, I'm sorry, you're my friend, but right now? Anything seems possible.'

'OK,' Leo concedes, pulling himself up onto a low brick wall that surrounds what was supposed to be a memorial garden for a girl who killed herself a few years ago, but is almost always overrun with weeds. 'I get that, I guess. I get what you mean about Rose too. But that phone, I forgot I even had it. Aaron asked me to get it when he was inside. He'd get hold of a phone sometimes, and we could talk. Sometimes I'd take stuff in for him, stuff he needed to get by.'

'You mean you smuggled stuff in?' My eyes widen.

'It's rough in there, you need contraband to get respect.'

'Contraband, like . . . drugs?'

Leo doesn't answer and I can't believe I had no idea that this was what he was doing. Maybe he's right, maybe we are all just play-acting being friends. Real friends know everything about each other.

'Fuck, Leo, if you'd been caught—'

'I wasn't even sixteen yet, it wouldn't have been a big deal.'

There's no way I can explain to him that the idea of doing something so dangerous makes me want to throw up, so I don't even bother trying.

'That still doesn't explain why you had Nai's number.'

'Because the first night we were looking for her, before I knew that her phone was switched off and missing, I thought . . . I thought maybe she might pick up her phone if it was from a number she didn't know. So I called her. But it went straight to voicemail. I tried a few times. I thought I'd try again in a couple of days, so I saved the number but by then we'd found out her phone was awol, so I didn't bother.'

Everything he says makes sense, but still, Leo is one of my closest mates, and he had a secret phone. That doesn't feel right.

'Can I have it back please?' he asks, and I hand it over.

'If Aaron's out why do you need it?'

'Because playing in a school band ain't real, bro. It's kid's stuff. And I got to start getting real about shit.' He rubs both his hands over his closely cropped hair. 'Aaron needs me, and sometimes he needs me to be off the grid. Anyway, I'll chuck it now. Get another one. Look, we had a good year, with the band. Maybe the best year of my life, and I'll play the concert for sure, but at some point I got to own the fact that this isn't my life, and I can't pretend it is any more. Someone like me, having a career playing guitar? It's just not gonna happen, Red. It just ain't.'

'This is Aaron talking, not you,' I say. 'Don't let Aaron tell you who you are.'

Leo gives me a look that if I were anyone else would probably end in a punch, but it doesn't.

'All I'm saying is, don't throw away what you are good at. You are a great musician, Leo. Really great. Don't waste that talent.'

'Fuck Red, I don't really know any more. The guy Aaron hurt. He's been taking over Aaron's patch when he was away. And now Aaron's got to do something about him, hurt him even worse than before, you know? Otherwise he says he'll lose face and no one will deal with him. And he wants me with him when it goes down.'

'Hurt him worse than before? He nearly killed him

before so . . . ' It dawns on me what he's trying to say. 'Leo, fuck no. You can't go anywhere near that.'

Leo shakes his head. 'You say that like it's easy, like it's choose right or left, but it's not like that, Red. It's not like that at all. I don't want to get into that shit, but he's family, right? And he looks out for me, and I don't know many other people that do.'

'I do,' I say. 'Rose does, Naomi . . . Mr Smith . . . your mum, Leo! Please don't do something stupid—'

'I'm not fucking stupid,' he growls at me. 'I'm working it out.'

'Well, before you decide can I tell you some stuff?'

'Might as well, I'm not getting lucky with Kasha now.'

'That's her.' Leo looks at me. 'That's Naomi singing. So Naomi is this DarkMoon?'

'Yes, or else DarkMoon was with her when she was missing. No one else could have known about the song, and the title? And the tattoos. And I might be going crazy but I think I can see a pattern here. I think that at some point after Nai ran away she was . . . abducted, trapped, I dunno. Kept somewhere she realised she didn't want to be, somewhere she couldn't just leave, somewhere she couldn't call for help.'

'Mate, that's a big leap.'

'I know, but the song, the words . . . she sounds like she's crying.'

'If you listen long enough you can imagine anything.' Leo is not convinced. 'She ran away with a bloke, she didn't want to be found and she made up a new avatar, that's what this is. Maybe that went wrong, maybe she got drunk and fell in the river, maybe she . . . maybe she jumped. Either way, much more likely than your story. I mean, if she had the internet, why wouldn't she just tell us to come and get her?'

'Because maybe whoever was keeping her was watching her too, and she was afraid of getting caught,' I suggest. 'It's easy enough to spy on someone else's internet history. Mum checks up on Gracie's iPad; it's linked to her phone so she can use her apps and not get up to anything she shouldn't. And Dad put an app on it that tracks every keystroke. If someone was watching Nai, to make sure she didn't try and escape or ask for help, well then of course she'd be trying to get us to notice her without getting caught.'

I struggle to find a way to translate my hunch into something concrete. 'If she didn't want to be found, why would she clone her old playlists? Why would she make sure that if someone looked they would find a link between Naomi and DarkMoon. When you think about it that way, do I seem so crazy?'

'I don't know . . . ' Leo is wavering.

Looking over his shoulder, I watch a butterfly find its way in and out of the weeds, never settling for more than a second, and that's how my head feels, like the answer is there, but I just can't settle on it.

And then something. Something catches at my thoughts.

'Do you remember Carly Shields?' I ask him. 'The girl they made this garden for?' Leo looks over his shoulder.

'Yeah, I'm not likely to forget the girl that threw herself under a bus. She was in my brother's year, they even went out for a bit. He was different when he was with her. What's Carly Shields got to do with anything?'

'What if . . . ' I take out my phone and look at the school website. Every year for the last few years the leavers make a video, lip syncing to a song and post it on YouTube and the school website. I go back three years, then four and there she is.

'Oh my God, it's her,' I say, watching a group of girls strutting down the corridor syncing to Beyoncé. Her hair is different, dark and short, she's wearing glasses, and there are no tattoos on her bare arms, but it's her, I'm sure it is.

'Carly?' Leo squints at the picture. 'That ain't Carly.'

'No,' I say. 'It's Danni Heaven.'

'Who?' Leo looks at me.

'The girl I met in Camden, she had a tattoo a bit like Nai's and when I mentioned it she freaked the hell out. Leo, she used to go to this school. And Carly Shields was a bright kid, school star, swimming champ and pro-level harpist. Everything was going right for her, and then she walks out in front of a bus, why? Why would she do something so out of character?'

'Nah.' Leo shakes his head. 'You're adding two and two and making fifty-seven. Running away wasn't out of Nai's character.'

'Not before, but since the band it was.'

'Yeah, maybe.'

'Maybe I am wrong, but these three girls went to the same school. One of them is dead, and two have the same kind of tattoo. There's something there Leo, I know it.'

'What are you talking about?' Ashira appears out of nowhere.

'Why do you care?' Leo snaps, before he catches my look. 'Look, I'm sorry all right? Red is chatting shit again.'

'You mentioned Carly Shields,' Ashira says. 'The girl that threw herself under a bus. What's that got to do with Naomi?'

Was she standing around the corner listening to us? That girl is intense. I kind of like it.

'It's nothing. I was just thinking about Carly, and thinking . . . what if there was someone she'd been involved with who'd pushed her into what she did?'

'Like a serial killer?' Ash asks me, deadly serious.

'No, I mean there's something else going on here. Something big and . . . invisible.'

'Like the Illuminati?'

'The what?' I blink at her. 'What did you find out about DarkMoon?'

'Nothing. Well, I found out her account is a sub-account linked to another email, but that's locked up real tight. I can't get to it. But it is definitely Naomi singing. Definitely.'

Her eyes drop to her feet, and it's like we all feel it at the same time. This is real, not a game, not a movie. It's real. Fuck.

'Danni Heaven went to Thames Comprehensive too.'

'Who the fuck is Danni Heaven?' Ash asks me.

'A girl I met. I thought it was nothing, my head playing tricks, but she had a similar tattoo to Nai's. We should tell the police,' I say.

'Fuck that,' Leo adds helpfully. 'You two, you've tied yourself up in coincidences. Say this to anyone else, and you'll sound like nutters. Let it go, concentrate on getting Nai better, yeah. And the gig.'

I look at Ash and she gives me the slightest shake of her head.

'Maybe,' I say. 'Yeah, maybe, you're right. Maybe it is all in my head.'

'Will you come to the hospital tonight?' Ash looks at us both. 'Please.'

'Yeah, sure we'll be there,' I speak for me and Leo without thinking.

'Thanks. Um, Red?' She walks away a few steps, and Leo rolls his eyes. Shrugging, I follow her and stand there as she whispers in my ear. 'Carly Shields. Danni Heaven. I'll see what I can find out about them. I believe you. See you.'

I watch her walking away and wonder if having the nuttiest girl in London believing in me is a good thing or not.

'I'm not sure if I can come tonight,' Leo comes up behind me, 'Aaron wants me around.'

'Leo, don't do what he wants you to do. Don't fuck up your own life for him.'

'He's my blood, bro,' Leo says, fierce.

'Fine,' I say suddenly tired. 'It's your life, what's left of it.'

'Fuck you,' he says.

I give him the finger as I head back inside, calling over my shoulder, 'Hey, will you ask Aaron about Carly Shields?'

'No,' Leo says. 'He liked her, he's never got over that. I'm not going there. If you want to do this whole conspiracy theory thing, do it yourself.'

He's right, it is a crazy conspiracy theory, it doesn't make any sense when you say it out loud. And yet . . . I can't let it go and pretend that everything is normal, everything is OK. Nothing is OK.

As I go back into class I realise I haven't seen Rose all day again.

And man, I really miss her.

Today 15.36

> Hey Kasha seen Rose today?

Read 15.37

Today 15.37

Nope.

Today 15.38

> Anyone know wotsup with her?

Read 15.38

Today 15.39

Naaaah, no one seen her 😮

Today 15.40

> Well, if you hear anything, give us a shout K?

Delivered

20

As the lift doors slide open, and the sharp-edged scent of the ward hits me, I come face to face with Max and Jackie, and they are both crying.

'What happened?' I ask. 'She isn't . . . is she?'

'No,' Jackie tries to smile, but sobs instead, 'No, darling. It's just she isn't improving as fast as they'd like her to. It's not good for her to stay under like this for so long and . . . it's just so much to take in. I'm sorry, don't you worry. It's all going to be OK, I promise you.'

She cries again, and hugs me, and I stand there for a long time breathing her in.

'Ash won't come home, she doesn't want to leave her side. Will you keep an eye on her for me?'

'Sure I will,' I say. I'd say anything to make her feel better, but that's an easy promise to keep.

She kisses my forehead, and instead of pulling away I lean into it for a moment. A mum hugging you, I miss it.

Stepping aside, I give them my best attempt at a reassuring smile as they get into the lift. Ashira is standing outside Nai's room, her head pressed against the window.

'Hey.' I stand next to her.

'Hey,' she says.

We stand there, side by side, looking into the room at this beautiful vivid girl we know so well, trapped in suspended animation, and I can't think of a single thing I can I say that's going to help. So I do something instead, something that somehow feels right. Reaching out, I take her hand and hold it. Ashira doesn't move, she doesn't say anything. All she does is squeeze my fingers briefly.

She takes a deep breath and lets go of my hand and turns to me.

'Right, so Carly Shields didn't have a tattoo, at least not the day before she died which is as close as I can get. I mean I could get into her autopsy report if I really wanted to, but that feels a bit wrong.'

'Yeah, a bit. But how did you find out the other stuff?' I ask her.

'School newspaper archive. She'd been in a swimming meet the day before she died and won it. And played harp at the school concert that evening. I mean I suppose that she could have had a tattoo somewhere we couldn't see in a swimsuit, but if both Naomi's and Danni's are on their wrists . . . Do you think we could try and meet Danni and ask her more?'

She hands me a printout of an old local newspaper clipping, and I catch my breath. I'm looking at a photo of my dad, in his role as school governor, putting a medal around Carly's neck as she stands there in her swimsuit. It's not a good photo, it's a bit grainy and he's got more hair. But it is definitely my dad. I stare at him with that dead girl, and something creeps down the back of my neck. It's one fuck of a coincidence.

'I don't think she'd want to talk somehow,' I say slowly. I don't tell Ash that it's my dad in the photo because seeing him there feels something like a secret I'm not ready to tell yet. 'But I'll try. I'll request to follow her on Instagram and send her a message.'

'OK. Will you go in and sit with Nai for a while?' Ashira's voice is flat, she's run out of places to look for her sister, even though her sister is right there in front of us. 'I'm going to get a Coke, want one?'

I nod, and steel myself before opening the door.

Every time I see Nai, she looks a little better. There's still a patch in place over one eye, but the skin around it looks less swollen and full of blood. If I squint and try and filter out the tubes and dressings, it's almost like she is sleeping.

'I heard your song,' I tell her. 'It's really good, Nai, your version is much better than mine. I wish I knew when you recorded it, and when you set up this weird account and why. Can't you just wake up, and tell us all what happened to you? How about that? How about you just wake up and tell us everything and then we can get back to normal. Get back to how things were. Since you left, it feels like everything is falling apart a little bit. Leo's getting all caught up with Aaron again, and Rose . . . Rose is just, I don't even know. She's somewhere else. If you wake up now you can play with us in the concert next week, it is on your birthday after all. Come on, Nai, just wake up and talk to me.'

The machines keep whirring and beeping and she keeps breathing and everything stays exactly the same, because of course they fucking do. She's sedated. I pick up her hand and I'm glad to see the bruises around her wrist have faded at least, unlike the tattoo. Lifting her arm higher I move so I can see it properly. It's strangely beautiful, with so much detail it would have taken hours and hours of sitting, a lot of pain for a girl who didn't like tattoos. Maybe I will take a photo of it to the tattoo shop, like Ash suggested. It can't hurt. Taking my phone out I take a couple of snaps, but every time I try, my shadow, cast by the harsh strip lights in the ceiling, falls across it, blotting out all the detail. Flipping the camera into selfie mode I gently hold her wrist up and take a snap, sitting out of the way of the light.

Fucking hell. It's as plain as day, and totally obvious. Suddenly I see it.

'What?' Ash sees the look on my face when she comes in.

'Here, look.' I pass her my phone and she looks at the image.

'What do you see, Ash?'

'Oh my God . . . ' Ash stares at it, and then at me. 'I see numbers, loads of them. Numbers and letters, dashes and dots all layered one on top of the other, but they are there. I think this might be code, Red. I mean it could be, it could be almost anything . . . and one of the things it could be is code.' She looks at me. 'I've got photos of the tattoo on my phone, so I'll just reverse them and . . . Red, this is massive.'

'Do you really think it could be?'

'I need to go home,' she says. 'If this is code then I can start trying to find a way to decipher it, this could be the answer to what happened to her.'

Her black eyes are bright and full of heat, like she has a fever.

'Ash, just wait a moment. There must be, I don't know, a hundred different characters in that tattoo, maybe more. It *could* all just be random,' I say. 'A private joke. Even if it was code, there are a billion different combinations of everything that's in there, it'd be impossible to make sense of them.'

'Well, I've got to try,' Ash dismisses me and starts to leave but I follow her to the lift, standing in front of the call button. The look she gives me is truly terrifying. Ash is not a girl who likes to be told what to do.

'Ash, I'm worried about you,' I say, and for some reason that surprises her, diminishing the fire in her eyes a little bit.

'You are?'

'I'm worried that you . . . me, we're going a little bit mad. Trying to find clues like Shaggy and Scooby and really there's nothing going on at all.'

'Am I Shaggy or Scooby in this scenario? Because I've always seen myself as more of a Velma.'

I smile, I like the way she can be so funny, even when she's being so serious.

'Either way, I don't want you to go home and lock yourself in your room, and drive yourself mad trying to make sense of a bunch of stuff that's senseless. I know right now it seems impossible, it is impossible, but Nai will wake up, and when she does, you'll need to have a life too.'

'Maybe,' Ash agrees. 'And thank you, for worrying about me . . . that's nice. But I have to do this. I don't think that the numbers are random. I think there has to be a pattern, there has to be, because if no one can read it, what's the point of it, the point of all that careful design.

It means something to someone. I can run it through some software I have at home, handy for cracking passwords. Will you stay with her?'

'Maybe I could help you?' I offer.

'Seriously doubt it,' she says, shoving me out of the way as she pushes past into the lift.

When she's gone, I feel weird. And I'm not sure if it's a good weird or a bad weird, so it's probably best not to think about it at all.

I look at my friend, oblivious to it all.

'Well,' I say. 'I asked you to talk . . . and you did.'

21

It's late when I leave the hospital, and I keep waiting to hear from Ash, though I guess whatever it is she is doing is going to take a long time. It's hard not to think of her, lost behind that veil of dark hair, chasing meaning, and I feel kind of guilty. It's me that sees all these connections, me that's feeding her need to discover a truth that may not be there. Me that looks at an old photo of my dad in a newspaper and wonders if he is involved. And every secret fear I have seems so possible.

And then I'm walking home, and the city looks like it always does, the other people on the street walking past me like I don't exist, like they always do, and that spider web of tangled thoughts in my head seems like a bad dream that's banished by daylight. I stop for a moment on the bridge, and breathe in the heat and exhaust of the traffic, as the lights of the cranes along the Thames shine in the dark looking like new planets just arrived in our solar system.

It's time to get a grip, Red, for your sake and Ash's. For Nai, and even Rose who seems to have checked out, without anyone making sure that she's OK doing whatever it is she is doing, with whoever it is. The trouble with Rose is that she is so much more fragile than she looks, and sometimes, just sometimes, I think she actively wants to get broken.

Are you OK?

Taking my phone out I send her a message and wait, but the minutes go by and there's no sign of a reply. At least she knows I'm thinking about her, that's something. Tomorrow, I'll make sure I find her, I'll make sure she's all right, because she needs to know that whatever happens, whatever she does or says, I'll always be there for her.

You can't help it, when you are as in love with someone as much as I am with her.

When I open the front door I see Mum sitting at the table. I can tell right away that she has been crying. I stand for a moment in the hallway, just hanging there with no idea what to do.

She sees me, and smiles. 'Fancy a cup of tea?'

'Er, yeah, thanks,' I say, even though it's warm and I'm thirsty for something like the bottle of Coke I know is in the fridge. I take a seat at the table, dropping my bag at my feet. 'What is this about?'

Mum puts a mug in front of me and sits down.

'Where's Gracie?' I ask.

'At her friend's for tea,' Mum says, resting her hands on the table. I notice for the first time they are raw, and dry. White pieces of skin flake and peel off her fingers and the backs of her hands. Her fingernails are bitten down until they are ragged and red. Mum's hands make me feel sorry for her.

'I wanted to say thank you,' she says, carefully, each word a tiptoe. 'For this morning. For getting Gracie up and getting her changed. I was a cow to you, I should have said thank you.'

'That's OK.' I watch her, warily. Her eyes look swollen and dark. 'I don't mind helping out.'

'Look, love,' she says. 'I know things haven't been right for a long time. And I know they are getting worse. You see it. You see that your dad hardly ever comes home any more, and that I . . . ' she hesitates. 'I know I'm not perfect and I suppose I take it out on you.' She looks at me then, and for a second I remember how when I was very little I used to sit on her lap and she'd put her arms around me and whisper stories into my hair.

'It's OK,' I say again, and I want it to be true, so badly. I want to make it OK for her. 'Things have been hard, and you've been managing on your own. But you've got me.'

'And it's no wonder you find everything so hard. What with Naomi and . . . I don't know, everything. There really hasn't been anyone there for you. Dad's . . . well he's not around much and I give Gracie much more attention than I do you, and that's not fair. I don't show you how much I care about you, love you. And that makes me a shit mum.'

I sit back in my chair, and of all the things I thought I might feel, it's relief that floods through me and threatens tears. Relief that my mum maybe doesn't hate me after all.

'So I thought I'd sort a play date for Gracie so that you

and I can really talk. Sort out a few things, get things back on track. Would that be all right?'

'That'd be great, Mum.' But when I go to hug her she backs away.

'If you really want to help me . . . ' Her eyes fall away again, her hands withdraw from mine. 'It's just that I worry for you, love, the way that you seem to be heading. I look at you, your hair and your earrings and how the band takes up so much of your life, and then I think about your poor friend Naomi and what happened to her, and I just . . . I get that you feel left out, overlooked. Who can blame you? But now it's time to stop. Time to go back to normal, please. Please. You're embarrassing me with all this nonsense, and I've got enough on my plate.'

Normal, that word slices through me, leaving an open wound.

'I am normal,' I tell her steadily. 'This *is* normal for me, Mum, don't you get that? I'm not trying to hurt anyone, I am just being me.'

'No.' Mum shakes her head, back and forth, back and forth. 'No, I don't get it. And you have to see that the way you are, it won't make you happy, love. It won't make you accepted or successful. For all your life, you will be on the outside, drawing attention to yourself for all the wrong reasons. And you think I'm saying this because I hate you, but I'm not. I'm saying it because I love you, and I don't want your life to be full of pain. Please, Red, please. That eyeliner, the black nail varnish. It's a costume, and it's the wrong one. You look like a kid who'd take a gun to school and start shooting. *Please*, Red, please listen to me and take out your nose ring, the earrings.' She wrinkles her nose. 'Please just be normal again. It might be the only thing you are good at, but *stop attention seeking.*'

'Mum,' I say very carefully. 'If I was attention seeking you'd know about my tattoos. Three of them.'

'Your what?' Her jaw drops.

'If I was any good at attention seeking you'd have noticed that I used to smuggle food into my room and eat in secret until I got so fat I could hardly walk without being out of breath, at *ten years old.* But you didn't notice, and you didn't notice when later I stopped eating and stayed in bed all weekend because I was too exhausted and depressed to get up. You didn't notice because it's all about *you.*'

'Three tattoos?' is all she manages to splutter.

'You want me to be normal, do you? But if I do that,' I say, my body springing up and out of my seat before I realise it, my mouth speaking before the thought appears in my head, 'if I could do that then what would I do about my drunk mother, about the woman who disgusts my dad so much he can't stand to be in the same house as her? Who passes out on the sofa without feeding her seven-year-old? Because if that's *normal,* normal can fuck off.'

I run up the stairs, up past Gracie's room and into mine, turn my music on loud, take the pads off the drums, grab my sticks and play until my arms hurt, my head hurts and the neighbours are hammering on the walls. I keep going, lost in the music, nothing more than the rhythm of crashes, high tops and bass drums and series of syncopations, and then when every one of my nerves twitches in time, when every cell leaps to the beat, I stop and switch the music off. She didn't even come up here to shout at me.

Gracie must be home. I can hear Mum running her a

bath, and singing 'Five Little Ducks' to her as she plays with the bubbles. She's in perfect mum mode. As soon as she is in Gracie's room reading to her, I go to get some toast. It seems like Mum is still sober as she sits on Gracie's bed, bathed in pink light. Her voice sounds normal, and she isn't hurrying over the pages in the story, desperate to be downstairs in the company of her TV and a drink. But then I see a tall glass of cold clear liquid, bubbles rising, waiting for her on the bannister. At least she's made herself wait for Gracie to be in bed, I suppose that's something.

I'm waiting for the toast to finish when the back door opens and Dad is standing there. Shirt crumpled, stubble. He looks fat and tired.

'Hiya,' he says.

'You're home?'

'Yes, don't sound so surprised, I do live here.'

'So I've heard.'

'You all right, school all right, working hard? Any news on Naomi?'

'Dad,' I grab the toast as it pops up, thinking about that photo of him with Carly Shields in her swimsuit, 'If you were ever around, you'd know.'

'Look, I know I'm away a lot right now. But I'm doing it for you and Gracie. And Mum. Putting a roof over your heads, paying for all of the stuff that you want.'

'Mum misses you,' I say. 'She gets upset. We know there is someone else, Dad.'

'There isn't,' Dad insists. 'It's work.'

'Fine,' I say. 'Whatever. Honestly, Dad, I don't care if you work with her or you are fucking her, I don't give a shit.'

Dad blinks, the muscle in his cheek tensing and I know he wants to shout at me, but he doesn't and that tells me everything I need to know.

'Well, I'm home now. I'll pop up and see Gracie and then how about a Chinese, hey, the three of us? You can have what you like, no lecturing you on ordering too much.'

'I've got toast.' Dad looks both disappointed and then relieved. I take my chance. 'Dad, you've been a governor at the school a long time haven't you? Since before I started even. How come?'

'You really want to know?' Dad asks me, frowning. 'They had this initiative to get more business people and local politicians involved in the school's development strategy. Full spectrum initiative, they called it.'

'Oh, I see.' I smile like that's interesting. 'Do you enjoy it?'

'Yeah.' Dad relaxes. It's rare that I ask him about his life, and he likes it which makes me feel bad about my next question.

'Do you remember Carly Shields?'

Dad sits up a little. 'I don't think so,' he says.

I press him further. 'Carly was the girl that stepped in front of a double decker. Killed herself right outside school.'

'Oh yes, of course.' Dad pushes his glasses up his nose. 'Terrible tragedy, she was having a lot of problems but kept them to herself. Very sad.'

'You gave her a medal for winning a swim meet right before it happened,' I remind him.

'Really?' He gets up. 'Well I don't recall that. I'm knackered, too tired to eat. I think I'll turn in.'

It's not even eight o'clock.

The same cold feeling that crept down the back of my neck finds its way into my veins. He remembered Carly, so why won't he say more?

'Dad?' Calling his name makes him start in the doorway. 'Look it's bad here. I'm worried about Gracie. Stay here tonight please. Stay with Mum, please. Don't bail on us.'

He stares at me, like he doesn't really understand what I'm saying. So I try again.

'You are the grown-up, Dad. You are the adult. It's not fair that you get to run away, do whatever the fuck it is you're doing and leave me and a seven-year-old little girl to pick up the pieces. You are the man, so act like one.'

'Now listen—'

'Oh fuck this.'

'Get back here, Red,' he shouts up the stairs after me, just as Mum comes out of Gracie's bedroom.

'He's back for his laundry,' I tell her.

The house is quiet, I stand on the landing and listen. Dad is here, I can hear him snoring in the spare room. Slowly I make my way down the stairs and go into the living room, his laptop is on the sofa. Holding my breath I open it. There's a password required to get past the lock screen, which I don't know. What would Ash do, I wonder? I think about Dad and the things he cares about and I give it a go. The 9th of May is Gracie's birthday, so I try Gracie09. I get it right first time.

But the smile freezes on my face as I get onto his desktop. Because the first thing I see is a photo of a girl, round about my age, maybe a little younger. A girl I don't know, a girl who doesn't know this photo has been taken of her. She's pretty, laughing, long, slender arms and a Hello Kitty backpack. I click on the photo and zoom in; she has dimples when she smiles. There doesn't seem to be anything attached to this photo, no document, no names. Just this pretty young girl, being looked at from a distance.

He has loads of folders on his desk and I click through them one by one. I'm knackered, my eyes are burning with exhaustion, but I keep looking, hoping not to find anything. And then I do. I find a folder full of encrypted files. I try the main password again but nothing. I try three or four times and I can't get in. I stare at the files, they don't have legible names, just a series of numbers – it's impossible to guess what's inside. But it crosses my mind.

The way Dad looked at Rose's legs.

The fact he was helping Naomi apply for Duke of Edinburgh right before she vanished.

Him putting that medal round Carly as she stood there in her swimsuit.

The smell of different women that's always there.

I don't want to think that those files contains photos of more girls. Girls like this one. Girls that I know.

I don't want to think it, but I have to. I have to know.

Rose
Awake?

 Rose
Red?

 Rose
Red?

 Red
Yeah. Groggy. Dude its late/early. K?

 Rose
I know but I'm sorry.

 Red
Wha?

 Rose
Was a bitch to you, don't know why

 Red
S'OK

 Rose
Nah. Not

 Red
Honest, I'm just glad u r OK. R u OK?

 Rose
Yaaasss. You are my Bae

 Red
😨

 Rose
Did you go see Nai today?

Red
Yah

Rose
I don't know why I can't go see her. I don't know . . .

Rose
. . .

Rose
. . .

Red
What? Something up? Talk to me

Rose
Nothing. Things good. All good.

Rose
Talk tomorrow?

Red
KK

Rose
Keep slaying the world, you rule.

Red
So see you tomoz?

Rose
YaaaSSS! ❤ ❤ ❤ Movies and junk food round mine?

Red
Sure thing

Rose
❤ ❤ ❤

22

I wake up to a message from Ash.

> Cutting school, been up all night. No progress, need more time. Will be at the hospital.

> OK, I need to see you, I reply and wait. Need to ask you something.

She's too busy to ask me what. I see the ellipsis rise and fall a few times and then disappear. Last night felt like a very dark and twisted place, but today the sun is up and nothing I saw or read last night feels as bad or as dangerous. It's amazing how much better I feel today than yesterday, and there is one difference.

Rose.

I can't explain how it felt to have her words and emojis filling up my screen again, after twenty-four solid hours of streak-breaking silence. Until my phone began buzzing under my pillow I hadn't really slept, I'd just closed my eyes and chased thoughts around and around in the dark.

But then Rose was there again and everything felt better.

The sky is clear and the day is warm and I love the look of London as it spreads out over the river, the London Eye standing out against the blue sky, the old buildings and the new jostling side by side, looking like they exploded from the earth at exactly the same moment, instead of over centuries. I love this place where everybody from everywhere can come and be whoever they want, and no one gives a toss. I love it because in this city you can never feel like you don't belong somewhere.

For a few minutes everything feels good. Like it used to before everything hit the fan.

Leo is waiting for me on the corner by the tube, and next to him is Rose. She's leaning against a lamp post, studying her phone and Leo is looking in the opposite direction. Together, but not together.

'Hey,' I say as I approach, feeling suddenly shy, like I used to back in the early days of the band.

'Mate.' Leo peels himself off of the wall, but Rose stays slouching until I am almost there, and I wonder if she can tell that there's heat in my cheeks and sees the way I find it impossible to look at her full on.

'Band's back together again.' Rose smiles when she finally looks up from her phone. 'Look, I'm sorry I went awol for a couple of days. Girls' stuff, you know. But I am fully on it now, OK? Fully here. I want to do well, for Nai, and I don't want to let you guys down. I love you both.'

Leo and I exchange a look, but it's Leo who shrugs.

'We've all let it slide a bit,' he says. 'I've been stressing about shit, too.'

'I know,' Rose touches his arm, 'I'm sorry I bailed on you. I'll do better, I promise. Forgive me?'

Something passes between them that I pretend not to notice. They could have said all of this before I arrived, but they waited until I was here to witness it, why?

'Red's coming over tonight,' Rose says. 'Movies and popcorn and shit. Wanna join?'

Leo glances back at me and I half shrug. Inside I am willing him to say he can't make it. I want her to myself for a few hours. If I can just get a few hours alone with her then everything will be all right.

'I can't make it,' he says. 'Aaron wants me around.'

'For what?' Rose asks, the crease between her eyebrows deepening in concern.

'Numbers.' Leo shrugs and tries to look like it's nothing, but it's not.

'Numbers?' Rose looks at me.

'He's going to see this bloke about this beef they've been having, and he wants numbers to have his back. I'm his right-hand man, he says.'

He lifts his chin as he says it; he's proud.

'Leo, seriously, don't go with him. His issues aren't yours,' I say. 'Guy's been out five minutes and he's already looking for trouble. Maybe that's just Aaron, but it doesn't have to be you.'

'Listen, Leo,' Rose says, surprisingly gently. 'Please.'

'Why do you care, anyway?' Leo asks her, but it's not an angry question. It's a serious one, one that hopes for a very particular answer.

Rose glances at me and I see uncertainty there. Leo isn't going to get the answer he wants, and the terrible thing is that part of me is glad.

'Because you are a mate, you dork,' she says. 'Plus if you get caught doing something you shouldn't right before the concert, we're fucked, aren't we?'

Leo rolls his eyes, like he doesn't care, but I know that he does. I feel it, exactly the same way he does. I know that if Rose told him she felt the same way about him as he does about her, he'd do anything for her.

'Did you ask Aaron about Carly?' I ask him.

'Nah, man, he's not been in the mood for nostalgia, know what I mean?'

'Carly who?' Rose asks.

'Carly with the remembrance garden,' I say.

'Oh that Carly,' Rose sighs. 'I thought you meant a *girl*. Why are we talking about Carly?'

'Red met a girl in Camden though,' Leo adds, deftly distracting her and Rose's mouth drops open.

'What? What happened!? Red? Have you suddenly got a sex life?'

'No,' I say firmly, enjoying seeing that the news, as over-reported as it is, annoys her little. I need to some-how talk to Aaron, even if he is the last person I want to be in the same room with. 'Look, Leo, can I come back with you right after school, chat to Aaron? And then I'll go to Rose's after. When you have to go off and be a number, whatever that is.'

Leo looks me up and down.

'I dunno, Red, you and Aaron aren't exactly . . . com-patible and things are a bit heavy right, now. You know. The thing with the numbers.'

'Jesus, I just want to chat to him, not marry him,' I say. 'And maybe me being around will give you a reason to not get involved with Aaron's shit.'

'Your funeral.' Leo shrugs and grins at the same time.

It's kind of menacing.

'Good plan,' Rose whispers as Leo jogs across the street to catch up with a mate. We've just turned into Dolphin Square, joining the steady stream of the hundreds of kids all heading in the same direction. 'Now you can keep an eye on him, make sure he's not getting mixed up in any heavy shit.'

And when Rose lags behind, to get in on the gossip going down between Kasha and the girls, Leo hangs back and waits for me.

'It's good you're hanging out with her,' he says. 'You can make sure she stays out of trouble. Try and find out who she is seeing on the side.'

'On the side of what?' I ask him.

'Us, doofus,' he replies.

Leo's estate is always bursting with life, twenty-four hours a day. This time of day it's little kids playing out after school, filling the green spaces under the trees with screeches and laughter. Bigger ones ride their bikes and skateboard over a makeshift obstacle course and down flights of concrete steps, risking the wrath of the old people on the bench making the most of the September warmth. Music drifts out of open windows, washing flutters on the tower block balconies, rising up as high as you can see towards the sky.

Leo's place is on the eighth floor of a long low block, with walkway balconies that overlook the patches of greenery below.

The lift is noisy and slow and smells of weed.

'So, you're all in for being Aaron's henchman?' I ask Leo eventually. He talked all the way home, about the usual shit we talk about, like how the rehearsals went, football, girls, music and then as we came into his estate, he just stopped. Not a word.

'That's not what it's about and you know it,' he says.

'What it is about, then?'

'People respect him, Red,' he says. 'For who he is, and what he's done.'

I manage not to say anything for one floor.

'For selling drugs and hurting someone so badly they nearly died?'

'That geezer, he knew the risks. It wasn't some civilian he went for. It's war out there on the streets, man.'

I want to laugh, but I'm not totally sure how he'd react if I did, and he's not wrong. In this last year there has been a stabbing in London every single week. We had an assembly on it at school. They are fundraising to put a metal detector in the main entrance, which is stupid because there are about ten other ways in and out of the building.

'You are a civilian,' I say instead. 'You're a guitarist, a really good one. It's not worth it, is it? Getting involved with that shit?'

Leo gives me a long hard look as the lift shudders to a stop.

'Red, you just don't know what my life is like. You don't even really know me.'

'Red!' Leo's mum beams when she sees me. 'You staying for dinner?'

I'm the archetypal good friend, the one that mums are always pleased to see because it means that their kids aren't getting into gang war on a Wednesday night after school.

'Thanks, Mrs Crawford,' I say, 'but I can't.'

Her face falls, and I see the worry etched into it. Leo

doesn't know how lucky he is having a mum who gives a shit.

'Tell me, how is Naomi? I called Jackie, but she's not picking up, I don't blame her, I can't imagine what's she going through.'

'No change yet,' I tell her, and she hugs me suddenly, whispering in my ear.

'It's good to see you, I haven't seen you for such a long time. You keep an eye on my boy for me, OK? I worry about him.'

She releases me. 'Well, nice to see you anyway.'

I nod a silent promise that I will do my best, but what if Leo's right? Maybe I don't know him at all.

Aaron is sprawled in a chair in the corner, one leg hooked over the arm, gaming. On the screen several CGI gangsters fall under the sweep of his machine gun.

'Yes! Bastards!' he shouts at Leo. 'Come here, bro, watch me slay these mothers . . . '

'Hi,' I say. Aaron slings me a sideways glance.

'What the fuck is that?' he says looking at me. 'Oh fuck, now I'm dead!'

'I'm Red,' I tell him. 'Leo's mate.'

'Red's in the band,' Leo adds, as if he doesn't quite want to own our friendship.

'Oh yeah,' Aaron says, looking me up and down. 'That's a strong look . . . Red.'

'Thanks,' I say and he smirks. He didn't intend it as a compliment.

'So how are you doing?' I try for small talk.

'A lot better if you stopped talking to me,' he says, dropping the console as he loses another life. 'Can you take it away, bro, please?'

It takes me a second to realise I am the 'it' he is talking about.

'Would you mind if I asked you something, about when you were at Thames Comprehensive?' I wish I didn't sound so fucking preppy, but I do. Thing is, even if I tried to go gansta I'd still sound stupid.

'Well, I tried not to be there so much, know what I'm saying?' Aaron laughs and Leo looks at his feet.

'Do you remember Carly Shields?'

Aaron looks at me with a tilt of his head. 'Yeah, nice girl. Proper sweet. We were something for a while. Yeah, that was sad.'

I'm surprised by the softness in his voice, his smile.

'Aaron!' Leo's mum calls from the kitchen.

'Fucking what?' Aaron calls back. 'Always nagging.'

'Look, it doesn't matter,' I say getting up. 'Leo, come with me to Rose's?'

'Yeah, maybe . . . ' Leo starts to get up.

'I was gutted when she topped herself, real sad. She was good, you know? Made me feel good for a bit. Then she dropped me, just like that and started getting well weird.'

'Weird?' I try not to sound too interested.

'She went mental, like a few days before. I remember that. Totally changed.'

'Really? How?' I ask him.

'Came to me, and asked me if I knew anyone that would kill someone for her. Said she had money.'

'*What?*' Leo questions.

'You calling me a liar?' Aaron challenges him at once. 'I was like, no, girl, but now I come to think of it I should have taken her money, she wasn't going to be around to collect much longer.'

She changed. She was scared. She wanted someone dead . . .

'Sounds like she went nuts, then,' I say. 'Coming, Leo?'

Leo gets up, but Aaron's hands stop him.

'Nah, Leo. You're not going anywhere bro. We got plans.'

'You don't need me, though, do you?' Leo shifts from one foot to the other.

'Don't matter if I need you or no, you're my brother. You are coming.'

'Right.' Leo sits down. 'Sure.'

'Message me later,' I say.

'Sure.' For a moment I wonder if I should stay, if maybe just being around might help. The last thing I want to do is let Leo cross a line he can't come back from, when I could have stopped him. 'I could—'

'You, freak, are not needed,' Aaron tells me. 'You bring me down, mate.'

'Leo?' Leo won't meet my eye. 'Tell you what, I'll call Rose and she could come over here, and we could do something, the three of us, yeah?'

'Red,' Leo shoots me a dark, warning look. He's telling me that hanging around isn't going to work out well. 'You gotta go.'

Still I don't move, I can't. Until Aaron springs up out of seat and is suddenly standing over me, his face in mine.

'My bro told you to get lost, so do one, before I take you outside and show how to get downstairs the quick way.' I see the spittle in the corners of his mouth, the mass of tiny red veins in his eyes, and I am shit scared.

'See you later, Leo.'

He looks at me, but doesn't reply. He doesn't have to, his eyes say it all.

23

Rose's street is quiet, all the children safely ensconced inside air-conditioned houses or playing in walled gardens. Cars that cost twice as much as most people earn in a year sit outside, polished and pristine, and if there had been anyone on the street, they would have looked at me twice, just so they could mention me at the next neighbourhood watch meeting. Her house is quiet, no sign of her dad or Amanda.

I feel a little guilty for not being with Naomi, but Ash says even she isn't going today. She seems to have been up all night crunching numbers that probably can't be crunched. But I need to be here, because, you see, Rose is more than a person, she is a place where I don't have to think any more, where I can just be me for a while, and it's just a relief. I hadn't realised how knackered I am, how much I just want to chill out for a bit.

And Rose's house is the perfect place to do it; it's a haven of order, insulated with cash. They have a woman that comes in four times a week, so there is never a pile of washing on the stairs, or unwashed mugs in the sink.

It always smells nice, and there are cut flowers in vases in the hall and the living room and upstairs, too.

As soon as we arrive, Rose goes upstairs to get changed, and comes back down in a baggy T-shirt and leggings, bare toes, her long hair loose,. I watch as she sets about making us bacon sandwiches, and gives me mine with a Coke in a glass bottle and a stripy straw.

'So are you worried about Leo?'

'Kind of,' I say. 'Yeah. Aren't you?'

'I'm not sure. He's got a dark side, you know.'

'What do you mean?' I look at her.

'I mean sometimes he's not the Leo we know. Sometimes he gets mad.'

'With you?' There's an edge in my voice, and Rose catches it.

'No, of course not with me. I've got him eating out of the palm of my hand. I just see it sometimes. He feels trapped.'

'I don't know,' I sigh. 'My parents hate me. You hate your parents. It's kind of normal hating your family, right?' I think how Leo looks more than pissed off though; he looks sad and afraid. And the way he acted, like he had to be someone else for Aaron.

'How is home?' she asks me, halfway through a mouthful, and I shrug.

'Not like here,' I say.

'Here's not like here when *they* are here,' Rose tells me. 'You know what it is, I think they are planning to have a baby, either that or she is already knocked up. Whenever I walk into a room, they stop talking. And you know, I don't actually care if they have a baby except I care about the poor kid, growing up with those fuckwits. There should be a law or something, a test that stops you getting pregnant if you don't have the intellect to sufficiently parent a human.'

'A what now?' I laugh.

'What?' Rose laughs too.

'That didn't sound like you, sounded like you've been reading a newspaper or something.'

'Are you saying I'm thick?' Rose peels the crust off her sandwich and throws it at me when I shrug, laughing, her eyes sparkling. This is the Rose I know, relaxed, carefree, not putting on a front for anyone. Not that distant, distracted and mean girl I saw the other day.

'Rose, can I ask you something a bit . . . disgusting.'

'Ha, yeah, go on.' Rose's eyes light up.

'My dad . . . he's never . . . I mean has he ever tried to . . . '

Rose keeps nodding, waiting for me to get to the point.

'Do you think my dad is a pervert?'

Rose laughs, 'Definitely.'

'Shit really, what's he done to you?'

'No, no, Red! I don't think your dad is a pervert. He's never done anything to me other than treat me pretty nicely, and try to look down my top.'

'Oh God!' I cover my face.

'I'm joking, you moron,' she laughs. 'Your dad is like all dads. Mortally embarrassing, but not evil. I'm pretty sure of it.'

'You are?' I must look worried because she puts her arms around my neck and hugs me.

'Stop talking nonsense and focus on the issue in hand,' she says. 'Movies downstairs or up?'

I look at the big telly on the wall in the living room, and

think of being alone with Rose, on Rose's double bed.

'You decide.'

'Up. Far more private.' She grins at me, as she grabs a multipack of crisps, and a couple more Cokes.

'You're not drinking tonight?' I ask her.

'I can go twenty-four hours without booze,' she says. 'I'm not your mum.'

Somehow when she says it, it seems funny.

Before the movie starts Rose turns off all the lights, except for the little fairy lights she has wound round her headboard and some scented tea-lights on a shelf over her bed. I sit on one side of her bed, folding a pillow to support my neck, keeping one foot on the ground. Before she died, my nan told me that in Hollywood, in the old days before sex scenes and nudity were allowed, there was a rule that even married couples shown on screen always had to have at least one foot on the floor, so that they couldn't possibly be having sex. Although of course it's totally possible to have sex with one foot on the floor, if you are really determined, at least that's what my nan told me. Anyway, tonight it feels safer to follow that rule myself, to keep myself in check, to not say anything that might give away what I'm feeling right now, which is something like being hideously tortured and deliriously happy at the same time.

'Your favourite.' Rose clicks through iTunes and sends a movie to the TV. '*The Breakfast Club.*'

'Really?' I grin at her. 'You don't even like this movie.'

'It's not like I don't like it, it's just I prefer my cinema to be dated after the birth of Christ, but you say it's the pinnacle of all teen movies ever made, and so I'm going to give it another go, because I'm sorry for being a dick to you and it seems like the least that I can do.'

'It's fine,' I say, trying not to beam at how perfect this moment is.

'So you're saying I was a dick, then?'

'No, I'm saying that you weren't like you, for a bit. And I worry about you, you know that.'

'I do.' Rose hugs me briefly. 'But you know what, I'm OK. I am A-OK. It's like I am finally getting to understand who I am at last. I'm becoming a woman, Red.'

I snort Coke down my nose. She whacks me on the head with a pillow and I think maybe, just maybe, this is the first time in ages that I have really been perfectly happy. If I could hold on to this one moment, and never let the clock tick on, I would.

We watch the movie, or at least I watch each frame flicker by as I try to take in how I am feeling, and fail.

Molly Ringwald does her lipstick trick, Judd Nelson punches the air and as the credits roll, Rose grabs my arms and pulls me further onto the bed.

She does do that. I'm not imagining it. I'm looking at her now as she pulls me over into the middle, where she is waiting, lifting my arm and tucking her head underneath, so it is resting against my shoulder.

Shit, what does this mean?

'You know what, Red,' she says. 'I really think you are the best person I know.'

'Oh shut up,' I say, glad that she can't see the goofy way I'm grinning at the ceiling.

'I really do, though.' Her head tips back and I crane my neck to look at her. 'You never give up on me, or let me down. No matter what fucking stupid thing I do or say, and that's really special, you're really special to me, you know that, don't you?'

She rolls over so that her chin is resting on my chest, and my heart stutters and strums, the weight of her against me makes my body fizz and pop, her arm across my stomach stopping me breathing. This really is happening, I really am on Rose's bed, and she really is lying almost on top of me. 'I worry sometimes that you don't realise how amazing you are,' she says, and her voice is so soft and gentle.

It's too much, I shift, turning onto my side, and tipping her onto hers so that we are lying lengthways facing each other, still just a few centimetres apart, but at least this way I can breathe. This way I might not die.

'I'm really not amazing,' I say. 'I'm just me.'

'Shut up,' Rose says. 'You're brilliant, funny, kind, loyal, the best drummer in the known universe, and the best dancer, and I love the way your hair falls in your eyes, and you wear those stupid checked shirts every day and . . . Red, there's something I swore not to tell you, but I can't keep anything from you . . . '

Time slows down to a trickle and then stops. I see the lights reflected in her deep blue eyes, and the tiny hairs of her soft cheeks and the way her top lip bows when she talks, and the silver scar just to the left of her mouth, and it's like everything in the universe, since the beginning of time has been reaching just for this moment, this one perfect beautiful moment.

And I don't need to hear what she is going to tell me, because I know, that something incredible has happened, and Rose feels like this about me.

She loves me back!

It all feels so right as I reach out, placing my hand on her waist, so destined to be as I lean over and kiss her. And even as it happens I see her eyes widen and her shoulders stiffen and feel her pull back as my lips meet hers, and yet my lips meet her lips, and for the smallest, fraction of a moment I am kissing the girl I love and I know what it feels like to be perfectly happy.

And then she's gone, and there is just cold air where she was.

When I realise what has happened I see Rose stand up, staring at me, eyes wide with horror. When time starts again, it's racing.

'Fucking hell, Red, what the fuck?' she says. 'What are you doing? Why are you . . . I didn't want that, why do you think I'd want that? You of all people. trying to force me to—'

'No. I wasn't, I didn't . . . I'm sorry . . . I thought . . . ' Everything rushes on without me, I'm still on a time delay, my mind, my body still catching up with that look on her face. Whatever I thought, I thought wrong. I got it really, really fucking wrong. Oh fuck, oh no, oh shit, oh fuck.

'I'm so sorry.' I spring off the bed. 'I'm sorry, I just thought . . . it just felt . . . I thought you wanted me to kiss you. I'm so sorry, Rose.'

I've never seen Rose look so upset, so angry, her face is patches of red and white.

'Oh my fucking God, Red, you are supposed to be my best friend! The one person in my life who isn't trying to fuck me. I trusted you, I felt safe with you. And . . . and . . . and . . . '

'I *am* your best friend.' I move towards her. 'Rose please—'

'NO! Don't come near me.'

I'm afraid to move or speak. I have no idea what happens to me after this moment.

'If you were my best friend you wouldn't have done that, Red. If you were my best friend you'd know . . . '

'Know what?' I say, dropping my head, knowing exactly what she is going to say before she says it, because I am her best friend, and I do know her better than anyone, and despite all that, I fucked this up about as bad as it can possibly be.

So I know what she is going to say next.

'Red, I'm not like you. I'm straight. I don't kiss girls.'

Ten months ago . . .

Our first gig was fucking brilliant. We'd only been together a couple of months, but we had all these songs, enough for a set – and you know what? We sounded good. Not like a school band, not like a bunch of kids. We were tight, we were awesome.

Playing together back then, the four of us, we couldn't put a note wrong. It was like we'd been destined to meet our whole lives and change the face of music history with our radical sound. It felt fucking exciting is what it felt like.

We were friends by then, laughing and joking. Hanging out, exchanging banter. I was part of it. I'd never felt like that before. Part of something so good.

Nai got us our first gig, she hustled and pestered this guy with a back room in a pub until he said we could play, but he wouldn't pay. We didn't care. We didn't even care if no one came. It was just the word, gig. Our first proper gig.

The room was empty when we set up. There was no lighting, just a couple of bulbs swinging from the ceiling. It didn't matter, it was our first gig. Fuck we sounded great. The floor was deserted, but we didn't even notice.

All we noticed was each other. Eyes meeting, feet tapping, bodies swaying, lips moving. I haven't ever had sex, but it would have to go some way to be better than that, four people so closely connected they know the beat of each other's hearts.

And then one by one people started to trickle in from the bar until there was a crowd by track five, and the heat built up so fast that sweat dripped off the ceiling like rain drops. We played every single one of our songs, and then as many covers as we could think of and by the end they were eating out of the palms of our hands, begging for more. The best drug in the world.

Eventually the landlord pulled the plug on us, and the whole pub booed and shouted for an encore. It was brilliant. Outside in the corridor I gulped down a pint of water and Rose came out of the loos.

'You are fucking awesome,' she said, grabbing me and kissing me on my closed mouth. 'I fucking love you, Red.'

And I stood there for a long time on my own after she left and tried to make sense of it all. Was my racing heart from the gig, or from her lips? Either way the adrenaline made me tremble and shake, and I was lost. I was lost to her, right in that moment and I knew it. I knew I was going to spend the foreseeable future in love with a girl who wasn't ever going to feel that way about me.

After they'd all gone, we were loading up my kit into Rose's mate's van when the landlord came out to see us, lighting up a fag.

'You can play again,' he said.

'Only if you pay us,' Naomi replied.

'Fifty quid,' he huffed.

We felt like millionaires.

24

I don't remember what happened after Rose told me she didn't kiss girls, I only remember the look on her face, and whatever it was, was the opposite of love. I remember leaving her house, though I don't remember putting on my shoes, or grabbing my stuff. I remember the cool of the evening air on my hot cheeks, and how, as I ran along the street the soft soles of my trainers barely made any sound. I don't remember going home, or anything else until this moment, standing in front of my mirror and looking at myself.

The me that is standing there, strong but not muscular arms, toned stomach concealed beneath a loose shirt that hides my small breasts.

And that other me, the girl who stands behind me, is the unhappy one, the one I could have been. The one who follows me around everywhere I go, my very own personal ghost.

For the first time I look over the shoulder of my reflection and into her eyes. She has long hair that she straightens every day, and just the right amount of lipstick for her age, peachy because that suits her skin tone. She's one of the girls, the girl who everyone likes because she isn't too pretty and she isn't too loud; she is the perfect BFF, studies hard and always does her homework on time. She does OK at school, she does OK at life, and if a boy notices her she pretends that she is excited. And maybe, in those skater dresses that her mum buys her, and the heeled ankle boots, she'd get a boyfriend before long, because even though she is ginger, she is pretty, with delicate features and big green eyes. That girl is everything on the outside that a sixteen-year-old girl should be.

And her mum is so proud of her.

But inside, inside that girl wants to cry every second. Inside she is screaming and she can't get out. Inside she is lost and lonely, and tired, so tired of faking it, that she wonders if she can even keep her heart beating it hurts so much to pretend to be everything she is not.

And I stopped looking in mirrors, while I remade my outside to match how I feel inside.

But now I make myself look.

I make myself see who *I* am, the shaved sides of my head, the explosion of hair that falls into my eyes. The angular face and beautiful green eyes.

Now I look in the mirror and I see myself, and it matches me on the inside at last.

I don't see weird or gay or straight. Or a girl who wants to be a boy.

I just see me. It's who I am, and I don't fit in to any category except my own, and why does that matter to anyone? All I want to do is be me.

I think about Rose, and the look on her face.

I feel the hurt of that ghost girl I used to know so well.

I let myself fall in love with Rose. Which was fucking bad. But worse than that, I let that feeling out at exactly the wrong time. Rose was telling me something big and important and I made it all about me, and I let her down when she needed a friend, not a lover.

What the fuck have I done?

Shit. Shit. Shit.

What the fuck have I done?

And then I look myself in the eye, and it helps. It helps to see me there, giving myself a look of compassion.

All I did was show how I feel.

I showed love, and longing, and desire.

But that's all. And that's not wrong. It's not wrong to be who you really are. And for a while all the anxiety drains away, and I stop looking at myself in the mirror, and instead stare at the backwards city I can see out of my bedroom window, the lights of millions of lives twinkling all the way to the horizon.

There is no need to despair over being brave, over risking everything to be true. Instead I feel free, because tonight I broke down one more barrier to truly being myself, crossed one more bridge towards the life I want. And for now, anyway, I feel good about doing that, even if I have burnt it down behind me.

I feel proud.

Ash is sitting there as I arrive at the hospital, and the moment I see her I feel better, anchored. Like the sight of her is the only thing stopping me from spinning out of control.

'Do you ever go home?' I ask her, trying to keep things normal. She relaxes against me, the warmth of her skin against mine. 'Ash, will you do something for me?' I ask her. She looks at me sleepily.

'What?' she asks.

'Will you hack my dad's computer?'

'Yeah, just give me his email,' she says.

'I love that you don't even ask me why.'

'You'll have a good reason,' Ash yawns. 'Because I only use my powers for good. But not right now, OK? I just need to close my eyes for a minute.'

I feel the weight of her head against my shoulder, and her breathing slows down.

'Ash, I think I might have fucked up my whole life,' I say.

She snores in reply.

Video
Posted 1 hour ago.

Last night I found out that @RedDrums is a liar and a pervert. I thought she was my friend, but all she wanted to do was to get it on with me. All this time, she's been trying to get into my pants.

87 rections
49 comments

Kasha: Fucking hell! Gross!
Gigi: Oh my God, I always thought she was looking at me
Kasha: R U OK Rose? You must be traumatised, pal!
Parminder: Don't worry I'll take care of that bitch for you
Maz: Want me to sort that cunt out?
Kasha: I'm going to troll her so hard
Gigi: She deserves everything she gets
Amy: What a slag!

Click to load more comments

25

I wake up early, before dawn, after an hour's sleep in my own bed. It's still dark outside, but I can hear noises downstairs. The second I open my eyes I am wide awake, my heart racing, my whole body restless, so I pull myself out of bed and check my phone. It's full of notifications. More than I can make sense of. I go to her Instagram, and there's a video. Of Rose crying. Angry and upset.

I watch it.

I drop the phone onto the floor.

Why?

Why would she do something like that, that . . . that isn't Rose.

I made a mistake, but I didn't do what she said, did I? I didn't. I know I didn't, so why is she lashing out like this?

Be pissed off with me, sure. Have a go at me, fine. But tag me and post that to all of our friends? All the people who thought I was a dickhead before the band. Now they have a reason to treat me that way again.

What do I do now?

Do I go to school, act like nothing has happened, when

I know that everyone will be waiting to stare and whisper and worse?

All the sense of pride and freedom I'd felt last night, that I took with me to bed, vanishes.

I always thought Rose was my friend, that she really cared about me.

Not the blood and bones that carries me around, but the me that's inside my head and my heart. But what happened last night must have been much worse than I realised. Because I've made her angry and I've hurt her, and if I made her feel even for one second like the scum that left her battered and used, then . . . oh my God, what if I *am* like them?

'Amy?' Gracie only uses my real name when Mum has sent her to fetch me for something. 'Amy?'

I don't answer, I just lie there. Not sure what to do.

'Red?'

'Come in, kiddo,' I call out, and she pads in, in her Scooby Doo PJs, screwing the ball of her fist into her sleepy eyes.

'What's up?'

'Mum says you have to take me to school because she's throwing up. But there isn't any milk for Cheerios and I don't know what else to have for breakfast.'

'Right, that's OK, I'm coming. Go see if there is any bread.'

I just want to make this right. I just want everything that happened last night, that post that is ticking through everyone's timelines to vanish, and for everything to go back to the way it was.

But I don't know how to do that.

It's almost impossible to tear myself away from the fear and anxiety that wants to invade every part of me, but I make myself do it, make myself get dressed and put on my trainers. On the way downstairs, I stop outside Mum's room. She's facing the window, her back hunched and tight.

'Want tea?' I ask. Groaning she rolls to look at me, her face all triangles, triangle eyes and mouth, sadness in every angle. My mum looks like shit.

'Please.' Her voice is hoarse and dry, the room stinks of something stale, I wonder if she might have wet the bed. I wait. I wish . . . I wish I could talk to her about this, but I can't. So I focus on the one thing I can take care of right now. My sister.

'I'll pick Gracie up today too, OK? I can cut the last ten minutes of school, make sure I get there on time.'

'Thank you.' Mum musters something like a smile, but it's barely that. She turns away from me, dragging the duvet over her head.

Gracie talks and I don't listen, I don't need to. All I need to do is hold her hand, feel the tug and pull of her on my arm as she skips and jumps, and to concentrate hard on not thinking about what waits for me at school. I could just not go, I could drop Gracie off and go to Camden again, but if I don't go I won't know how bad it really is. I won't know if Rose is OK.

Gracie has to tug at my hand to make me let go of her as we reach the school gates.

'You're coming to pick me up?' she asks and I nod.

'See you later!' I watch her as she runs into class, and the playground empties and the school mums and dads leave. And then there's nothing else to do but turn around and face whatever comes next.

Ash
What the fuck is going on, whole school calling you a rapist?

Ash
I hate Instagram

Ash
Fuck. I mean clearly you didn't do that . . .

Ash
Or maybe you don't know her as well as you think you do . . .

Ash
Look don't worry. It's fine

Ash
Do you feel like disappearing and then throwing yourself off a bridge?

Red
Fuck. You saw her Instagram?

Red
Go look

Red
Something else is going on. This isn't Rose . . .

Red
I know her. I really know her and . . . I can't explain it, but this isn't her

Red
How is it fine?

Red
OK, I take your point. Any luck with the tattoo?

Ash

No, although the more I look at it the more I think I'm right about it being code. But I need help. So I'm getting in touch with some people

Red

What sort of people?

Ash

People. Dark Net kind of people. The less you know the better

Red

Fuck Ash, you aren't bloody Edward Snowden you know

Ash

Who?

26

Everyone is in class as I walk quietly down the corridors, hoping that the constant buzzing and pinging in my pocket will eventually stop. Like that time that Tally Lawson sent a pic of her boobs to Clarke Hanson and he screenshotted it, and it went all around school. Some people called her out as a slut, and some people called him out as the dick he definitely was, and they were both off school for two weeks after the police cautioned her about making an indecent image.

And then, when news got round that Naomi had vanished, no one cared about Tally's tits any more.

Everyone hates me and that old uncertainty that I used to feel comes back, like my ghost girl stalker had suddenly run up behind and thrown herself back into my body, filling me up with the pain and anxiety that she carried around in her chest.

Maybe I *am* a liar. I was never honest with Rose about how I feel about her.

Maybe I'm *not* the decent person I thought I was.

Maybe I *am* a monster after all.

I walk into Music and sit at the front of the class. I can sense the bitching going on behind my back, I can feel it vibrating in my pocket. Pulling my phone out, I quickly suspend my accounts.

'Red, what are you doing?' Mr Mark shouts at me, taking me by surprise. 'Give me your phone!'

He doesn't wait for me to offer it, snatching it up from my desk, and tossing it in his desk drawer.

'Come and get it at the bell,' he says.

But not having my phone any more doesn't make any difference. I can still hear it vibrating in his desk drawer, and see the flash of screens all around me, a swarm of electronic words massing and multiplying in thin air, each one a needle-sharp sting.

The bell sounds and I sit in my chair, trying to show I hear every one of the muttered insults that hits the back of my head as everyone else leaves.

When the room is clear, I go to Mr Smith.

'Look, I'm sorry I shouted at you,' he says. He looks flustered, ruffled. I know how he feels. 'That class really winds me up sometimes. But you're one of the good ones, you didn't deserve that.'

'It's OK.'

'What's going on?' he asks me, taking the phone out of the drawer, but holding it back as he waits for an answer.

'Nothing.' I shrug, and look at the door. I don't want him to be nice to me, I'm afraid that if he is, I'll cry.

He gets up from behind the desk and comes around to stand next to me.

'Hey.' I feel the reassuring weight of his hand on my shoulder as he looks into my eyes. 'If that lot are giving you grief, then speak up, all right? I don't want anyone keeping stuff to themselves. Nothing is that bad, Red. You can come to me, OK?'

'Thanks, sir,' I say. I stand for a moment longer and wonder if I really could tell him about how the second time I ever kissed a girl, I ruined everything with my closest friend. And I look up into his green eyes, and I decide that the answer was no.

'I'm here for you,' he says. 'You're a great girl, Red.'

Which is funny, because I feel like a terrible one.

'Fucking sleaze,' Kasha says as I walk past. 'What, you trying to look at my tits, dyke?'

I keep my head down, for the first time regretting losing the mass of hair that I'd had scissored onto the floor of the barbers. Nowhere to hide now.

'You heard of consent?' Parminder asks me as I walk past. 'Dickless rapist.'

I stop, and remember the reason that I had my hair cut off was because I wanted to be the sort of person who didn't hide who they were behind a curtain.

'That's not what happened,' I turn around but now it's not just Parminder and Kasha standing there, another six or seven of my year group have joined them, arms crossed, chins jutting.

'Look, I don't know why Rose has done this,' I begin and it comes out wrong. I try again. 'I just . . . I made a mistake that's all. I got it wrong. I don't know why she's reacted like this—'

'Oh yeah, sure, blame the victim.' Kasha takes two steps towards me and I take two back. 'Next you'll be saying she was asking for it.'

'Fuck's sake, it was nothing, barely anything!' I feel my

throat tighten and I know that if I speak again I will cry. If I walk away I'll look like I don't care, if I stay I'll look pathetic.

'Fuck off the lot of you.' Leo appears at my side. 'Go on, fuck off and go and cackle somewhere else, witches.'

'So you're on her side?' Tasha raises a brow. 'You think it's OK, what she did to Rose?'

'No, I'm not on anyone's side, because there are no sides, you fucking child. Now fuck off.'

Kasha and Leo stand eye to eye for a moment, and she sneers at him, turning on her heel, and Parminder and the others follow.

'What the fuck?' Leo shakes his head at me.

'I d . . . don't know. I thought. It seemed like . . . '

He puts his hand on my shoulder and marches me down the corridor, through to the music room, and I'm not sure if he is protecting me, or taking me somewhere private to beat the crap out of me, but at least no one messes with Leo, no one stops him, or says anything. They just watch as we walk by.

'What the fuck, Red?' Leo asks again as he shuts the door hard. 'What did you do?'

'I didn't . . . ' I say. 'I . . . I just tried to kiss her.'

'What the fuck?' Leo stares at me in disbelief, like I am a moron, and the thing is, I think he is probably right.

'I know Leo, I know, OK? I know how it sounds. I got it wrong, I got carried away and I thought the things she said meant something they didn't, and it lasted for about a second and then she told me to go, and I went. I tried to kiss a girl and got brushed off. Don't tell me you haven't done the same, without all of this shit?'

'But Rose isn't a girl, Red.' Leo shoves me in my

shoulder a little, and I have to fight not to falter backwards. 'She's not some woman you met in a bar. It's Rose. *Rose*. Fuck, don't you think there have been times when I've wanted to tell her how I feel about her, never mind trying to fucking kiss her? But I don't. Because it's Rose. And she doesn't need you and me to fancy her. We're supposed to be more important than that. She needs us to be her friends. Why do you think I haven't ever tried to kiss her, as much as I'd like to.'

His voice softens with the admission, his head dropping. He's angry at me and he's right to be.

'Dude,' he says, shaking his head.

'That's the trouble though, isn't it,' I say. 'I'm not a dude.'

'Dude,' Leo says again. 'Red, no one cares that you're a girl. No one cares that you are gay. This isn't about that.'

Sitting down on the platform where the drums are set up, I run my fingers over my head, and feel twisted inside, out of kilter, jangled and mismatched.

'Jesus, Leo, what am I going to do?'

'Find Rose,' Leo sits next to me. 'Front it out, face it and sort this shit out. But before you do that, Red, you got to get your head round who you are. You got to own it. You look like you own it, you dress like you own it, but really you are just playing a part, with your hair and your clothes. You hide who you are, what you want. You live life in neutral, and neutral doesn't work. You can't go around just hoping that no one will notice your skinny little arse, because if you do, they are always gonna be freaked out by you just being who you really are.'

'Oh fuck off, Leo,' I retort, because he's hurt me with the truth. 'I don't need you to mansplain my sexuality to me. How would you know what it's like to be gay or anything like it? You have got it easy, you're a straight boy, you play guitar, you are taller than all the girls. You haven't got anything to worry about.'

'Seriously?' He stares at me. 'You have noticed where I'm from, right?'

'It doesn't matter to me where people are from, what colour their skin is or how much money they have, or if they like boys or girls or . . . or . . . any of that shit. Why can't people just be people?'

'Because people are arseholes,' Leo says. 'And the world is supposed to be getting a better, fairer place, but it isn't. And it ain't gonna any time soon. So the only thing we can do is look out for ourselves, Red. And that's it.'

Neither one of us says anything for a moment. I think we both sense that one false move could mean another friend down, and neither of us wants that.

'So,' Leo says adjusting his tone. 'Have you seen her since?'

'No, is she at school?'

'I don't know, I ain't seen her this morning.'

Ugh, it feels like I've ripped down the world around me, and I'll have to start again from scratch.

'Do you think she'll come to rehearsal?'

'Do you think we've even got a gig, any more? We were supposed to be doing this for Naomi, and now . . . why did you have to kiss her? Your band mate! We said right at the beginning, that we have to keep it mates between us. This is how bands break up!'

'Right, so if Rose walked in here right now, and said Leo, will you go out with me, you'd say no, right? Right?'

'Yeah . . . I don't know. Yeah.'

The door opens and slams shut and there she is. Rose.

Hands on her hips, hair tied back from her face, no make-up, jeans and a T-shirt. And she is mad as hell.

'It's Red or me,' Rose says looking at Leo but pointing at me.

'Rose . . . come on, really?' Leo shakes his head. 'Red is an idiot, but you know she didn't mean to upset you like this, you know her, right?'

'Are you telling me that what she did to me is OK?' Rose's eyes flash, and I see not only the anger on her face but pure hurt, and my gut twists in anguish. 'I thought I was with a friend, and she puts the moves on me? That's like . . . that's like you putting the moves on me when all we are is mates. It's creepy, and it's wrong.'

I don't think Rose knows how much she's hurt Leo with those few words because although I see it – the tightening in his jaw, the sigh – she isn't looking for it. The only thing she is looking for is a fight.

'Really, the only thing Red has done is fallen for you, and been a bit of an idiot.' Leo stands up as he talks to Rose. 'She tried to kiss you, a dick move yeah. But she doesn't deserve to be trolled for it.'

'Are you calling me a liar?' Rose takes a step towards him, sparks flying off her.

Leo frowns clearly expecting Rose to back down, or at least soften a little. He looks at me and then back at Rose.

'It *was* just a kiss, right?'

'Fuck you,' Rose says. 'If I didn't want it, it doesn't matter if it's a kiss or a grope or a fucking handshake. You don't do that, you don't just grab a person like that, it's not right.'

'Rose, please. I'm so sorry, I didn't mean to upset you like this, I got it so wrong . . . but I really care about you and . . .'

'I thought you did.' Rose stares at me, and the look of fury and hurt on her face makes my blood run cold. 'I thought you cared about me, but you are just like the rest, pawing at me like I'm a piece of meat. I trusted you.'

'I love you!' The words explode out of my mouth. 'I love you, because you aren't just "a piece of meat", because you are funny, and clever and talented and kind, because you care about me, and sometimes it feels like you are the only person that does. And yesterday I felt overwhelmed with those feelings. I made a mistake, I should have kept it a secret. I made a mistake, Rose. If you were my friend you'd understand.'

Rose looks at me for a long, cold moment.

'If *you* were *my* friend you'd understand why I can never forgive you for what you did. Gig's off.'

'Rose . . . ' Leo calls after her but as she opens the door Mr Smith appears. Rose stops dead in front of him, her eyes on his, her shoulders moving with every breath, and I can't tell if she's going to shout at him too, or burst into tears. She does neither, she just stops dead.

'Where do you think you're going?' he says, putting his hand on her arm. 'Guys, we need to talk.'

I expect Rose to push past him, but she doesn't, instead she steps aside to let him into the room and leans against the closed door.

'Look,' Mr Smith says. 'Us teachers aren't immune to the gossip that goes around the school. Are you two OK?'

He looks from me to Rose.

'I've apologised,' I say. 'It was a mistake.'

'Good.' Mr Smith nods. 'Look, Red, I think what's happening to you at the moment is pretty disgusting . . . '

Rose snorts and shakes her head.

'And what about what happened to me, *sir*,' she says. 'You're OK with that, are you?'

'Rose, just dial down the drama queen act for a moment please.' Mr Smith gives her this look, and amazingly Rose stills, her head drops, her cheeks ignite.

'Act? She forced herself on me, is that OK in your book?' Rose takes a step towards him.

'Of course it's not OK,' Smith looks at me and I want to die on the spot. 'That is never OK, Rose. But was there malice, anger or hate when Red made that mistake? You pushed her away and she didn't try again, did she?'

'No,' Rose's shoulders drop, some of her anger fading. 'No, I guess not.'

'Look, school bands break up all the time because the kids fall out or get involved and then fall out.' Mr Smith looks at each of us in turn. 'It's boring, it's predictable, and who the fuck cares, because none of you are going to make it as musicians anyway. In a couple of years school will be done, and you'll live off your dad,' he says to Rose before switching his gaze to me. 'You'll go away to uni, and find a nice girlfriend and you . . .' His eyes land on Leo. 'Well, hopefully you won't follow in your brother's footsteps.'

Leo's expression darkens.

'That's what I *could* say,' Mr Smith adds. 'That's what I'd say if you lot were like any of the other school bands that I've worked with. But you aren't. You are actually good, you can play, and write and sing and you might be able to do something with this. *If* you can stick together. *If* you can keep playing despite this . . . squabble. And at the very least, I would have thought all of you would want to do this for Naomi. Or are you really OK with letting down her family, her mum and dad who have been so looking forward to the concert, to seeing how much her daughter means to people and having some little shred of hope that something good has come out of something so terrible.'

Rose sinks down onto a chair, burying her head in her hands.

Leo turns away, staring out of the window.

I'm the only one who doesn't look away from Mr Smith.

'I want to play at the concert,' I say. 'I will.'

'Leo?'

'Yeah.' Leo nods. 'I'm in.'

'Rose?'

Rose doesn't move for a while and then she pushes her hair back from her face.

'I'll do it,' she says. 'For Nai, after that . . . I don't know.'

'Thank you,' Mr Smith says. 'Rose, calm this stuff down about Red, OK? Say what you have to to take the drama out of it. It's the last thing the school needs.'

Rose sighs, pressing her lips together.

'Seriously?' Smith looks hard at her. 'You are better than that, Rose. At least I thought you were. You're not a bully.'

For a moment it looks like she might challenge him, but then she stops herself, and shrugs.

'Fine,' she says. 'But only for Nai, for the concert.'

'Right, better get on with rehearsal then,' Mr Smith replies, opening the door to the corridor, pushing his way through a small crowd that had gathered to peer in through the window.

'Show's over,' Rose spits at them. 'Everyone fuck off.'

'Even me?' Leckraj's voice comes out of the press of faces.

'No of course not fucking you . . . get in here, idiot.'

I pick up my sticks and sit at the drums.

Leo picks up the set sheet.

'I think we should go over "Left Overs" – it's the one Leckraj has rehearsed the least.'

'Fine, let's get on with it.' Rose adjusts her mic stand.

'Rose,' I say. 'Thank you for not walking out.'

'Fuck you,' she says, without looking at me. 'This changes nothing.'

Red's Fuck You Playlist

Psychosocial/Slipknot
Please Don't Go/The Violent Femmes
Ride a White Swan/T-Rex
Girls Like Girls/Hayley Kiyoko
Make Me Wanna Die/The Pretty Reckless
Death of a Batchelor/Panic! At the Disco
Smells Like Teen Spirit/Nirvana
Heathens/Twenty One Pilots

27

As soon as the rehearsal finished I ducked out of school and headed for the hospital. Another two hours of all that shit is the last thing I need.

Ash is sitting outside Naomi's room, headphones plugged in, laptop open.

In Naomi's room I can see Jackie and Max sitting by her bed. Jackie holds Nai's hand, and Max holds hers, and they both sit in silence, watching the rise and fall of their daughter's chest.

Sitting down next to Ash, I tap her on her shoulder and she slides off her headphones as she looks at me, her normally poker-straight hair a little mussed up and tangled.

'Any news?' I ask her.

'They are going to start weaning her off the drugs after the weekend,' Ash says. 'They say the swelling has all gone, no bleeding, all the other injuries are healing, so now it's just seeing what happens when she wakes up. If she can breathe for herself . . . if she can still talk, see. That sort of thing.'

'Fuck. That's heavy shit.' It still seems impossible even after the last few days, even after sitting by her bedside, that this is real. I can't get my head round the idea that she could wake up damaged, or even not at all.

'In a way . . . ' Ash looks up from the laptop. 'In a way it'd almost be better if she stayed like that forever, at least when she's like that there's hope.'

'Dark,' I say.

'I feel dark.' Ash sighs, and I do the same in solidarity. Really what I want to do is go and sit next to Naomi, and just hang out with her for a bit, but I don't want to intrude on the silent vigil taking place in her room. Does she dream, I wonder, or feel the touch of her mum's hand? Does she know they are there? I hope she does, otherwise being shut inside her head with all those secrets that she is keeping must be a very lonely and frightening place to be.

'Your dad took the bait on my phishing email this morning,' Ash tells me, and that's another dark thought that comes crashing back in. 'Old people are so easy.'

'You looked at his computer?'

Ash nods. 'Yep, been all over it, do you know your baby photos are on there? Mate, you were an ugly baby, like all red.'

'Ash, don't fuck with me please, not today.'

The corner of her mouth twitches with a tiny smile.

'Red, your dad is a good man. Like a better-than-average man. Apart from all the women he is cheating on your mother with, he's basically a stand-up guy.'

'Seriously?' Blood rushes to my face, my cheeks burn with relief. 'But who was the girl?'

'He's working with a local charity to try and rehome

families made homeless through domestic violence. That girl, that was a photo taken by her dad, who found out where she was living and sent it as a threat to her mum. That's why the folders are numbered. No names for safety. You really need to get him to update his software and give him a basic tutorial on not clicking on a link in dodgy emails.'

'My dad is a good man,' I repeat the words.

'He's not perfect, but he's not evil.'

'Good because how awkward would that be?' I say, and we smile at each other, a moment of warmth passing between us. If there is one good thing to come out of this, it's getting to know Ash, spending time with her. Seeing the humour that she normally keeps so carefully hidden away.

'I've been looking at this tattoo for hours.' Ash turns back to her screen. 'I managed to separate out eight layers of numbers, punctuation and letters – see?'

'How?' I ask, peering over her shoulder. 'I mean how do you decide which number is part of which layer?'

'Because even though it looks really messed up, there *is* a pattern.' That hint of a smile again. 'I told you there would be. My theory is that each number or letter directly touches part of the other number and letters in its layer. At least that's what I'm hoping. If it's not that, then . . . fuck knows.'

Ash shows me eight separate semi-circles that she has separated out from the original design.

'So now I'm looking at them for another pattern that makes sense. Something that's going to enable me to crack the code, but I don't have the key. I don't have any way of knowing where to start. I've tried as many combinations as I can and I'm no further on, and there are a billion potential combinations here. So I ask this group of activists I know, they are all like, what the fuck? I'm stuck, out of ideas, and maybe I'm trying to decode something that isn't even there, know what I mean?'

She looks at me and I shrug, this kind of thing isn't really my bag. Now, if she wanted me to upset and alienate one of the people I care about most in the world, that I can do.

I peer at the images, one after the other. They are like those annoying tests you get sometimes on websites when they want you to prove that you are human. The more you look the less you see.

'I mean, are they even in the right order?' I ask her, 'Like left to right?'

Ash shrugs. 'Fuck knows.'

'Because that third circle. That's looks like it could be . . . No, I'm probably being ridiculous.'

'What?' Ash looks at me. 'Go on, there are no stupid ideas. Much.'

'Well, that could be a dot com, right? A dot and C O M. Could it mean dot com?'

Ash stares at the circle.

'Fuck me,' she says.

'Look, you're the tech-head, I'm just saying . . .' I feel stupid for saying anything.

'No, I mean in some types of malware there's a kill switch, right? A fucking stupid long random website address and if it's live, it turns off the virus. But a fucking stupid long random website address would be a great way to hide something really dark. Something you could only know was there if you had exactly the right combinations of letters and numbers that make up the address. But even the longest and stupidest website addresses have to finish with dot something. Red, I think maybe you've figured it out!'

'Really?' I stare at her.

'I could kiss you!' she says, and this time her smile is full, bright and brilliant and for one crazy second I want to say, yeah, OK then. But then I remember how it worked out the last time I kissed a girl, and she realises what she's said, and her smile freezes into a grimace. It's all kinds of awkward.

'I mean maybe not,' Ash looks hard at her screen and I stand up. 'But maybe, and there are still a fuck of a lot of combinations to go through, but . . . it's a start. You are not as stupid as the selfies you take on your phone and never post on the internet make you look.'

'Great,' I say, glad we are back to normal.

'Red!' Jackie and Max emerge from Nai's room. 'Did Ash tell you they are going to try and wake her? On Monday! The same day as the concert. Won't it be wonderful if she wakes up and we can tell her all about it?'

'It really will,' I say. 'Do you mind if I go and sit with her?'

'No, please do.' Max smiles at me. 'You're a good friend to her, Red. The best.'

I go and sit down next to Nai, and talk for a long time about the good times. The times when everything seemed right.

The night before Naomi ran away . . .

All we wanted to do was dance.

It was the end of the school year, it was hot and we were free. Nothing to do, nowhere to go, nowhere to be, no one to be except ourselves and it felt so good that we wanted to go out and get fucked up and dance.

Even Nai, who wasn't ever really that into going out; she didn't like crowds and people looking at her, was up for it. She wore a yellow sundress and strappy sandals, and Rose put some daisies in her hair. We set off, taking a couple of pills each as we walked along the river, up past the Houses of Parliament and across Trafalgar Square, heading towards Soho. We could have got a bus, it would have taken half the time, but why be stuck in the heat with a load of strangers when we could be free, the breeze coming off the river, the blue sky arcing overhead, and the smell of the city summer in the melting asphalt and exhaust fumes. We walked and talked and laughed, and with every step the world around us got a little bit brighter and shinier, covered in gold. The feeling of joy in my chest rose and expanded until it seemed to reach my fingertips and toes; a rainbow-filled bubble of happiness.

Don't ask me how we got away with what we did, and where we went, because I don't know, but we did. In and out of the bar and pubs we went, buying drink after drink, Rose flashing her dad's credit card, picking up the tab. Fearless and ageless, we took it in turns to play chicken with the bar staff, to ferry out vodka and bottles of beer for those three and Red Bull for me. I didn't drink, but I felt drunk, laughing louder, flinging my arms around my friends and telling them how much I loved them. We did that a lot that night, declarations of love fell from our lips with every other sentence.

Down Wardour Street there are some basement steps that lead to an underground bar. It used to be an illegal drinking den, but Soho is almost all for tourists now, hardly anything really dirty left. Another round of pills and we headed down there, following the sound of grime that was blaring out onto the street. The bar was full, shoulder to shoulder with every kind of human you could imagine, black, brown and white, gay and straight, and no one cared about anyone else, we only cared about the music, letting ourselves fall in between the beats, moving to the heavy bass. Skin rubbed against skin, hips, arses, my body, his body, hers, all one great moving sweaty happy mass. It got dark while we were dancing and it took Rose to get bored first and drag us back out onto the street to make us leave. I think I would have stayed there until dawn if I could have, I liked being lost in all of those bodies.

We weaved in and out of the crowds, down to Soho Square where the tramps stunk of beer and piss, and men kissed men on the benches, and we sprawled out on the grass, Leo producing the joint he had in his back pocket, a little dented, but still good. I don't know if this happened, or if it's just how I remember it, but I felt like when I lay back on the grass, the moon was really close, almost within touching distance, that I could push myself off the surface of the earth and land there with barely any effort at all if I wanted to.

'It's so weird that the end of the school year comes in July,' Nai said. 'This doesn't feel like an ending, it feels like a beginning.'

'Good, because I don't want us to ever end,' Rose had said. 'We are the best things in this world.'

'Me neither,' I added. 'Us four, forever.'

'Yeah,' Leo agreed. 'They'll write about this time in our lives in *NME*, the time we were getting around to being fucking famous. We're never going to be over, not ever. Not us.'

The fact that Naomi didn't say anything, the fact that she just lay in the grass in her yellow dress, looking up at the moon, and smiling from ear to ear, didn't seem to mean anything at all. That was just Nai, being Nai.

But the next day she was gone, and everything started to fall apart.

And it's only when I look back at it now I realise, that was her, saying goodbye.

28

I'm almost home, head lost in music and memories, before I realise I didn't go and pick Gracie up. School finished more than forty minutes ago for her. Fuck. I take my phone out of my pocket as I turn around and start to run back.

I ring Mum but no one answers, so I try and run while Googling the school and calling the number. It goes to voicemail.

'Hello?' I shout and run and pant into the answerphone. 'Hi, I'm supposed to be picking up Gracie Saunders but I'm running late so—'

My phone beeps to tell me there is a call waiting, and I stop.

'Where are you?' Mum says, as soon as I answer it.

'I had a bad day at school,' I say, wishing so hard that I could turn to my mum and ask her for a hug. 'I went to see Naomi after and . . . I'm sorry, I forgot.'

'School phoned,' Mum says, her voice like ice. 'Gracie was crying her eyes out. Luckily Mrs Peterson from up the road dropped her back, but she hasn't stopped crying since. You better get back here now and try to explain to her why you forgot about her.'

She hangs up the phone.

Fuck.

Mum opens the door as I come up the path.

'I thought you at least cared about Gracie,' she says.

'I do care about her, I am the only one that does,' I say. 'I just had a really, really shit day. Where is she?'

'A really shit day isn't a good enough reason to leave your seven-year-old sister standing on her own in the playground.'

'Unlike vodka,' I snap back, and she grabs hold of my arm tight enough to hurt.

'I'm getting just about sick of you, Amy. You forget that you are a child and I am an adult.'

'Who was too hungover to pick up her own kid?' I say, breaking free of her and running upstairs.

'Get back here!' Mum shouts after me.

Gracie is lying on the floor with her dolls, white-socked feet waving in the air.

'I'm sorry, kiddo,' I say.

She turns to look at me and smiles.

'I cried,' she says. 'Snot tears and everything. I got a biscuit.'

'I'm a terrible sibling.' I sit on the floor next to her.

'You aren't, I got a ride home with my teacher in her car, and no one else gets that. What's a sibling?'

'A brother or a sister.'

'Oh well, then, you are the sibling!' Gracie hugs me hard.

'So you don't hate me like everyone else?' I ask her, and

there are tears in my voice. I'm tired of being strong, and now it feels almost too much to not just cry.

'No,' Gracie says. 'Who hates you?'

'Not you,' I say, 'and that's all that matters.'

I hear the doorbell ring downstairs, as Gracie climbs into my arms.

'Want to play tea party?'

'No,' I reply.

'Too bad, you owe me,' she says cheerfully. 'I'm the queen and you're the princess.'

I haven't even started my cup of imaginary tea when Mum starts shouting from downstairs, each word getting louder as she thunders up to Gracie's room.

'How could you? HOW *COULD* YOU?'

She just stands there in the doorway, thrusting a piece of paper towards me.

'How could you?' she says again. 'I know you have no shame, but do you really not care about anyone else in this family?'

'What are you talking about?' I look at the paper; it looks familiar but I can't think why.

'My God, Amy, It's one thing to look like that . . . ' She gestures at me. 'But you force yourself on your friends? You are disgusting.'

Carefully I remove my tiara, and get up.

'Be back in a bit, your majesty,' I say, curtseying to Gracie who watches us with big round eyes going onto the landing. I pull the door closed behind me.

'What is that?' I say, keeping my voice low.

'It's bad enough, that you . . . you can't be normal.' She hisses at me. 'But this? Her father is a lawyer; you know that, don't you?'

She balls the paper in her clenched fist and throws it at me. It lands at my feet. Slowly I pick it up.

Your daughter tried to rape Rose Carter.

'Are you on drugs?' she asks.

'Mum, it's not like that,' I say, trying to keep my voice steady, even though I can feel the tremble building in every muscle. 'This is a lie.'

'So you didn't do that to Rose, then?' She grabs my wrist; it hurts when she drags me into her bedroom, the scent of stale breath and unwashed clothes hitting the back of my throat. Carefully I keep my face still, expressionless.

'No, of course I didn't. I'm your daughter, don't you know me at all?'

'This has got to stop, Amy. This stupidity, this phase. You are not a boy. You are not a . . . a *lesbian* or whatever it is you think you are. This is attention seeking, it's desperate. It's *pathetic!*'

She spits the word out like it tastes of poison, just the act of her saying it that way hurts me more deeply than I thought possible. I tug my arm free of her grip and go to the window, pushing it open and sucking in the evening air.

'Don't call me Amy. I'm not her. I did kiss Rose,' I say without looking at her. 'But she didn't want me to, so nothing happened and I left. I tried to kiss her because I've fallen for her, and it hurts and I'm upset and lost because she doesn't want me. And hurt and upset and lost because for some reason she wants to punish me for caring about her. And I'm hurt and upset and lost because if it had been a boy that had treated me that way, a boy I had tried to kiss, I could have talked to you about it, and you would have been kind to me. But instead you think I am repulsive, just for being me. And that's all I want to do, Mum, is to be comfortable in my own skin, and to love the people it feels right to love. I don't want to hurt or disgust anyone. I just want to be me.'

'No.' Mum shakes her head. 'This isn't you. It's filthy, *you* are filthy. Perverted! What's wrong with you?'

'What's wrong with *you*?' I can't keep the anger and sadness inside any more, and the words explode out of me. 'Who can really hate their own child so much for just existing?'

'You aren't my child,' Mum says bitterly. 'Not any more. I don't recognise you.'

'Stop it.' Gracie pushes the door open, her face crumpling. 'Stop talking to her like that.' For a moment I'm not sure who she is talking to, but it's me she runs to, putting her arms around my waist.

'Go downstairs, darling.' Mum tries to smile at Gracie, it looks like a death mask. 'Go and watch TV.'

'No,' she says. 'No, I'm not leaving Red. Why do you hate her? I love her. And I hate you!'

'Get your hands off of her!' my mum screams, dragging Gracie off me, toppling her onto the floor. Gracie screams and cries, but as I go to her, Mum blocks my path.

'What the hell are you doing?' My face is in her face, fury fuelling every breath. I'm skinny and short but I am just as tall as her and twice as fit. 'What's wrong with you? The things you say to me; the way you treat Gracie? When did you stop giving a damn about anything except yourself and where the next drink is coming from? Do you know what the neighbours gossip about? It's not me, your dyke daughter. It's you.'

The blow comes from nowhere, and it's not a slap. It's a clenched ball of knuckle and bone that strikes, detonating pain across my face. A crack sounds as my head snaps back and the room blurs. I will my feet to stay planted on the floor, my knees not to buckle, and I weld my balled fists to my legs, determined not to touch the place where she's hit me, licking the blood from my lips.

'Red!' Gracie shrieks, and Mum steps out of the way as I crouch down to my sister and pick her up.

'It's fine,' I say. 'I'm fine, are you OK?'

Gracie hides her hot snotty cheeks in my neck and I carry her away from my mother, keeping my eyes fixed ahead as I take her into her room and shut the door. I call Dad.

'Red?' He answers straight away and I'm so grateful that I almost cry.

'Dad, we need you to come home now. Right now.'

'The thing is, love, I've got a few more . . . '

'Dad, it's Mum, she's lost it. Gracie is scared of her and . . . it's bad. We need you to come back now. We are your kids and we need you.' I pause. 'Gracie needs you.'

'OK.' When he says that, when he doesn't argue or try and delay, the tears come, rapid and hot. I wipe them away as quickly as I can.

'How long till you get here?' I ask.

'Depends on traffic so . . . '

'Make it quick,' I say, hanging up.

I sit with Gracie, behind her shut door, and pour imaginary tea, and serve imaginary cake, and admire her tiara, and sparkly plastic shoes, until I hear a car pull up out-side, and the front door open and shut. I hear Mum's voice and then Dad's, and eventually he opens Gracie's door, and she runs into his arms.

'It's all right, darling,' he says, 'I'm home now.'

Getting up, I try to walk past him, but he stops me, tilting my face to show the bruise that's forming there.

'She did that . . . ?'

I nod.

'Red—' He tries to hug me too, but I rip myself away from him, unable to take comfort from the man that let it get this bad. Knowing that Gracie is safe is enough. 'Where are you going?'

'Out,' I say, turning to look at him. 'Just out.'

And I don't know if it's the way my face is swelling and bruising or the look in my eye, but he just nods and steps aside.

Downstairs Mum is crying on the sofa, her face buried in a cushion. When I look at her, I hate her, I mean I really hate her. For the first time in my life, I hate her so much my blood burns. I wish I could get in there and rip the hair from her head. I need to get out of here before I do just that.

Sticking out of the top of her bag, which she's left on the coat hook by the door, is the familiar cap of a half-bottle of vodka, this evening's entertainment. Without thinking, I grab it and leave, slamming the door behind me as hard as I can.

The park is empty, thank God, and I scoot under the slide, only touching my fingers to my swollen lip once I'm out of sight. It hurts to wince, the pain shooting into my teeth and up around my eye.

My whole body hurts, like every bit of me is bruised, inside and out. And I just want this feeling to stop.

Twisting the lid off the bottle I lift it to my lips and drink.

It tastes vile, like watery medicine, and it stings my lip where it's cut, and the inside of my mouth around my gums. I swallow against my will and my stomach buckles and bubbles. Still I drink again, and again. And again. One steady gulp after another. Outside my little metal shelter, with kids' names and outsized dicks scratched into the paint, it starts to rain, diagonal streaks of water turning the dry ground around the slide darker, and still I take another gulp and another. Gradually my tongue gets used to the taste, and the pain in my face fades. More, and a little more, and the pain in my chest and gut falls away, almost out of sight now, like nothing living or dead in the universe has a single thing to do with me.

Warmth spreads through my body from my belly outward, and then all over, and even though my cheeks and fingertips are like ice, I don't feel cold. When the world tilts, I slide over onto the hard concrete with it. I hear myself laughing, and even that seems a long way off, like I am outside looking in, looking in at a girl with a half-shaved head, and a smashed-up face lying on the ground and laughing hard. As I rest my head in the dirt and fag ends, I see myself do it. As I tip the last of the bottle into my mouth, spilling it down the side of my face where it runs into the cut on my cheek and lip, I see myself lying there, like I'm somehow not in my body any more. I see the tears, as clear as the vodka, running down towards my ears. I see myself cry and cry, my body shake, my chest contract tight as a balled fist, and from very far away I hear the sobs, ripping out of me one after another, but I don't feel them, and that's good, that's very good. I look up at where the top of the slide makes a kind of a roof, strung out with dirty spiders' webs and globules of chewed gum, and something else. Something strange that shouldn't be there but I can't quite figure out why, and it begins to twist left and right until I'm not sure if I'm standing up or lying down. I don't care, I'm not afraid. All I want to do now is close my eyes, and let the world rock and shift behind my lids, until I don't even notice that any more.

29

Some kind of force is trying to propel my guts out of my mouth, so I sit up abruptly, waking up to a world of pain, just in time to avoid throwing up on myself.

I struggle to my knees, my head following a few seconds later, and I shudder and retch again, a pool of clear fluid forming in the dirt.

'Fuck. Shit. Fuck.' I know I say those words out loud, but they don't sound like me, they are deep and rough. Fuck. It's properly dark and I'm freezing. I wind my arms around myself trying to hug some warmth into my painful bones, but there isn't any. Everything hurts; my face throbs, my head pounds so hard and worst of all, I think I must still be drunk, as when I try and stand the world does its best to fling me out into space.

Christ. I climb out from under the slide and force myself upright, holding onto the rough rusty metal as I suck in the cold air. That's when I see that I am not alone any more. There's a figure on the swings, dressed in dark clothes. I might not have noticed them except for the squeak of the rusty chain as the swing moves back and forth. Hood up over baseball cap, shoulders hunched. I should feel a prickle of fear, a sense of danger looking at the kid. Because no kid is ever out here at this time of night to have fun on the swings.

Still not afraid. So that's what vodka does to you.

It takes away every last emotion and leaves you fearless. Stinking and in pain, but fearless anyway. For one fleeting second I almost feel sorry for Mum; if this is what she needs to be able to get through the day, she must be terrified all of the time.

I sit down next to the kid on the other swing, and I feel like a dick because the other swing is a baby swing and I can only really perch on the top of it. It's awkward and uncomfortable, but I can't move now. If I move now then I'll look like even more of a dick. The kid doesn't move, their face hidden, lost in the dark of the hoodie, but I can't see a weapon, just pale, slim, familiar-looking fingers wound around the chain. And then I realise where I've seen that daisy ring before. It's Naomi's, she was wearing it just before she went missing.

'Naomi?' I whisper her name. Has she died? Is this her ghost? I look back at the slide, in case my body is still there, but it's not; it's me, and it's her, her long fingers exactly. 'Nai?'

'Oh you fucktard.' Ashira turns to look at me, her face crumpling into disgust as she does. 'Jesus, what happened to you? No wonder you think I'm my sister's fucking ghost; you're pissed. And, FYI, she ain't dead. Yet.'

'What are you doing here?' I ask her. 'It's not safe!'

'No, not when you're here. I came here to think,' Ash says. 'I can't think at home, or in the hospital and I'm trying to figure out the tattoo.'

'What?' I seem to be lagging behind reality by one or two beats and nothing she says makes sense.

'I know why you are fucked up,' Ashira says, when I don't reply. 'I didn't bring it up at the hospital because, well, you looked like you were handling it. Now . . . Anyway, that shit's been going round and round in circles all day. First you kissed her, then you grabbed her tit, then you stuck your hand in her pants. Best of all, last post I saw, it said you made yourself a fake dick, whopped it out on the bed.'

'Oh God,' my whole body seems to cringe itself sober in horror. 'I made myself a dick, out of what? Some toilet roll tubes and a washing-up bottle? Christ, I'm a girl who fancies girls, why would I want to get anywhere near a dick?'

Ash laughs. 'Trolls never get that sort of shit.'

'Fuck, I can never go back to school. Never.'

'You can.' Ash looks straight ahead, between the tower blocks where lights of the fancy penthouses, and the cranes that are building even more of them, twinkle high in the sky. 'Try having your sister disappear and maybe attempt suicide, and see what crazy shit gets chatted over that, and then you'll know that you can go back to school. Trying to snog fucking Rose Carter, isn't anything. Fucking everyone's snogged her anyway.'

'Not everyone,' I say. 'Shit, now I feel like even more of a dick.'

'I thought you said you don't like dicks?' She laughs and so do I.

'That's the worst thing.' Ash looks at me, and I see the pain in her face. 'I can't move on, Red, I can't see a way out of this. Not until I figure out what happened.'

'Look, it's Friday, and she might wake up on Monday and tell us,' I say. 'Maybe it would be better, saner to just wait. Because she's going to wake up in a couple of days.'

Ash is quiet for a very long time, the chains of the swing stop creaking as she stills.

'Or she might not.'

'Wait a minute . . .' Something comes back to me as my brain starts to sober up. A flash of an image, of something where it shouldn't be. I get up off the swing and turn around, staring at the slide.

'What?' Ash frowns.

'I'm not sure if it was real or imagined but . . .'

Turning on my phone torch I go back to the slide, careful to step over what I threw up a few minutes ago.

'Bloody hell, you're disgusting,' Ash says as she follows me. 'To think I wanted to kiss you.'

'Wait. What?' Did she say that or did I imagine it?

'What?' She holds my gaze, and I'm trying to figure out what happened when something occurs to me.

'Oh my God, I just remembered. . .' I crouch under the crook of the slide and look. We sit here a lot, talking and messing around, but we never look up, never even thought about it. I never would have if I hadn't been unable to stand up any more.

Shining a light right up into the crook I see it, ducttaped into the narrowest angle of the triangle.

'Oh my God,' I whisper, sending spiders and bugs scurrying down my arm as I reach up and rip it off, carrying it outside to look at it in the torchlight.

'What is it?' Ash asks me and then she sees and her face changes.

'It's Naomi's phone. It's her phone! She must have hidden it there!'

We stare at each other in the dark.

'This changes everything.'

I don't want to face either of my parents, so I guide Ash through the alley to the back door. Hopefully they are in the living room, ruining each other's lives.

'Take your shoes off,' I whisper to Ash, before we go inside. 'And try not to make any noise.'

'This is your house, right?' Ashira asks me, her eyes widening as I shush her. 'Drama, much.'

The door jams, something is caught underneath it and it's not until I dislodge it that I see it's Mum's purse; coins are scattered across the floor and her bag is upside down, lipstick with a lid off, her keys. Her empty upturned bag thrown against the wall, slumps against the skirting board, like it's been knocked out for the count.

'I think she was really pissed off that I nicked her vodka,' I whisper as we creep through the kitchen. The living-room door is slightly ajar. Mum is asleep on the sofa, no sign of Dad. Did he go out again?

I jerk my head up the stairs, and Ash follows my lead walking upstairs in her socks. Gracie's door is open, her nightlight on, a sure sign that she was upset before she went to sleep, because Mum only ever lets her keep her door open if she is afraid of something. I'm about to go in when I see Dad stretched out on the floor next to her, eyes closed, phone resting on his chest.

For a second I remember when it used to be my bed he slept beside when I was scared to sleep on my own, and I feel something stretch and snap inside, happiness and sadness mingled into one moment of loss. There was a time when everything in my house was warm and safe, and good. And I'm pleased that Gracie went to sleep feeling that way tonight. I wish I could, too.

Ash looks around my room, the drum kit in the corner, the clothes on the floor, and sits on my bed and stares at the phone.

'Do you think she put it there?' I ask her.

'Yes,' she said. 'Yes. I think she put it there and I think she thought you'd find it weeks and weeks ago.'

'But why?' I sit on the floor, leaning my back against the bedroom door. 'If you were running away, why would you do that?'

'Because whatever it was she was doing, she had doubts. Not enough to stop her going through with it, but enough to want to leave us a way to find her. Only we didn't fucking find it, did we? Not until it was too late!'

'I don't know how many times I've sat under that slide since she vanished,' I say staring at it. 'Will it still work?'

Ash presses the home button. It's dead.

'I can try and charge it, but she didn't put it in a bag or anything. It's pretty good at keeping the rain out, that slide, but it's not watertight. Before I can charge it, I'll take it apart and dry it out in some rice.'

'Should we—'

'No, we aren't calling the fucking police!'

I exasperate her.

'For a rebel, you are very keen to get the pigs involved, but they don't give a toss, Red. You got to remember that.'

'I . . . well . . . maybe.'

'She was leaving us clues, laying a trail of breadcrumbs to be able to find her.' Ash gazes at the dormant phone as she talks. 'The playlists, the song she recorded and uploaded after she left. The phone, DarkMoon's Insta account. She must have had a new phone, or an iPad or something, something to keep her busy while she was locked away, maybe at first it even seemed exciting, an expensive gift.'

'Oh yeah, her Instagram account,' I say at once. 'I forgot about that, but I checked it out and . . . '

Picking my phone up I search her profile.

'There's nothing. Just these drawings and boring views of London. Virtually the same photo every time.'

'Let me see.' Ash takes the phone out of my hand, and slowly scrolls through the photos. 'You're right. These are the same. Same angle, same view every time, just different times of day . . . Oh fuck it, Red. We are morons.'

'Why?' I stare at the grid of photos.

'Because she was trying to show us where she was. She had one view from the place she was kept in and this was it. But we didn't see it in time to stop her being hurt.'

'She must have had access to the internet, but it was being controlled and monitored by someone else,' Ash continues, angry and excited in equal measure. 'That has to be it.'

'Shit,' I say. Ash's eyes glitter as she looks at me. 'It all fits.'

'Maybe, it *maybe* fits, Ash . . . '

'I'm taking the phone home, and I'll work on the tattoo code. There must be more clues. More answers that might help us crack the tattoo.'

'Ash,' I stop her as she heads for the door, 'what if we let her down by not finding her phone until now?'

'I can't think like that,' Ash snaps. 'And neither can you.

And look,' her voice softens, 'those fuckwits at school will be on to the next big drama before you know it, but if they aren't, and if they keep getting at you, I've got your back . . . and all of their passwords, OK?'

'OK,' I say. 'Thanks, Ash.'

She frowns as she looks at my face in the bright light of my room, her hand rising to my face, fingertips touching my cheek just below where it hurts the worst.

'Shit,' she says. 'I'm sorry this happened to you, Red. I know she's your mum, but if you like I could probably frame her for some kind of fraud, get her sent away for a few months, cheaper than rehab?'

It's so typically Ash, and so weirdly sweet that this time it's me who smiles, even though it makes the break in my skin crack afresh and sting.

'I'm not quite at the putting-my-mum-inside stage yet,' I say. 'But it's good to know you are on my side.'

'For now.' She hugs me tightly, and we hold each other for a moment, and I feel her thighs against mine, the small of her back against my hand, and something in my chemistry fizzes and pops in a most unexpected way. When we let each other go, I can feel the heat in my face, I only hope my bruises mask it.

She walks downstairs, slamming the back door behind her. Once she's gone I miss having her around.

When I go back to my room, Dad is waiting for me on the landing.

He reaches out to touch my cheek and I back away.

'It just hurts, that's all,' I say.

'Who was that, in your room?' he asks me.

'Ashira, Naomi's sister. She's a friend.'

He nods. 'Look, love. I'm so sorry. I'm sorry I haven't

been around. I had no idea how bad it was getting here.'

I just look at him, and his shoulders drop.

'I know how that sounds. I realise that. I realise I've failed you all.'

Nodding in the direction of Gracie's open door, I motion for him to follow me into my room.

'Dad, it has got to change. We can't go on like this.'

'I can see that,' he says. 'She really hit you.'

'Yes, she really did.' Even so, the hate I felt earlier is all but gone, and I want to make excuses for her, I want to find a reason behind what she did that I can understand, but despite wanting that, I don't try. I can't hide how bad this is. I love her, but I can't help her now.

I am still just a kid after all.

'I don't know what to say . . . ' Dad shakes his head. 'Gracie wouldn't stop crying, and your mum, she wouldn't talk to me. What have I done to you all?'

'Don't feel sorry for yourself, Dad,' I say. 'She drinks. Because she misses you. She hates herself for not being enough for you. She knows you've got someone else, more than just one. It's bloody obvious. And it's not just that . . .' I struggle. 'She hates me, too. Because she hates who I am, Dad. I disgust her. Some stuff has happened recently and she . . . she looks at me like I'm dog shit on her shoe. And I've got to tell you, it fucking breaks my heart. Because sooner or later the way I feel about her, it will be gone for good. Sooner or later, I'll just hate her right back.'

Finally, I let him hug me, pressing the sore side of my face into his shirt, and I cry, because I'm sad, because I've missed him so much, and more than anything, because I miss the way he used to make me feel so safe, safe in a way I haven't felt for the longest time.

'I miss you, Dad,' I say. And I don't just mean him, but the idea of him I used to have in my head, before I realised he was normal like everyone else.

'I miss you too,' he says. And we stand like that for a minute or two and when we step apart I feel like I know who he is again, in a new way. In way that I will be able to like one day.

Back in my room and my head hurts like a bastard, but I can't sleep, not after finding Nai's phone. Instead, I pick up Nai's notebook and I read every single song through again. They are love songs, lust songs, call them what you want, but there isn't anything in any part of them that could tell me who they are about. Then stuck in between the pages I see the tiny corner of a ripped cigarette packet. And I remember all the other stuff that Nai kept stuffed in this book. I assumed it was disposable, and shook it out on my floor. I never even looked at it.

Thank God Mum never comes in my room. On my knees I scour the carpet picking up everything I find, throwing it all back onto my bed. When I'm sure I have everything, I lay them out on my bed in a kind of grid.

Fragments of lyrics.

A ticket to Hampton Court.

More of her words written on the back of a torn cinema ticket for exactly the kind of romantic movie she hated.

A label from a beer bottle.

An empty packet of Maltesers.

As I look at them I begin to see they aren't just ideas scribbled down, they are mementoes. Moments that belong to one story. The story of whoever it was Naomi wrote those songs for.

Finally I see the rest of the cigarette packet, the one that left its corner still lodged in the book, and at least I know something about whoever it was that Naomi was seeing, because she doesn't smoke.

When I turn it over I know something else, too.

There's a handwritten note on the back, and it's not Naomi's handwriting.

'You belong to me now. Remember that, whatever else happens, you are mine.'

I take a photo of it and I send it to Ash.

'That's him,' she sends back. 'That's the bastard that took her.'

And I'm starting to believe that maybe she's right.

That's him right there.

But who is he?

30

Morning, but it's dark under the pillow and if I press it down hard against my ear, it's almost quiet except for the sounds inside my head, but if I do that the dull throb in my cheek turns into a sharp stab that seems to radiate through my body. But it's more than just the pain from being hit, it's everything. And there are so many things that are out of place and wrong, it feels impossible to imagine how life might be normal again. Stop. Open your eyes and feel your heart beating, feel the pain in your face and remember *you are alive.*

There's a way out of this mess, and I am going to find it, not just for me, but for Naomi. Because even though I don't know what happened to her, I know it nearly killed her and even if she thought she wanted it at the start, I know she was terrified.

I want Rose, I need to talk to her about this, I need her help. Which means I need to fix us, to show her that her friendship means so much to me, more than the way I feel about her.

But when I unlock my phone she's not there, not in

any of the places where she always is, only a few seconds away from any message. I go from account to account and I can't find her anywhere, and for a moment I think, oh fuck, she's left social media because of me, and then I realise, of course she's blocked me. Everywhere.

This hurts much more than a slap, or a punch. This feels like an invisible wall has been built all around me. I'm frustrated and confused. Rose is always there, I rely on her to be always there, I hate this space between us.

Sitting up in bed, my thumb finds Rose's number on my phone.

I never make calls, hardly ever. It's just not the way I talk to my friends, or to anyone if I can avoid it. Pressing her name on the screen, waiting for the long moments it takes the phone to connect, and then even longer while it rings. I'm expecting her voicemail, and so I'm surprised when there is just silence, and the sounds of her being there, not speaking.

'Rose?'

'Hi.' It's a short word, and I can't tell anything from it. There isn't a handy emoji to go along with it, just one word, flat and unreadable. Just the silence that comes after she's spoken.

'Are you OK?' I ask her.

'Yeah.' Short again. But she is still there. She hasn't hung up, not yet.

Breathe, and think. Don't put one word wrong.

'Look, I am sorry about what happened. I made such a dick of myself. I never meant to fall for you, and I certainly never meant to ever tell you. It was . . . I was stupid for doing what I did, but I'm not stupid for caring about you the way I do. You are amazing, the most amazing person I have ever known. And I feel the way I do about you because I do know you. Not because of what you look like, or anything else. But because you are you.'

Silence still. Take a breath, try again.

'I think I know why you are so angry with me. And I get why you've blocked me from everything, but . . . well, I hope you will change your mind one day. Because I miss you. And not in that way. I miss my best mate . . . I need a best mate more than anything else.'

'So we are going to rehearse on stage tomorrow, yeah?' she says.

'Yeah.' I say. 'But . . . '

'What I did, that post. That was dickless and I hate myself for it. I've tried to fix it. I think it will be OK at school now.' She pauses, I hold my breath. 'But the truth is, Red, I thought we felt the same way about each other. And now I know we don't. And that makes me feel weird, like we're not honest with each other, like what you say and do isn't because you are my friend, it's because of how you feel.'

'It doesn't have to make you feel that way because—' I begin to say but she cuts me off.

'It does have to, it should have to. What you feel, it matters. You should want it to matter. And I . . . I just need a break from us for a bit. A break from what we used to be. I don't hate you, OK? Not at all, I just need a break. I've got . . . stuff. Something important happening, and I think it's better if we don't hang out so much. I'll do the concert, but then I'm leaving the band.'

'But—'

'I'll see you at rehearsal tomorrow.'

'Rose, please, can we talk about this some more?'

'Stay out of my life, OK? I just need some distance right now.'

'But . . . ' But she's already hung up by the time I say it, I didn't even get a chance to tell her about Nai's phone.

Collapsing back onto my bed, I have no idea what to do next. Outside grey sky smothers every trace of blue, and it feels like winter. A whole day with nothing to do but sleep seems like torture.

So when my phone rings, I almost fall out of bed trying to reach it, hoping that it's Rose calling me back, that she's changed her mind and we can laugh about all the drama and get over it. But it isn't.

'Red, I need help.'

It's Leo.

I sit up, feeling at once anxious and uneasy because Leo hates talking on the phone even more than I do. And more than that, even more than that the anger, the swagger; it's all gone. Now all I can hear is fear.

'What's up?'

'Red, I think I'm fucked.' Leo is whispering, and I can barely hear him. Somehow at once I understand this is serious, he means this. 'I'm in deep and now I can't get out.'

'What, why? What's happening?' I ask.

'Wait, wait a minute.' There are shuffling noises on the other end of the phone and I hear a door slam, footsteps.

'I had to get out for a minute. I can't talk in here. Fuck, Red, I am so fucked. I don't know what to do.'

'What is it, Leo?'

'Aaron. The guy he has business with, the one he thinks made a fool of him, whose fault it is that he is inside. Aaron's had his mates around here all night. Staying up taking hard shit, music turned up so loud you can hear it across the estate. Mum tried to get them out, and Aaron locked her in her bedroom. I tried to let her out and he . . . he got real mad, Red. Him and his mates, they have been winding each other up, getting ready for shit to go down. And now. Now they're gonna do it, Red. They found out where this bloke is gonna be, and they are going over there, he says I'm going over there with him, I've got to be more of a man, and I don't know what to do.'

'Leo, do what?' I ask him. 'What are they going to do?'

'I saw a gun,' he says. The moment I hear that word my mouth goes dry, and fear races down every nerve ending at high velocity.

'He's going to *shoot* someone?' This time I am the one who's whispering.

'He wants me with him, Red. If I don't go, I don't know what he'll do. He won't let Mum out, not even now. He took her money, her phone. I heard her crying all night and I can't get near her to talk to her. He's had zero sleep, he is fucked up, paranoid and angry. I don't know what he'll do.'

'Hang up on me. Call the police now, tell them,' I say.

'I can't, I'm not a grass, if he even knew I'd phoned you . . . and anyway I don't know where it's happening, or when. All I know is that I've got to go with him.'

'Leo, you can't go. That's not you. Just don't go!'

'I don't know what else to do . . . ' Leo's voice wobbles in a way I have never heard before. 'I'm scared of him, Red. I'm scared of what he'll do.'

'Just leave, now. Keep walking and come to me. We can talk to my dad and get help.'

I hear a distant shout.

'He's calling me. It's time. I gotta go.'

'Leo wait . . . don't go!' I shout. The call ends. I stare at the phone, my mind's gone blank. Did my best friend just hang up on me to go and take part in a murder?

31

The seconds go past, and I run that thought around and around in my head until it solidifies and becomes real. It's fucking real, and I can't let this happen to Leo, I can't. But I can't stop it either. Somehow I need to find Leo, get him and drag him away from Aaron before it's too late.

But how? Where do I even start looking? Dragging on my jeans and a T-shirt, I think again of going to my parents but what's the point? What can they do for me when they can't even take care of themselves? Then it hits me, Find My Friends on my phone. When we first got it, it was a laugh, a game. And then the novelty wore off because I always knew where they were, but now? This could work.

I open the app and look for Leo, and see him, a small pulsating dot. He's still at home. Shoving my feet into my trainers, I shrug on my hoodie and stuff my keys into my pocket, running out of the front door towards Leo's estate, keeping my eye on my phone, wanting to get as close to him as I possibly can before that dot starts moving.

I am about halfway to his place when it does.

Slowing to a jog, I keep my eye on the dot trying to work out where he is going, cutting back and forth through streets and side streets to try and meet him head on, but as quickly as I go, he keeps moving just out of reach. Then my phone rings again.

Fuck's sake. It's Ash.

I reject the call, but she rings again, and somehow I know that it's going to keep ringing, so I just put her on speaker and keep following the dot.

'Where are you?' she asks, without bothering with a 'hello'.

'I'm not totally sure,' I say looking around me. 'I'm trying to find Leo. Ash, he's in trouble. It's serious so I can't really talk right now.'

'What kind of trouble?' She sounds annoyed, not concerned.

'Big trouble. I need to get to him before something bad happens.'

'Like actual bad, or mega teen drama bad, because I've got something to tell you. Something really fucking huge.'

'I'm talking about something really serious,' I say. 'Leo's brother has a gun, and I think he's going somewhere to use it.'

'Fuck,' she says. 'OK, where are you?'

'I don't really know,' I take a left down one road, and see that Leo is two parallel streets away, still ten minutes or so ahead. 'Going towards Brixton tube, I think.'

'OK, I'll get there and then track your phone.'

'You're not on my Find My Friends list,' I say.

'I don't need to be.'

I choose not to think about that. Stay focused on the bigger picture.

'Ash, it might not be safe.'

'Which is why I'm not letting you go in there on your own,' she says. 'Naomi always makes a big deal of how important friends are. She's not here to rescue you, so I suppose I'll have to.'

How an eighteen-year-old tech-head is going to stop a gang of men with weapons I don't know, but I haven't got time to worry about that now.

One more left turn, one right turn and then I stop dead and step back into a shop doorway. I can see them, a group of young men – around ten of them – standing together under one of the archways of the railway bridge, laughing and talking. People walking past see them and cross the road, or keep their heads down. Searching Leo out, I scan the crowd until I see him. He's on the edge of the group, head bowed, scuffing the toes of his trainers on the pavement, like a little kid.

I need a plan. I don't have a plan after getting here. So . . .

This is what I'm going to do. I'm going to just walk up to him all casual and be like, hey, Leo, fancy meeting you here, want to come to do something with me? And then he and I can just stroll off, just like that and at least whatever happens after that won't be happening to him.

Taking a breath, I shake out my shoulders, running my fingers through my hair. Act cool, Red; look casual, Red; just be normal, Red.

Leo sees me as I approach and starts shaking his head, covertly gesturing for me to go the other way, but I just keep going, minding my own business, playing it cool, like I haven't noticed more than ten massive guys crowding by the bridge.

Until I'm almost on the top of them.

'Hey, Leo, man,' I say, trying to sound casual and surprised. 'Oh hi, guys.'

(Oh hi, guys? I couldn't sound more fake if I tried.)

I look around at the rest of the crew, all of them older and bigger and scarier than me, and more importantly suddenly all looking right at me, like I'm a skinny, ginger little insect they could squash with a single stomp.

'Fuck's sake,' Aaron grabs Leo by the arm, and drags him away from the main group. I follow, determined to stick to Leo like glue.

'Did you tell it what we were doing?' He kind of growls, and when I see him up close I can see why Leo is so worried. He's out of it. Strung-out wired, you can see it in his face, which is kind of twisted. There are spots of spit around his mouth and his pupils are huge and black, wiping out every trace of colour from his eyes. Like a zombie, almost. A really angry zombie.

'What? No!' I say, playing the idiot. 'What *are* you doing? Hey, is there a party or something? Leo, you didn't tell me there was a party, dude, not cool. Where is it? Can I come? And oh, by the way, I'm not an "it" I'm a she.'

My theory is the more annoying I am, the more disruptive and challenging I am, the more likely it is that Aaron will just tell Leo to go just to get shot of me.

But my theory doesn't work.

'Listen *Thing*.' Aaron gets right up close to me. Close enough for me to see the tiny rim of colour that encircles his dilated pupils, the sweat oozing out of his pores, and smell his rancid breath. Close enough that my heart thunders in my chest and I wish I was anywhere else but here right now. 'Now you are here, you ain't going nowhere.

You're with me until this is done and afterwards, if you say anything to anyone about this, then I'll be introducing you to my mate.'

He sounds so much like a soap opera villain that I'd laugh if it wasn't for the fact that he doesn't have to do much to reveal the weight and shape of the gun in his tracksuit bottoms. That piece of metal makes it all very real.

I nod.

'Now stay out of the fucking way.'

He turns back to the others and Leo pulls me deeper under the archway, as far away from them as we can get, shaking his head.

'What the fuck are you playing at?' he asks angrily. 'I told you not to come. Now we are both fucked, Red.'

'You didn't actually say don't come and I'm trying to help you,' I say. 'Of course I have to help you. What's going on here? What are they waiting for? Cos they aren't exactly inconspicuous, are they?'

'See that snooker club over there?' Leo nods across the road and I see what looks to me like a run-down bar or something, but with a sign made of a snooker triangle filled with balls. 'They are waiting for a guy to come out of there. Then . . . then I don't know, Red. Look, when it kicks off just go, OK? Just leg it in the other direction.'

'Come with me,' I urge him.

'I can't. Aaron will kill me.'

When he says it, it doesn't sound like a figure of speech.

Aaron gets a text on his phone and suddenly the whole group is alert, tuned in to what could happen next, like a pack of wolves about to go on the hunt.

'Right, this is it.' Aaron eyeballs the group. 'Get ready.'

Nobody pays that much attention to the regular city background noise of the sirens until they are really close, just across the road, and I see traffic pulling out of the way to make way for . . . fire engines. Two of them. They come to a stop in front of the snooker hall, and a team of fire fighters rush out, running inside the club.

'What the . . . fuck?' Aaron's shoulders drop, he shakes his head. 'What the actual fuck? You couldn't make it up!'

The tension and aggression that knits the group together gradually disperses, as they stand around, watching as people come pouring out of the club and onto the street, slowly realising that whatever they had planned is not going to happen now.

'Well fuck that.' Aaron turns to us. 'Fuck it. Who's holding?'

'I got something,' a voice comes.

'Let's get fucked up, then,' Aaron says and just like that, he stalks away, his mates in his wake. But the only thing I care about is the direction that he is going in, which is away from us.

Three or four beats pass and I breathe out.

'What just happened?'

I look at Leo.

'I mean what are the chances of that happening, just then?' Leo says.

'Pretty high when someone you know calls 999 in order to save your arse,' Ash says, appearing at our sides.

'You did that?' I laugh, drunk with relief. 'Ash, you're a genius! You just defeated a bunch of tooled-up gangsters.'

'Yeah, well.' She shrugs. 'Someone needs to take care of you all . . . Nai's going to need you when she wakes up. And anyway, it really didn't take much effort. After I spoke to you I got the tube to Brixton, located you and then when I saw the situation, because – no offence Leo, your brother and his dickwads have got all the subtlety of a fucking nuclear explosion – I called in the cavalry. Not the police, because that's snitching. Fire Brigade. I checked the scanners to make sure and there weren't any major fires happening in the area, first, otherwise I'd have had to have thought of something else. Bomb scare, maybe.'

Leo and I both stare at her and she stands there, her long hair neatly plaited, her too-new denim jacket buttoned all the way up to the top. She's like Wonder Woman, the awkward years.

It's crazy how high I am, how much I feel like laughing my head off or running around. All of a sudden I feel invincible, powerful and that is fucking stupid. If that's what being in danger and not dying does to you, then evolution has got a lot to answer for. I am a stupid fucking kid who got into a stupid fucking situation and I feel brilliant. That can't be right.

'I got to get home to Mum,' Leo says, 'and then we got to get out of there, Aaron's out of control now.'

'Yes, good, let's do that, I'll come with you,' Ash says. 'But just stop for a minute. Just stop. I need to tell you both something. Something important.'

'What are you talking about?' I reply. Ash doesn't give much away, but I know one thing about her for sure. She doesn't do drama for the hell of it.

'This morning I got a hit from one of the combinations of the tattoo.'

'You mean you found a website?'

'Yeah.' Ash nods, her face is grey. 'On the dark web.

It wasn't too hard to get in once I found it, I guess most people don't look. It's a . . . it's a site where men post about children, the kids they groom and rape. The tattoo. It's a secret symbol, half of a design that is part of a whole, semi circle becomes a circle, triangle a diamond. The other half is tattooed on the person that owns the girl, but in white ink, so only he'd know it was there. It's a slave stamp. Someone tattooed a fucking slave stamp on my sister.'

'Oh Christ.' Leo turns from hammering his fist into a wall.

I shut my eyes, trying to close out the images of just some of the things that Naomi might have been through. 'Oh God, oh no.'

Ash's face is wrought with pain, but still she has more to say. 'Sometimes, if the images of the girl are very popular and in demand, they persuade her to run away with one of them. The guy tells her he loves her, he isolates her from her friends and family and says they have to leave to be together and then . . . Then the guy imprisons her and lets the other men on the site know when and where they can take a turn.'

'I'm gonna kill someone,' Leo says. 'Someone is going to die.'

'I can't even imagine . . . ' I look at Leo and he puts his arms around me, more or less holding me up.

'I found Nai's story.' When Ash speaks it's automatic, like a robot, like she has to force out pre-programmed words. 'Everything that happened between her and the man that groomed her, MrMoon he calls himself. Photos . . . videos. Every detail, everything. And there are photos of twenty other girls, just on his feed. One of them was

Carly Shields, and yes . . . Danni. When they get bored with a girl they sometimes let her go, scare and shame her into not talking, I guess. There are tips on what to say to make a girl keep quiet. But also there were some names on there. . . and when I looked for them they had died, killed themselves, been in an accident, or were just listed as missing. There's another girl on there now. His latest project, he's still grooming her. It's still a romance as far as she is concerned and nothing more. It hasn't gone that far yet.'

'Who is it?' I ask her the question, but I already know the answer.

'It's Rose,' she says.

32

Leo's place. The moment Ashira told us what she had found, it had started to rain, cold slices of water coming down that soaked us through to the skin. As Aaron and his mates drifted away in small groups, we three stood there, the water pooling in every pore, caught in a loop of uncertainty. When you know something that massive, that devastating, where do you go next? How do you push into the next second and the one after and still make sense of the world around you?

In that moment, standing there in the rain, we didn't know. And in this moment, as we arrive back at Leo's flat, I still don't. The only thing we can do is react, and the first thing Leo thought about was his mum, still locked in her bedroom. We did the one thing we could think of to do, we came back to help her.

It seems to take forever to get there, the last leg – travelling upwards in the creaky old lift – the longest of all. As we approach the front door my heart is pounding out some serious bass. I fear the worst, no that's not right, I expect it. I'm overwhelmed by the feeling that someone has just dragged away the last veil of protection that was left over from the world of my childhood. A world where the sun was always bright and the sky was always blue, and now, now I'm left with this wash of grey and dirt and the realisation that bad things happen, not just out there, but to people I know, people I love. To me.

And it's terrifying.

The flat door comes into view and it's been left open, Aaron probably too high to care about checking if it was shut when they left. For a moment it's pinned against the hall wall for a second by a sudden rise in the wind, and then it slams shut in our faces.

Leo unlocks it, and stops on the threshold, looking down the corridor. Inside it's dark, very quiet, even though someone has left the TV on in the front room. At least Aaron isn't there.

'Mum?' Leo calls out as he goes inside. 'Mum?'

'Leo?' She replies at once, her bedroom door rattling as Leo races to it.

'Hold on!'

She begins to cry from the other side of the door as Leo fumbles with the padlock, trying a few times to open it, even though the key was left in the lock and really only needed turning, but even easy things are hard to do when you are trembling.

The second the door is open, Leo is enveloped in his mum's embrace, his arms coiling around her in return.

'I've been going out of my mind!' She speaks between gasps. 'Where have you been, what did you do? What did he do?'

'Nothing, Mum.' Leo tries to reassure her. 'Nothing.

It was all talk. All show, he hasn't done anything, it's fine, everything is OK.'

'He wouldn't listen to me, and when I wouldn't shut up like he wanted me to, he hit me and he locked me in there. I was so frightened.' She looks up at Leo, grabbing him by the face. 'He can't live here any more, Leo. He's my son and I swore to love him from the day he was born, but I can't keep that promise while I am afraid of him and afraid for you. We can't stay here if he's here. I know he's your brother, but . . . '

'I know, Mum.' Leo nods. 'We need to get out of here. You need to get some stuff together and go to Aunty Chloe's, yeah? For a couple of nights.'

'And you, too,' she says. 'I need you with me, Leo. I need to know you are safe at least.'

'I'm going to stay with Red.' Leo looks at me, and I nod. 'We've got band practice tomorrow, haven't we? So I'm going to stay over. And after we've had a couple of days away we'll figure out what to do. Maybe we can try and talk to Aaron, get him away from the people and the drugs. Because do you remember, Mum, what he used to be like? How he stepped up when Dad died, and how he used to spend hours making model planes, remember that?'

'I remember.'

'There's still got to be a way to get him back,' Leo says. 'The way he used to be when I was a little kid. We just got to figure out how. Go and pack your bag, Mum, phone Aunty Chloe, tell her you're on your way.'

'You are a good boy, Leo,' she says kissing him on each cheek. 'You'll be OK, with Red?' She looks at me, and then at Ashira. 'You'll be safe?'

'He'll be fine,' Ash says. 'I promise.'

And for some reason that reassures her.

'Fuck.' Leo drops his head in his hands, the moment she leaves the room, and we all collapse into the same moment, the same how-has-this-happened madness. 'What's going on?'

'This time, the only answer is we go to the police, Ash. Tell them what you found. You have proof, they'll believe you.'

'No,' Ash says, and for the first time since she found us under the arches, I see how this discovery has dragged through her, taking a good part of her away with it, draining her of almost all the rainbow of colours that makes her who she is so that I am looking at someone who is more or less a monotone girl. 'If I can charge up Nai's phone and unlock it then we might be able to find out who MrMoon is. And I want to get him. *I* want to. I want him and all those other . . . scum to know it's me that ended them.'

'Ashira,' I begin to say cautiously, 'you can't really want to kill him . . . '

'No, I'm not going to kill him, I'm not violent. I can do better than that,' she says. 'So. Much. Better. I'm going to bring his life down in ruins and then I'm going to make sure he has to live with it.'

'I'm ready, I think.' But Leo's mum appears just at the moment Aaron throws open the front door. If he looked bad before, it's a hundred times worse now. I like to think I'm a bit street, a bit cool, that living in London means I know what life is really about, but I've never seen someone this gripped by drugs before, like there's a fist squeezing him in the middle, sending all the blood and guts to his face.

'I didn't say you could let her out.' Aaron grabs Leo by the neck of his hoodie, sticking his face in his. This is where I step in, I think distantly, where I tell him to lay off my mate. But that's not what I do, I find myself shrinking back from his fury, sensing that the danger is real. The air around him stinks of booze, smoke and something else. I've seen angry, and I've seen hurt, I've seen drunk and I've seen drug-crazed. But looking at Aaron, I see all of those things, mixed up in a swirl of something more, something terrifying. And I just want to run.

But there is no way out.

'You can't keep her locked up.' Leo does his best to look unconcerned, straightening his shoulder, jerking himself free from his brother's grasp. And all I want to do is to cry out to him, stop, don't talk to him, don't move, don't even breathe if it might risk triggering the trip wire that is stretched so tight, arming a bomb that could blow any minute.

'Aaron, no.' Leo's mum's voice is very quiet, very afraid.

'She's our mum, not an animal, bro,' Leo says.

'It's OK son, let it go,' Leo's mum replies.

'You telling me what I can do?' Aaron's clenched fist is drawn back, locked and loaded. 'YOU TELLING ME WHAT I CAN DO?'

It happens so quickly that when I see Leo sprawled on his back at Aaron's feet, blood exploded across his face, it takes me a while to make sense of what happened, like a bad jump-cut in a horror movie. This is not me, this person frozen to the spot in terror, who doesn't go to their friend, this is not who I am. I want to go to his side, step in front of Leo, but I don't. I can't move. I can't breathe.

'Let me tell you something, *bro*,' Aaron takes the gun

from the pocket of his joggers and levels it at Leo's head, the muzzle touching his forehead, 'I'm getting tired of people telling me what I can and can't do. I'm getting bored of fools who don't show me any respect. *You* respect me, you got that? *She* respects me, and you both do what I tell you to do, because I own you. I own these freaks, I own this fucking town, and if I want to burn it down to the ground with you in it, I will. Don't you think that I won't, because I will. I fucking will.'

'Oh please, boring,' Ashira says.

I hear her voice, I'm aware of the shape of her, but I can't stop looking at the muzzle of the gun as he releases it from Leo's forehead and searches her out, staring her square in the chest.

'Do you want to die, bitch?' Aaron asks her. 'Who the fuck are you anyway?'

'Sometimes I do want to die.' Ashira takes a step closer to the end of the gun with every word. 'Sometimes I think oblivion might be the easy way out. But you know what? You are so lucky to have a family that care about you, to have a brother who's trying to take care of you. If my little sister was around, if she was awake and undamaged and I had the chance to do things differently, like you do, the actual very last fucking thing I would do is try to intimidate and scare the shit out of her with a fucking gun, *arsehole*.' She takes another step closer and my knees give way, I fold onto the floor, my body feels like it's disappearing around me, and only my eyes remain fixed by fear.

'Ash.' I try and whisper her name, but nothing comes.

'You must be a very scared man,' Ashira says, and even

though that bullet is aimed right at her, her voice is gentle now, and tender. 'You have to be. You have to be very scared and very lonely for the idea of respect to mean more to you than the love of your family, the life of your brother. And I get that, I think. What it means to feel that fucked up. I feel that fucked up. But there are still choices to be made, to live or die. Kill or care. So if you need to pull a trigger to feel like a man, go ahead. You'll end up back inside, for good this time, and maybe that's the only place you will ever be anyone. So put my brains on the wallpaper, if it makes you feel any better. I really don't give a shit.'

Despite everything I thought I'd learnt about Ashira since that day when I found her hacking traffic cams, I never really knew her until this very second, when suddenly I see so clearly the vast and unlit ocean of sadness she has to navigate alone, every day. So raw, so real that she looks at a man half out of his mind – with a gun in his hand – and feels some kind of recognition, some kind of hope, even.

Aaron doesn't move, not for one, two, three, four, five, six seconds. By ten seconds and with the gun still pointed at us, he walks out of the flat, slamming the door to a close behind him.

DarkMOOn
Locked In

There's nothing but dirt here, nothing but dark,
Animals in shadows
That want to rip me apart
There's nothing but hurt here, nothing but pain,
Cold cruel hellos
Again and again and again...

You told me there'd always be sunshine,
You told me there'd always be you,
You made me believe in believing
And then you locked me in.
You locked me in.

You tell me I have to smile, even when I taste blood.
You say they want to see teeth
It's a sign of love when you hurt me so hard
There's not love here, just pain.
You say I am your own private feast
You bite me again and again. And again...

You told me there'd always be sunshine,
You told me there'd always be you,
You made me believe in believing
And then you locked me in.
You locked me in.

33

The sun is high enough in the sky to come cutting through the narrow gaps in my curtains and dazzle me awake. Very, very slowly I open my eyes, my lashes tugging as they untangle. My phone tells me it's almost midday, so why does my body feel so heavy with sleep? And so sore, like I've been beaten up from the inside out. As I register the sound of breathing from the floor, every moment of yesterday comes back in one chaotic crazy rush. Rolling over I see Leo, still out of it, in his sleeping bag on the floor, eyes closed and looking like a little kid. Leaning against the wall, Ashira is sitting with her legs stretched out in front of her, a deep line between her eyebrows as she stares at her laptop screen. The last thing I remember from last night is her sitting exactly like this as I went to sleep. She might have been like that all night.

We didn't have to stay together last night. Leo could have gone with his poor, tearful mum to his Aunty Chloe's, and Ashira could have gone home to her mum and dad. But when it came down to it, not one of us wanted to say goodbye to the others. It felt safer to be together, that's all. We didn't talk about what Aaron did, we didn't talk about what Ashira did. We just wanted to stick together. And the easiest place to do that, and to do what had to be done, was at my house.

Even so we felt the presence of the missing. Naomi, who would have been so freaked out to see her big sister hanging out in my bedroom, and Rose. More than twenty-fours have passed, and I have no idea what happened to her in any of them, and that is so strange and so different that it feels like she's left for the moon.

Watching the rise and fall of Leo's chest, I wonder what Rose is doing now. On almost any other day of the week in the last year I would know exactly, within seconds of waking up. But today she isn't here. So much has happened, so much that would matter to her too, just as much as it matters to any of us. She isn't here and . . . she could be with him. He could be using her right now and the thought of that kills me. Ash said that it wasn't at that stage yet, but Ash is obsessed with bringing these creeps down herself. What if Ash is wrong?

Leo's phone is on the floor next to him, one end of it poking out from under his sleeping bag. Glancing up at Ashira I see she is still staring hard into her laptop screen, and Leo rolls onto his side, facing away from me. After a moment's hesitation I pick up Leo's phone, turning it over in my hand. I don't know the code that unlocks it, but I can see the notifications on his screen. Sure enough there are five messages from Rose. I can't see all of them, just the preview.

Hey loser, what were you up to yesterday, everything OK? I've been . . .

Leo, are you around, I could really do with talking to you about
something . . .

I'm not sure how I feel about today. I don't really know how
to . . .

I wish you'd answer me, have you got a problem with me?

Leo WTF! Are you OK? Where are you now?

'The code is probably his birthday,' Ashira whispers, and
I drop the phone, pushing it back in place. When I glance
up she is watching me, with half a crooked smile. 'If you
want to get into his phone.'

'I don't want to get into his phone,' I say. 'I thought it
was mine for a second, still half asleep.'

'Rose put up a thing on all her media, saying to lay off
you and that everything was OK between you.'

'Did she?' I brighten, sitting up. 'Does she seem all
right? She doesn't seem like . . . like . . . you know?'

'Not as far as I can tell,' Ash says. 'This guy is locked
up pretty tight here, I can't ID him. I have to hope that I
can charge Nai's phone today and see if there's anything
on that.'

'Ash . . . what if we are putting Rose in danger by not
going to the police?'

'We aren't, he posted on the dark site last night saying
they are still just kissing and holding hands, that he wants
to prove to her how much he cares about her. He said
another week of that and she'll be eating out of his hand.
He said that's when he'll nail her. Set up a video link and
everything.'

'Oh God.' I press my hands over my mouth, bitter-tasting acid rising in my throat. This is real, it's happening, but it feels like being trapped in the last fifteen minutes of a horror movie which just keeps looping over and over. 'Oh God, Ash . . . '

'Look, don't worry.' She smiles at me briefly, it's gone almost before I see it and yet somehow it helps. 'I'll have him by then.'

'What are you doing, anyway? Did you even sleep?'

'There's no way that I'm going to sleep properly until this is done,' she says, looking up at me. 'I mean yeah, I got my head down for a little bit, I don't want to lose my edge. But I need to stay on this every minute I can if I'm going to track him down. I want his email, I want his cloud, I want his internet history, I want everything.'

'That's illegal, you realise that.'

'Obviously.' Ashira lifts her chin. 'Are you afraid of breaking the law?'

It's a challenge, I see it there in her dark eyes, and I know whatever I say next will affect the way she thinks of me.

'No,' I say very carefully, and deliberately. 'But I am afraid of you getting caught, and him getting away with what he's doing.'

Ashira's mouth curls into a dangerous smile.

'That isn't going to happen, Red,' she assures me. 'You – you are brilliant at playing the drums, you don't question if you are good, you just know that you are. Well, that's me, and this shit. I'm good at it.'

'I know,' I return her smile, 'I'm just saying if we go to the police today, talk to them today, then they have people who can do all of this, and get him. It doesn't have to be us. It doesn't have to be you.'

'It does,' Ashira says. 'It does have to be me.'

'What does?' As I speak, Leo sits up, rubbing his eyes.

'I have to be the one to get him. I want to be the one to make him feel trapped and scared with no control over his life, unable to see a way out. I want vengeance. And what I've got planned means we can't fail. But I need you two on board to make it work. If you're not OK with it, if you can't keep what we know to yourselves – no matter what – for a few days then it won't work. But if you trust me, and let me do my thing, as soon as I find out who he is we can make this bastard pay. And pay hard. But to do that, you can't tell Rose anything.'

'Are you kidding me?' Leo shakes his head. 'We can't use Rose as bait.'

'We aren't doing that, we are making sure this bastard doesn't close any loopholes I might be able to get through. If we spook him, that's what he'll do, or he'll run and pop up again with a different username and then how many other girls will there be? It's really important he doesn't know that we nearly have him.' Ashira closes her laptop, to show how serious she is. 'I get that you want to talk, I want to. I want to go to Jackie and Dad, and tell them. But we can't, not yet. We can't run the risk of him finding something out about us, before we have everything on him.'

'But couldn't we just tell Rose and explain why she can't tell anyone?'

'No.' Ash narrows her eyes at me. 'Look, when you think you are in love with someone, someone who's told you to keep your relationship a secret because the outside world wouldn't approve, then you expect to be told something bad about them, you expect people to try and split you up. If it was you and Rose, and someone said you can't see Rose, what would you do?'

'But I hate lying to her,' I say. 'Because eventually she'll know that we lied to her, and what then? And what if we had a chance to save her from something really awful, and it's too late?'

'She's not even really talking to you now, so maybe you won't notice the difference.'

'She's talking to me.' Leo picks up his phone, and shows us another message from Rose. 'What do I say to her?'

'Tell her almost everything about yesterday. Just not about me being there, and not about what I found out, OK?'

Leo nods and unlocks his phone, I see how his mouth curls into a smile when he sees her messages, and I flop back down onto the bed.

Nothing feels normal.

Nothing feels safe.

Everything feels kind of awkward, a puzzle that's been put back together wrong.

I don't know why I am surprised.

This is my life after all.

Rose
Where you at, fam?

Leo
It all went down last night, with Aaron. Red got me out. Close thing, but I'm OK and I think maybe Aaron's gone

Rose
Fuck. You all right?

Leo
Dunno yet, really. It got pretty heavy. Where you been?

Rose
Stuff, you know

Leo
Rose . . . I care about you, you know

Rose
I care about you too

Leo
I'll see you at rehearsal

Rose
In a while crocodile. Got to go, am getting breakfast in bed!

34

School is always weird when it's out of hours and there's no one around, and on a Sunday it's especially strange, like it's watchful and awake, waiting for the life and energy that will come surging through its doors again tomorrow morning.

Even so it's may be the only time that I really like being here, when I feel like I'm not supposed to be.

I like how the corridors are dark and empty, the classrooms quiet and full of shadows. It's when no one is here that you hear the secret sounds you never notice when it's full of other people's lives. The creak and squeak of your shoes on the floor, the echo that bounces off the walls when you shut a door behind you, the whisper of the ancient heating system, or at least that's what I think it is.

There's something about this place when it's empty. It stops being a place of work where dull-as-fuck hours of your life slip away, and starts to be a movie set.

But not today. I've got no idea how I am going to get through the next two hours.

I take a breath outside the double doors that lead into

the school hall and remember what Ashira said.

'If you agree to the plan, you have to stick to it. You have to act normal around Rose, OK? No matter what. It will be hard, but it will be worth it.'

Hard doesn't touch it.

Rose is there already, standing on the stage by the mic stand, walking through each track while Smith and the kids from drama club go through the lighting plan. They're up in the gallery, the sort of balcony that runs along the back of the hall where the school's sound, vision and lighting mixing desk is situated. I walk down the centre aisle, flanked on either side by the chairs that have been set up in readiness for the concert. I'm about halfway when the lights drop. Rose sees me and her smile falters and fades, she hooks the mic back in the stand, and walks off stage.

'Red, come up here a sec.'

I look up at Mr Smith and he waves at me, I wave back, turning on my heel to go up to see him. It crosses my mind that I could tell *him* everything, that maybe if I told him, he'd take all this worry off our shoulders and everything would be sorted. All I want is for someone else to be in charge of this, because I don't want to be any more. I want to go home and go to bed and stay there until all of this has gone away.

'Come and have a look at the stage from up here, it looks great,' Mr Smith says, his face beaming, as I arrive in the gallery. He's right. He's managed to sweet talk a professional audio-visual hire place into lending us loads of equipment and it looks amazing. The lighting rig looks properly pro, and there is a screen almost as wide as the stage, right behind where my drums are set up, and small screens up and down the auditorium. The plan is for a multi-platform event, with videos and photos of Naomi growing up that her dad has carefully put on a USB stick for us. Her words, song lyrics, all of that combined together with our music. It was meant to be the perfect way to make sure no one forgot the missing girl. But now instead I suppose it will be a kind of a prayer, a wish that the girl we love will open her eyes.

'This is great,' I say to Smith. 'I've had my head so stuck in the band that this part kind of passed me by, but it's really good. Thanks, sir.'

Mr Smith grins. 'As much as I'd like to take the credit, it's Emily and her team who have done most of the magic.'

Emily, the same Emily that didn't make the band, grins at me proudly. I know that I look like an idiot the moment I realise she is there, sitting behind the light mixing desk. The sight of her takes me by surprise.

'You're in charge of all of this?'

'Don't sound so amazed.' She smiles at me.

'No . . . I didn't mean . . . I just thought it was the drama club.'

'I am the drama club, well a bit of it anyway. I asked Mr Smith if I could help with this to go on my CV, and because I just wanted to . . . '

'Amazing.' I turn back to the stage, wondering if Emily was maybe even flirting with me a bit. 'And you'll be able to see the performance on the screens all around the hall?'

'Yeah, more than that,' Emily says. 'We'll be cutting between you, live on stage, and the videos and photos of Naomi. It's going to be a total blubfest . . . oh fuck, sorry.

I mean it's going to be really moving. How is she, by the way?'

'No news yet, and this – it's great,' I reassure her. 'Really great. So how do you know it's not all going to go wrong on the night?'

'Well, no one but me will be here between now and tomorrow. I'll run a rehearsal tonight alongside you, and then just cue it up to start over again.'

'Can I get a picture of you?' I ask, and Emily beams. 'For our Tumblr?'

'Sure.'

'Move to the side so I get all your tech in,' I say, and she does, though she leans forward a little in the frame and smiles right into my eyes as I focus my phone camera.

'I hate to interrupt, but Leo and Leckraj are on stage now.' Mr Smith makes me jump, I'd actually forgotten he was there for a moment. 'Better get down there for a sound check?'

'Sure, see you, Emily.'

'See you, Red!' She calls after me as I trot down the stairs and realise that Mr Smith is right behind me.

'Red?'

'Sir?' I stop and turn on the bend of the stairs.

'I couldn't help but notice your face, I hope it wasn't a student that did that to you, because of that video Rose put online?'

'Oh no,' I touch my finger to my cheek. 'No, that was . . . well it was my little sister. Jumped into my arms, knocked me off balance and I fell against the corner of our coffee table. It could have been worse.'

I've no idea where the story comes from, it's just there, and I tell it with ease, because even after everything she's done, I still want to protect my mum, our home, my sister from the prying eyes of outsiders, even Mr Smith.

'If you say so.' He smiles, but his eyes don't stray from my bruises and I know he's deciding whether or not to believe me. 'What's the situation with Naomi? Any updates?'

'They are waking her up tomorrow,' I say, feeling a flash of anxiety when I think about the uncertain outcome. 'Or they hope to, anyway. It's her birthday so . . . well, I just hope she's OK. It would be great to know she was awake when we were onstage, you know? It would really mean something.'

'Yes, of course. I think I'll pop and see her tonight, check in with her folks and update them on tomorrow.' He walks down one step towards me. 'I just wanted to check before we go out there, how you are holding up? I mean I know you and Rose were very close, it must have been hard for you when you fell out like that. If you need someone to talk to, or confide in, then you can always come to me, right?'

'Thanks, sir,' I say. Just for a second it almost all comes out, and then I think of Ash, and that look in her eye, and her quiet determination and I know that I have to trust her. No, that's not right, I don't have to. I want to. 'Everything's cool.'

'No problem, Red.' He smiles at me. 'Anytime.'

A few seconds later and I am climbing up onto the stage, taking my place behind the drums.

'OK?'

I nod at Leo. 'Yeah, I just need to get going,' I say.

I nod at Leckraj, who plays a riff for me to join in with

for a few bars while I loosen up. Rose stands by the mic, right in front of me, her head bowed as she reads over the set list, her foot tapping to my bass drum. And seeing that is just enough to lift me, as I find my way into the music, syncing my body to the beat.

There will be several long dull minutes of sound checking ahead, adjusting levels, working out the mix in the PA and my in-ear monitors, but as I sit there going through the motions I feel excited to get started on the full set. I can't wait actually, because right now all I want to do is beat the shit out of these drums until one of us bleeds.

'Dude, you were on fire,' Leo says to me moments after the last number, and I love the way his eyes are alight and his smile is so wide, and that just for a moment everything that happened is erased by everything that used to be. Rose skips up next to him grinning, hooking her arm around his neck and planting a kiss on his cheek.

'Wow, that was great, we sounded great, right?' She looks at me, for a second her face open and full of joy before she remembers she doesn't know how to feel about me any more, and she looks away. 'And you were great too, Leckraj. Really on-point.'

Leckraj, who is already on his knees, quietly packing away his stuff, smiles.

'Thanks,' he says. 'My dad's picking me up, so I'm just going to wait out the front. See you tomorrow.'

The three of us watch him go and then burst into laughter.

'That guy is ice,' Rose giggles. 'Nothing phases him.'

'He's on it, for sure.' Leo smiles at me. 'This was good, guys, it was really good to play with my two best mates tonight, to play the whole set without one fuck-up or bum note. It was good. And I know shit went down between you two, that was weird, but . . . well we're us, right? We're stronger than that.'

Rose smiles.

'This was great, really good,' she says, half smiling. 'But I better go, I got a thing so . . . '

'Oh, I thought we could hang out, get a pizza before I have to trek halfway across London to my aunty's to check up on Mum.'

'Can't, thing,' she says, shrugging.

'What sort of thing?' I ask before I can remind myself that I am exactly the wrong person saying exactly the wrong thing at exactly the wrong time. Her tentative smile vanishes.

'Really none of your business. See you tomorrow.'

'Wait!' Leo calls after her. I look away but I can just about hear what they are saying.

'Rose, look, you don't need to tell me who you are seeing, but I need to say something to you.'

'What?' Rose sighs.

'You're the most amazing girl I ever met,' Leo says. 'I never have the guts to say it, but now I'm watching you slip away from me, and I got to tell you, in case I don't get another chance. You are more than just a mate to me, if you change your mind about this guy, you just got to know that. You got to know I'd treat you right. I'd care for you.'

Careful not to get caught watching, I see Rose's eyes hold Leo's for a long time and her hand reach up to his cheek. I see her stand on her tiptoes and kiss him on the cheek and then she is gone, waving a hand as she disappears through the doors.

'Why now?' I ask him. 'Why tell her all that now?'

I expected jealousy and pain, but that's not how I felt when I was listening to him open up to her, it was . . . admiration. That took guts.

'Because it's true,' Leo admitted. 'Because if making a fool of myself means there is even just the smallest chance that she might think twice about whoever this creep is, then it's worth it. I mean, if she knocks me back, my life is basically over. But if it keeps her safe for five more minutes, then who cares?'

35

The unexpected smell of cooking when I walk in through the front door stops me in my tracks, I lean into it, and it takes me back to being a kid. There's something about the night getting darker, the yellow of electric lights behind closed curtains and the smell of our family's traditional Sunday evening roast that makes me feel not quite sad, not quite happy, but lost for a moment in remembering what family life used to be like. When it was always like this smell, familiar and warm.

'You're home!' Dad opens the kitchen door and I see he's set the table, four places, salt and pepper in the middle along with a massive bottle of ketchup because there is no food that Gracie will eat without it. 'Thought I'd do dinner for when you got in, as we didn't really see you yesterday.'

'Great,' I say, hanging my jacket on the end of the banister. Of course, I'm not great; I'm thinking how tired I am, and how my face still hurts and how very much I want to talk to Ash to see what she has found out – if anything – and check in with Leo to see if Aaron really has stayed away, and that this family dinner will be hell with roast potatoes.

'Red!' Gracie comes thundering down the stairs and leaps into my arms with such force that I stagger back.

'Kiddo!' I kiss her faintly sweet-tasting cheek. 'Had a nice day, I see. Enjoyed some candyfloss?' Gracie's mouth makes an astonished 'O'.

'Yeah, how did you know? We went to the zoo!' She looks as surprised as I am by the news. I look at Dad who shrugs slightly. You have to say this one thing about my parents, nobody goes from family apocalypse to pretending everything's just peachy quite as easily as them.

'Go wake your mum up from her nap, Gracie,' he says, and my little sister runs up the stairs with just as much enthusiasm as she walked down them.

'Trips to the zoo, Dad?' I follow him into the kitchen, as he begins to carve up a chicken.

'Look, I'm just trying to get some normality back, for Gracie. For your mum, for everyone. That's why I made dinner, it's nice, right? Like old times.'

'But it isn't old times, is it?' I'd barely thought of the bruise and cut on my cheek for hours, but now it suddenly throbs as I remember how it got there. 'Pretending everything is happy families isn't going to make Mum stop hating me, or stop drinking. Or fix the fact that you have a girlfriend, is it?'

'I know that.' Dad turns suddenly, lowering his voice. 'But we've got to start somewhere. Give me a chance, love. I'm trying.'

'OK,' I say. 'Can I help?'

'Pour some glasses of water for us?'

As I take four glasses out of the cupboard Mum comes in, led by Gracie.

'Red's here!' Gracie says, when Mum doesn't look at me. She sits down at the table, and so does Gracie, patting the chair next to her for me.

'How was your dress rehearsal?' Mum asks. Still her eyes don't meet mine, but at least her voice isn't hard or cold. All I want is for everything to be OK between us, to be like it used to be when she was my mum and I was her little girl. I don't want to have to find it in myself to forgive her, or for her to need to forgive me for being who I am. I just want us to be us, so hard it hurts, much more than my face.

'Good,' I say. 'Really good.'

'I asked your mum if we had tickets, and she said no, so I said we'd get some on the door, hey, Gracie? We've got to see Red strut her stuff, right?' Standing next to the oven, Dad stretches out the oven glove taut and does some mortifying air guitar.

'You're coming?' I didn't realise how much it had hurt me to assume that they weren't until that moment.

'You bet we are coming!' Dad says. 'We wouldn't miss it, would we, love?'

'Course not,' Mum says, and this time her eyes do find my face, her steady gaze making me look down as she studies the bruise. Dad brings over plates piled high with steaming-hot food.

'What a treat,' Mum says. She doesn't sound like she means it.

Gracie talks for us all through dinner, giving me a minute-by-minute catch-up on the zoo. The food is good, hot and homemade; I've been craving vegetables and didn't even realise it. The kitchen window steams up and for a little while it feels cosy, safe in there, You could almost forget that everything has fallen apart.

You could if it wasn't for the fact that Mum barely touches her food, and that she is restless and anxious, her eyes constantly straying to the door.

'Back in a second,' she says as soon as Dad clears the plates away.

'There's pudding,' Dad calls after, 'Sticky toffee!'

'Back in a second!' she repeats, this time her voice comes from the top of the stairs.

'Everything's OK now, Red,' Gracie says suddenly touching her hand to my cheek. 'Everything's fine.'

I look at Dad, and he turns away from me.

'Course it is, kiddo,' I say. 'Course it is. It always will be while I'm around.'

Mum didn't come back down for dessert, so it's me sitting on the floor next to Gracie's bed, my head leaning against second-best teddy as she drifts off to sleep, her small hand in mine, holding fast in case I have any ideas about leaving her to sleep alone.

As it happens, I don't really feel like going anywhere. The adrenaline that has kept me going must be draining away now, leaving trembling muscle and aching bones in its wake. In the last few days I've felt every emotion there is, and God only knows what will happen tomorrow. So for now, with my little sister's hand in mine, I just want to rest, to close my eyes and give up thinking or feeling or caring for a little while.

'She asleep?' Mum's whisper disturbs me.

'Yes.' I stretch, sitting up, tucking her hand under the duvet.

'Get into your own bed then, love, you look shattered.'

She called me love, and it feels like a peace offering.

Clambering upright, I my screw my eyes up against the bright landing lights. She stands there, and I realise she wants to say something else. So I wait.

'I'm so sorry,' she says, at last. 'What I did to you. It was unforgivable.'

'It's all right,' I say. 'It doesn't matter.'

'It does matter, love,' she takes a step towards me, 'I'm your mum, I should never have raised my hand to you, I should be trying to protect you but I was . . . I wasn't myself.'

'OK.' It's not much, but it's enough. It's the best start I can think of or hope for, and I want to go to bed with those words in my ears. ''Night, Mum.'

'I think it might have worked out for the best though,' she adds, and I hate how much hope there is in her voice. 'I mean, your dad is home. He's home and things are already much better. I didn't know what it would take to get him home, but . . . well he's back now.'

My bedroom is just a few feet away, bed and oblivion for a few hours. And God, I have never wanted that more. But I can't just nod and say, yeah, so it's all worked out for the best. I just can't.

'Mum, nothing is fixed, you get that, right?' I have to say this. This fake OK is not OK.

'No, I mean not overnight, of course not, but it's a start.'

'It isn't a start,' I tell her as gently as I can. 'Dad being here, it's good, it's brilliant, but it's not the answer. Dad loves us . . . but he can't save us, he doesn't know how. I thought maybe he could, but he can't. He's not back here for good, he's not back here because he wants to be. He's back here because he loves us as much as he can and he feels guilty that he's left us to fall apart. But Dad won't fix that you can't sit through dinner without sneaking off for a drink, or me being a lesbian and you hating me for it.'

Bracing myself, I wait for her to kick off, to shout and accuse and slam and maybe even hit again, but she doesn't. She is just still for a moment, and then she nods.

'I know that,' she says. 'But I'm not strong right now, Red.'

For the first time ever she calls me by the name I chose, and it's maybe the kindest, most loving thing that she has ever done for me.

'I know.' Ever so slowly, very carefully, I put my arms around her and hug her. As she rests her chin on my shoulder, I can feel the last snapshots of my childhood falling away from me, like a cascade of old-fashioned photos. Mum feels small and thin and short, and more like me than I had ever guessed. All this time I have been growing up and she has been getting older and somehow only now, here on the landing under the electric light, we have met in the middle.

'I know you aren't strong,' I say. 'But I think I am, Mum. I think I am really, really strong. Much stronger than you know. I can help you.'

Her arms tighten around me, and I close my eyes and there is sunshine and bedtime stories and knees kissed better.

'We'll help each other,' she says. 'But there is one thing you have got wrong. I don't hate you, Red. I love you, I love you more than I can say. And I'm afraid for you and what you have to face in a world that won't always welcome you. I'm afraid and I let that look like hate, because maybe it's me that I hate. But not you, never you. I love you, my little girl.'

And for me, that's good enough, it's better than good. For the first time in a long time, when I climb into bed I feel at home.

And then Ash calls me.

'I've got into Nai's phone,' she says.

'And?'

'Everything we needed to know was in WhatsApp. If we hadn't found her phone it would have taken a lot longer to find out who he is. If she'd really thrown it away he would have been safe, but she didn't. There must have been something, some tiny doubt about him that made her hide it in a place she thought it would be found by you. Because now we know who he is.'

36

'Who?' I hold my breath.

In the spilt second before Ash answers, a million different scenarios play out in my head, a million different answers and outcomes, and none of them are the one that becomes blindingly obvious the moment she says it.

'It's Mr Smith, Red,' Ash tells me. 'It's Mr Mother Fucking Smith.'

'It can't be,' I whisper. 'No, Ash . . . it can't be. Because . . . it can't be, you've made a mistake . . . '

'I'm sorry, Red, I am, but once I had the WhatsApp messages it was clear who she was talking to. He talked about getting out of school early, how she looked in class. But I double-checked, I got into all his less secure stuff, and I found the pathways that led to the truth. He thought he covered his tracks. The front door was a bog-standard Facebook page, but after that, there were levels. Secret Facebook groups, where the members posted photos of girls they'd taken, and talked about what they'd like to do to them. Forums. Chat rooms, and I followed the trail he left, down to the lowest, deepest level, to the basement of the dark web where I found his other name: MrMoon. It's him, it's undeniable. It's him.'

I can't speak, it's like I've been winded by a punch in the gut, so hard it's stolen my breath. Not him, I don't want it to be him, because that means . . . that means that every kind thing he's ever said to me about Nai and Rose and Leo, every word, everything he's ever done, the concert, the band; every single thing that has meant anything to me over the last year is a lie.

Ash keeps talking, and the more she says the worse it gets. I can hear the tremble in her voice, the fear and the fury, and I wish she hadn't called me. I wish I was with her now, because if I was, I'd put my arms around her and hold her tight, and hope she'd do the same for me.

'I know how she ended up in the river, Red. He wrote on that sick site, boasting about it. She tried to get away from him, she tried to come home, and he beat her up. So badly he thought he killed her. It was him who dumped her in the river. He'd been keeping her in a block of old flats less than half a mile from home. All those weeks, she was his prisoner.'

'Oh my God.' I'm not sure if I say the words out loud or not, my mind suddenly crammed with images of what Nai was forced to endure. No, I can't even think it. 'Oh my God, Ash. Oh my God. No. Are you sure?'

'I'm sure, I've got all the proof, and I'm going to hand it over to the police, just like you want me to. But before I do I've got a plan that's going to ruin him for good, it's going to blow you away. What we're going to do is—'

My brain, frozen in shock, reactivates in a rush of fear. 'Ash, wait, he said he was going to visit Naomi tonight.

And . . . and he knows they are planning to wake her up tomorrow.'

'How does he know?' Ash asks.

'Because I told him.'

'Fuck, I got to go.'

'I'll see you there,' I say. Trainers on, grab my oyster card. I run out of the door and all the last traces of sleep fly off me as I run for the tube.

Matt
Nearly time for us to really be together. Excited?

Naomi
Yes, I am . . . I just wish . . . Do I have to leave home? Mum and Dad and Ash will be really worried, and I've put them through so much already. Couldn't we just carry on like we are?

Matt
Look if you don't really love me Naomi then just say, OK? Don't make me think you care about me the way I care about you if you don't

Naomi
I do, I do care about you, more than anything, but . . . you get to stay in your home, and at work. What if we ran away, caught the ferry to France?

Matt
Then I'd be caught, and probably go to prison. In another couple of years it won't matter who knows how much we love each other, but right now – no one would understand. They wouldn't see us, they wouldn't know what we know.

Naomi
I guess . . .

∨

Matt

Look, all of this, everything I've done, the flat I've found you, the rent I'm going to pay for you, it's all because I want you so badly, all to myself, all the time. If you don't want that, then let's call it off right now. And the next time I see you, I'll try to pretend that you aren't the only thing in my life worth anything

Naomi

No . . . no please, don't do that. Matt, I love you

Matt

I love you too. Be ready where I told you to be, and remember throw away your phone

37

We don't know how long he has been there, sitting next to her and staring. Or why the nurses let him in, because he's not on the list. But that's Mr Smith for you, he's charming and well-spoken. Good-looking and kind. When he looks you in the eye, you feel like he really cares about you and what happens to you. He's the kind of man you look up to. The kind of man you trust. The worst kind of monster.

And I trusted him, more than my own dad. I've never wanted to hurt another person until tonight. Tonight I want to hurt him really badly.

'We'll confront him,' I snarl. 'We go in there and we tell him we know what he is.'

'No!' Ash takes my hand and squeezes it. 'We act like we don't know a thing.'

'Why?' I stare at her. 'I want to kill him. Everything he's done to the people I love, to me. I told him stuff about me, Ash. I thought he cared. I *need* to hurt him.'

Ash puts her hands on my shoulders and makes me look into her eyes, and when I do, I feel a little better, a little more grounded and centred.

'I know it's hard but I need time. Time to get every last little bit of evidence from his stuff. And because he's standing right next to the machinery that is keeping my sister alive.'

We stand there, toe-to-toe, eye to eye, her hands steadying my heart, and we stay that way until our breathing steadies and the shaking in my legs stills, and finally without having to say a word to her, I know that we are ready to face him.

'Hey, sir,' I say as we walk in.

'Oh, you girls are here late.' He withdraws his hand from Naomi's and I want to throw up.

'Yeah, it's not really visiting hours, is it?' Ash says. 'I'm surprised the nurses haven't thrown you out yet?'

'The night nurse was very understanding.'

We go and stand by Nai, and I wonder what's going on now behind those lids. Less sedation, we know that much. What if she can hear his voice? What if she feels his touch, but isn't able to move, isn't able to scream?

'It's OK, Naomi,' I say picking up her hand. 'Me and Ash are here. We've got you.'

'Where did you two come from?' A tired-looking nurse shakes her head at us. 'Come on, out. Naomi's got a big day tomorrow, she needs her rest.'

'Yeah, come on, sir.' I force a grin. 'We've got a big day tomorrow too. It's concert day!'

'I'm not leaving.' Ash shakes her head. 'I'm her sister. And I know other relatives get to stay here on a mattress. And maybe . . . well, we don't know what's going to happen tomorrow, do we, so I just want to be with her tonight. Please. I won't get in the way, I just don't want her to be alone.'

The nurse purses her lips. 'I'll have to phone your parents, make sure they don't mind.'

'They won't,' Ash says.

'OK, then.' She looks at me and Mr Smith. 'But you two, out.'

'Want a lift?' Mr Smith asks me once we are outside. I look into his kind eyes and dream about ripping them out.

'I'll walk,' I say.

'Are you sure?' He smiles, and it's sweet and gentle. A smile I've trusted for a very long time. 'You're safer with me.'

'I'm sure,' I say. 'But I'm much tougher than I look, sir. You don't want to mess with me.'

He's chuckling as he gets into his car. He has no idea how deadly serious I am.

38

I'm waiting for Leo by Vauxhall tube station, as he's had to take a couple of trains to get here from his Aunty Chloe's. People stream in and out of the entrance, parting only to go around me, like fast-running water around a rock.

This is the day that I have been working towards for weeks. This is the only thing that has made sense, the concert, the fundraising. Making sure we were doing everything for her that we could. And it was his idea. All the time that he was telling us we could make a difference, we could help Naomi be found, Mr Smith had her his prisoner.

That takes a special kind of evil.

There's something else about this day that's important. The reason we chose to stage the concert on a Monday in September, when almost all the other days of the week would have been better.

Today is Naomi's birthday.

We do this thing on each other's birthday that we call The Edit, compiling photos that we've taken over the year, and making a collage, dicking around with stickers and emojis, and just doing something stupid and kiddish and fun. This morning, when I woke when it was still dark, the reminder that it was her birthday popped up on my phone.

There was no more sleeping, not with this dark day hanging over me. There might never be sleeping ever again.

So I made Naomi an Edit. Going back through my photos, going back to the months after her last birthday. There were photos I hadn't looked at in months, loads of them. Bursts of her mucking around in the park, when we were having our first go at cosplay. Stupid photos taken at school, at the movies, all the places that we used to go together, without thinking that those places and those moments meant anything at all. At least one photo of her, of her and me, or all of us together taken every single day, right up until the last one before she went missing.

So I made her an Edit and I posted it anyway, like I would have done if she had been here. And it wasn't until I stood there outside the tube station waiting for Leo and checked my Instagram that I realised Rose had added me again to all her accounts – her name, her heart-shaped 'like' right there under my post. And I'm glad, because today of all days we need each other. I just wish I didn't know about the dark shadows that are lengthening over her. Right now, she must feel so happy, so special and loved. And all of that is about to be ripped away from her.

'Hey,' Leo says, as he is thrown up out of the mouth of the tube station along with everyone else.

'Hello.' We fall into step alongside one another.

'I liked the Edit you made Nai,' he said.

'Yeah, thanks. I was thinking about the last time we saw her and if we could have done something, anything . . .'

'There was nothing,' Leo says. 'I've gone over and over it a million times. Nothing. She didn't want us to know, Red. I guess we just have to deal with that. Because if she'd wanted us to know, we would have. Somehow. But you know what? Today you, me and Ash are going to nail that bastard's balls to the wall.'

'Fuck knows what shit is going to hit the fan, so you know what we should do today?' I say as we reach the school.

'What?' asks Rose, closing her dad's car door behind her and joining us.

And at exactly the same moment that I am happy to see her, I feel sick with nerves, too. I want to stop what she's going through right now, this second. And yet, I don't; I'm doing what Ash wants, we all are. And soon we are going to pay the price for that.

'We should celebrate her birthday,' Leo says, he too seems unable to look right at Rose. 'Whatever happens today when they try and wake Nai up, she deserves that.'

Rose touches his cheek with her fingertips, tears shine bright in her eyes.

'Yes,' she says, turning to me and sliding her arm through mine. 'I loved the Edit, Red.'

As we near school I see Ash and beckon her over, but she shakes her head, and instead sits down, choosing not to look at any of us in the eye as she hurries by.

'Ash, you OK?' Rose calls after her. But she just keeps going.

'It's hard for her, today,' I say, my eyes following Ash as she disappears inside. A few seconds later my phone buzzes in my pocket and I take it out as we walk slowly to registration; it's from Ash.

I need to see you and Leo. In the hall, third period, cut class. Don't bring Rose.

It's easy for me to find a reason to leave R.E., all I have to do is mention girl's stuff, and Mr Grimes waves me out of the class before he has to think about it. I tell him I'm going to see the school nurse for some paracetamol, but of course instead I head for the main hall. It's supposed to be locked up tight to keep curious kids out, and all the borrowed equipment inside safe and primed ready for tonight. I was never sure how Ash was planning to get in there, assuming that she'd be able to somehow externally hack the mixing desk and the laptops that were running the video, but when she sees Leo and I approaching from different directions she jerks her head, indicating that we should follow her, so we do, trailing her into reception. The school secretary is on the phone, gazing out of the window. Seeing her chance, Ash darts to the door that leads to the gallery stairs and, slipping a key out of her pocket, unlocks it. She disappears inside, reopening the door just a crack, beckoning us to follow her. We wait. Mrs Minchen puts the phone down and turns back to her computer monitor. Seconds tick past – before long the bell will ring for fourth period and then we won't have just been excused, we will be missing.

Then Mrs Minchen gets up, going out the back, heading for the ladies. We both run, bolting through the door and up the stairs. When we get upstairs, Ashira is sitting with a torch between her teeth working on the laptop that's wired into the mixing desk. I feel a moment of regret, remembering how Emily smiled when she showed me the desk, and how proud she was of it. I'd felt bad when I'd sent Ash the photos last night, and I feel bad again now. I like Emily, she always smiles and she never cares what other people think of her. It's a shame that all of her good work is going to waste and she doesn't know a thing about it, won't know a thing about it until she sits at this desk tonight. I hope she understands. I hope she gets why we are doing what we're doing.

Ash looks up when she sees us, and takes the torch out of her mouth.

'What do you need us for?' I ask in a whisper. The hall is large and empty but still it doesn't feel right to talk at normal volume.

'I got him, last night,' Ash says. 'I got right inside his world. Everything, everything there at my fingertips, every grubby little secret. And there are some things I need to tell you. Dark things.'

'OK.' I sit down on one of the plastic chairs that have been left up here.

'Carly Shields, she was one of his first,' she says. 'I found photos, videos, emails. And Danni, Danielle Haven, that's her real name.'

'God.' I cover my mouth with my hand and look at Leo, who shakes his head, his fists clenching.

'Look,' Ash says, 'I know better than anyone how this makes us all feel, but we are so close now. So close to getting him, for the sake of Naomi, Carly, Rose and the other girls. Keep your cool, we are nearly there.'

I look at Leo, and see the way his jaw is clenched.

'It's going to be really hard not to just punch his lights out . . .'

'I need to know.' Ash's voice is steady, her expression laser focused. 'Are you up for this?'

Leo looks at me, 'Fuck yeah.'

'Do it,' I say.

For a second we are silent, because we each of us know that there is no turning back now.

39

I think I'm going to be OK when I go into music class, but the second I see her, standing next to him, talking in a low voice, everything falls away, and I don't care about one single thing except getting between them.

'Hello.' My voice is brittle, made of cold metal. I try hard to melt it into something softer, less obvious but it's impossible. 'Sir, I was thinking that maybe Rose and I could be excused because it's lunch next, and we were going to just run over the set one more time.'

'I thought you were going to rest today, so you are fresh for tonight.' Mr Smith frowned. 'You don't want to kill the vibe, besides, this is your GCSEs, Red. You need to be in this lesson.'

'Yeah, sure, we don't need to do any more practice.' Rose frowns at me, and the truce between us is so fragile, so tender, that I don't want to do anything to break it, but not as much as I don't want him to lay a fucking finger on her ever fucking again.

'Actually, Rose, if I'm honest this whole thing is kind of getting to me. It's Nai's birthday, the concert, the doctors trying to wake her up. I just need a bit of time, will you come with me? Please.'

Rose looks from me to him, and I can see the anxiety in her face.

'Can I?' she asks. And it's not the way a pupil asks a teacher, it's much more intimate than that. The shift in his body language in response is minute, hardly there, but I see it. A proprietorial shift that makes it hard to let her go with me, and suddenly I understand why. I'm not just some loser kid to him, I'm a rival.

'Course,' he says, but he doesn't smile. 'It's a hard day for you both. Go and have a moment. Back in ten, OK?'

I find the nearest exit and suck in some deep breaths of cold air.

'Red, I mean I'm glad things are getting back to normal between us, and yes, we said we'd talk about Nai today, but that was a bit . . . intense.'

'I just . . . I just want you to be safe.' I blurt out the words before I can stop myself, and of course they make no sense to her. Of course, she frowns and looks uncomfortable, stepping away from me.

'Red, stop it, OK? Look, you're feeling upset, we all are today. It's going to be hard, but I *am* safe, I'm really happy actually, happier than I've been for a long time. I feel like I've met someone who understands me, who sees me for who I am. Who really cares about *me*, you know? I get you have feelings for me, and well, there's part of me that's very touched by that, but at the end of the day, Red, we can't ever have that kind of relationship. So if you can't live with that, and be happy for me then . . . I think maybe we'll have to stay apart.'

Every word is killing me slowly, chewing chunks off me

and spitting them out. Not the rejection, that part I can take, I've been ready for it. It's the hope in her eyes, the smile on her lips. The love that she believes in, that she is so ready to give, to feel safe and cared for. That's what I can't bear. But I have to just hide it away, all of this. For a few more hours, I have to hide away. One wrong word now and he will have won.

'I know, I get that. I just want what we had back then, Rose. That other stuff, I kind of just lost it. It wasn't real, it was a moment. A stupid moment. But I've lost one of my best friends and so have you. Let's not do that to each other again, OK?'

'Right.' She hesitates for a moment and then hugs me. 'You look broken, pal, she says. 'But it will be all right. Tonight we are going to be amazing, and I know it feels like we've got to live the rest of our lives stuck in this rat trap, but you know what? It's going to go by so quickly, and who gives a fuck about GCSEs, there are so many more important things, like travel and adventure. And running away to the other side of the world, exploring the Amazon!'

'Exploring the Amazon?' I make myself smile. 'You do realise that you can't even stand to be near a woodlouse.'

'Because they're evil,' Rose replies very seriously and I can't help but smile.

'So are we going to go back to class now?' she says.
'I guess so.'
The look that passes between Smith and Rose as we walk back into the classroom is lost on everyone but me.

40

The hall buzzes with chat and laughter already, and the audience hasn't even begun to arrive yet, it's just the lighting crew and Emily, and some of the teachers who've come in early to wish us luck. Nerves knot and double knot my insides, my mouth is dry and I couldn't eat anything after breakfast today. If this was just a gig, then I'd be nervous but excited, pumped up, ready to go. But this isn't just a gig. This may be the most important thing that I will ever do.

It's strange to know ahead of almost everyone else that the clock is ticking downwards towards something terrible, something that will change everything. I just hope that Ash, Leo and I have got it right. I hope that it's a disaster for him, and not us.

'OK?' Emily appears at my side.

'I think so. And you?'

'Yeah, all the hard work is done to be honest,' she says. 'I pretty much just have to press play and cross my fingers now.' Her smile is sweet, her voice light. I like looking at her.

'Red,' she says. 'Listen, I was thinking and I—'

Before she can say any more my phone rings, and when I see the number I know I have to answer it.

'Sorry,' I cut her off, waving the phone at her like a total dickhead. 'Sorry, I've really got to take this.'

'Really? We start letting the audience in in about four minutes!' Emily calls after me.

'Got it,' I reply, but really I'm already listening to the person on the other end of the line.

'OK,' I say, 'we're on.'

We stand behind the curtain, just the three of us, because Leckraj is suffering from a serious case of pre-gig nerves and is still on the loo, listening to the hall fill up with voices. There's a tiny gap between the curtains, and every now and then we take turns to peep through. I see my parents and Gracie and I hope that my dad has the good sense to get them out of there when it all kicks off. Ash is here, but not her mum and dad. They are still at Nai's bedside. Still waiting for her to come back to them.

When I see Ash, taking her place in the front row that I reserved for her, I try to study her face, looking for some sign of how Nai's doing, but there's nothing there. Nothing at all.

'Be back in a sec,' I say.

'Red, where are you going?' Rose calls after me.

I climb down the stage, crouching in front of Ash.

'How is she?' I ask her. When she looks up from her hands, her eyes are full of tears; she doesn't speak only shakes her head once.

'Do you have to be here?' I cover her hands. 'You could

go, you don't have to sit through this.'

'I do,' she whispers. 'I do. It's all set up to roll, but I still have to be able to take control of the system with my phone and override anyone who might try to pull the plug. Anyway, I want to see him go down. I have to. For her. I'm OK. A couple more hours and I'll fall apart, but until then, I'm OK.'

'Love!' Dad has spotted me and is beckoning me over. Squeezing Ash's hands, I glance back at the curtain and run over to where my family is sitting. 'I got to go,' I say. 'Look, Dad. A lot of this isn't really going to be right for Gracie. Swearing and stuff, talk about death and depression. The first song is really good, then I think you should take her home. Right after the first song.'

'Don't you want us to watch you?'

'I do,' I say, 'but I don't want to upset Gracie. Mum will stay, won't you, Mum?'

Mum looks pale, and drawn, clutching on to her bag very tightly, but a light dawns in her eyes when I ask her to stay and she smiles.

'Yes, I'll stay,' she says.

'I don't want to go home,' Gracie begins to moan.

'Red!' Leo shouts to me from behind the curtain. 'Hurry up!'

'Listen,' I say. 'When this is done, you and me we can form our own band, OK?'

'Can I be the singer?' Grace demands.

'For sure.'

'Daddy, I'm going to be a singer!'

As I run back to the stage, I glance at Ashira, she nods at me once.

This.

Is.

It.

Sound explodes out of the P.A. systems, filling the hall with noise. I close my eyes and I let myself fall into the music. Every part of me, every atom tunes into the music, vibrating at the perfect pitch. Leo burns a path with his guitar, Rose sings her heart out, and Leckraj is there under it all, pinning it all together. But in my heart, in my head, it's not him I hear, or even see behind my lids. It's her. Standing next to my kit, turned towards me, like she always did, shoulder hunched around her ears as she directs every bit of energy she has into the music, her head punctuating every beat. For three amazing minutes she is back on stage, large as life, haunting this song that she wrote, making it hers again, and they are three minutes of magic. I know I'm not the only one to feel that way, I know the others do too, I can see it in their smiles, in the way they move, in the rise and power in Rose's voice, and I get it suddenly; the way to deal with all this shit is to beat the fuck out of it with my sticks.

Cymbals crash, my bass drum vibrates and the song comes to an end. The audience are on their feet. Rose turns around and beams at me as Mr Smith walks across the stage, and she steps away from the microphone.

'That was a very special start to this very special evening,' he tells the crowd. 'And how wonderful to be here tonight to honour this remarkable young woman.' Naomi's photo appears on the huge screen behind us, and we all turn to look at it.

'I've had the pleasure of watching Naomi grow up,' he continues. 'Of seeing what an incredible young woman she has become. It's clear to all of us that she was going through some difficult times, that she didn't feel she had anyone to turn to. And that's why we've staged this concert today, for Naomi, to show her how many people love her, and also to show every kid who feels like that. Because we want them to know that they are not alone.'

Catching Leckraj's eye, I signal for him to come over to me.

'Don't play the next track, OK? We've got a surprise planned. Tell Rose too.' Leckraj shrugs and goes over to Rose, whispering in her ear. She turns around and looks at me with a questioning look on her face. I get down from the drums and walk to the front of the stage and stare at Smith. He sees me looking at him, watching him, and falters for a moment, before going back to his speech. One sick lie after another. Leo puts down his guitar and stands on the other side of him, and stares too. And after a moment, Smith stops talking, and half laughs.

'I get the feeling that these two are trying to tell me something.'

'We are,' Leo says. 'Tonight is a night not only to remember Naomi, but to try to understand what happened to her. And to protect other teenagers like her, like us, from going through the same thing. And we know that you took an interest in her, sir. A really close interest. So we made a special video. Just for you.'

I look at Ashira and she presses play from her phone.

Naomi laughing, running in sunshine, there's snow on the ground and she's smiling, looking back at the camera, and blowing kisses. Her hair is loose, her eyes glitter. There's a tussle, a moment of confusion, the ground, the sky, a blurred face and then it's clear that Nai has the phone, as she turns it around on the filmmaker. The room gasps as they see Mr Smith.

'Tell me you love me, say it!' Naomi laughs. 'Go on, say it! I want to hear you say that you love me one more time.'

'I love you,' Mr Smith says right into the camera. 'Now give it back, will you!'

The film jump-cuts to a room, bright with electric lights and Naomi sitting on an unfamiliar bed, her shoulders hunched, her arms wrapped around her, trying to cover herself. She is crying. This time he speaks.

'Tell me you love me,' he says, voice robotic, emotionless. 'Go on. Tell me you love me.'

There are gasps, shouts from the audience as Mr Smith turns to face the big screen, transfixed by the innards of his life being ripped right out for all to see. Photos, dozens of them, fill up the screen in quick succession, the faces and bodies of the girls pixelated out. There are screen shots of his secret groups, close-ups of his comments.

'Look at this one, she's ripe for the picking.'

His email list comes up and opens, his chat rooms, his photo library. It's all there, images of him with arms around girls, girls who look scared, girls who look lost, girls that I know. But no images of Rose, we'd agreed on that. No one needed to know about Rose.

As the images continue to stream the crowd falls silent, just watching. Some have their hands clasped over their mouths, some are crying. Some stand up in their seats trying to make sense of it all.

And then I see Rose, see her take it all in, and what it means. I see her realising what Smith is, and what his promises were made for. I see her realise that she was on the point of being lost for good, just when she thought she was found. She turns away from the screen and looks at Smith, and the hurt in her face is unbearable. Shaking her head, she turns on her heels and runs. I try to go after her, but Smith blocks my path off the stage.

'Who's doing this?' Mr Smith is shocked into action as Rose starts pulling at cables trying to disconnect the power, tearing down the huge screen just as his WhatsApp messages with Naomi flash up.

'What's going on here? Why are you doing this?' he screeches.

The video keeps playing out against the back wall and a light from the gallery shines right on it, somehow I know it's Emily, making sure that nothing is missed.

'Whoever is doing this, it's lies, all lies.' He's pathetic suddenly, face red, voice strained. But this isn't even close to what he put these girls through.

Just as the video stops, the doors at the back of the hall open, and I see her. The police constable I met in the park, P.C. Wiggins. She stands there watching as I nod at Ashira who gets up from her seat and passes a packet to the police officer. As Ash gets to the doors she looks at me and smiles.

And she leaves.

The film lasts a few seconds more and then there is silence and shock reverberating around the room.

'Matthew Smith?' Police Constable Wiggins and two of her colleagues walk down the aisle towards him. 'We'd like to ask you some questions down at the station.'

Smith stares at me, and I see it. I see exactly what I wanted to see. The terror and confusion, the dread and horror, and the certainty that his life is ruined. Which is when he turns on his heels and makes a bolt for the wings.

It's not like Leo and I decide to run after him, it just happens. I feel Leo at my side, the two of us leaping down the old wooden stairs that lead into the maze of corridors. We catch sight of him going around a corner and skid after him, faster and fitter, on his heels by the time he careers out of a fire exit and spills out in the night air outside, tripping and rolling over onto his back. He puts his hands up to protect his face as Leo stands over him, but Leo doesn't hit him. He just stands there, looking at him.

'I think you are going to be very popular in prison,' Leo says. 'I got a few contacts inside, so I'll make sure they know what you are in for.'

Smith starts to sob as the police come around the corner and grab him before he can get up.

'It's a mistake,' Smith cries as the officers pull him to his feet and put him in the back of the car. 'It's all a mistake, this isn't me, I don't know how this has happened. It's a vendetta, it's a frame job. These kids clearly hate me. Can I phone home? What's going on?'

As he is put in the back of the car, Constable Wiggins comes over to me.

'What are you doing here?' I ask her, deadpan.

'I was coming anyway, my kid is really into your band, and then I got a tip-off and a load of very incriminating anonymous information. We'll be seizing all of this computer stuff now, and taking it in for evidence.'

'Who tipped you off?' I ask her.

Wiggins smiles, ever so slightly. 'No idea, but if I did, I'd tell her that this son of a bitch is going to pay for what he's done. And I'm going to make sure of that.'

*

'Where do you think she is?' Leo asks me as we watch the police car pull away.

'I don't know, she was upset, do you think . . . ?'

'Come on.'

We break into a run, a jog at first, but as we near our destination our feet pick up the pace and we're flying, both of us flying towards our friend, determined to keep her safe from harm.

We only stop when we have her in sight, sitting on the very top of the slide.

Of course she'd come here, to this place where we always hang out. This is the safest place we know, even in the dark, even tonight.

I look at Leo and he looks at me, and together we go over to her. Leo climbs up the steps behind her and I sit at the bottom of the slide.

'When did you know?' she says.

'Yesterday,' I say.

'We both did,' Leo says.

'And neither of you told me? I mean my God, why the fuck wouldn't you tell me? Why would you let me make such a fool of myself, stand there in front of all those people and see all those things, those awful things. Naomi . . . '

'Because . . . because we knew we had one shot to get him and . . . '

'You thought I'd warn him?' I can just about see the whites of her eyes as she stares at me, the rest of her made out of a combination of orange and black shadows, cast by the streetlights.

'Rose, you told me that you were in love, that it was special. And different. If I'd told you, outside of music class today, would you have believed me? Sided with me? The needy lesbian who has made a fool of herself over you? Or would you have run to him, and told him how crazy I'd gone. And believed whatever he said, and given him the chance to go home and wipe all of his sick stuff away forever. I wanted to tell you, so badly, we both did. But this was . . it was bigger. We needed you to understand what sort of a man he really is before we told you anything. We needed you to see with your own eyes.'

Rose says nothing, she just seems to curl up on the top of the slide, hugging her arms around her legs into a tiny ball. I see Leo behind her and she leans into his arms and sobs. I sit there for a while, under the moon and the twinkling lights of the planes that criss-cross the orange sky and I listen to the sound of the traffic and Rose's crying gradually fades away into something close to silence.

Eventually I get up.

'I'm going home,' I say. 'I'm so tired. And Rose . . . I'm so sorry. I really am. I know how hurt you are, because I'm that hurt too. And sad, and broken. We all are.'

Just as I get to the gate that leads out onto the road, I hear footsteps behind me and she catches up with me, flinging her arms around me.

'Thank you,' she says. 'Thank you. I'm hurt and stupid, but at least that's all I am. I feel so lucky, so thank you, all of you. Thank you.'

I hug her back hard, and as I do it's like a fog clears. Because I still think she is the most amazing and wonderful person I have ever known, stronger than I could ever have guessed. And all those feelings I had for her, that I thought were love, well they were, because I do love her:

she is my very best friend, but I'm not in love with her. I don't think I ever have been.

And I think it's taken me falling in love for real with someone else to realise my stupid mistake.

'See you tomorrow, buddy,' I say.

'See you then, old pal,' she replies.

My phone rings in my hand and I answer it, putting it on speaker.

'Ash?' The three of us stand there, waiting for her to talk.

'It's Nai,' she says, her voice heavy with tears. 'It's Nai. She's woken up. She's groggy. But . . . but she's going to be OK.'

41

Mum is waiting for me when I come in.

'I looked for you everywhere, I was so worried. What happened? Tell me everything, from the beginning.'

I sit at the kitchen table with her and she makes me a cup of hot chocolate and some toast, puts it down in front of me, and I start talking. I don't know where the words come from exactly, but it's somewhere deep down inside me, and once I start I can't stop. Every single moment I have lived through alone just comes pouring out of me. Everything about Naomi, about Rose, about me and who I truly am. About how I want to be that other girl for Mum, that reflected girl with the long hair and the pretty dress, how if I could I'd be that girl, I would. But I just can't, because she is as much part of me as the moon. And I talk, and I cry, and I tell her about what happened to Naomi, and how very sad and scared she must have been, and how she felt so alone, because that's what Smith did to her. He lied to her for so long, and so well, that she didn't see she could have talked to her friends or her sister or her mum and dad and everything would have been all right. And as I talk to Mum she puts her arm around me, and Dad comes downstairs and sits down and puts his arms around me too.

Eventually there are no more words, at least not for a little while; I've used them all up and I'm quiet at last.

'You've been very brave.' Dad's big hand covers mine.

'You've handled all of this on your own,' Mum says. 'We've let you down.'

I shake my head, because I don't want them to feel bad. I just want them to understand, who I was and who I am now. And to let me be who I want to be.

'You are amazing, Red,' Mum says, pulling me closer to her. 'So much stronger, so much braver than I ever realised. And you are my daughter. And I'm proud of you. And everything you stand for. When I had kids, I never thought that I'd be looking up to them, but I am.'

I look at her, 'Really?' I whisper.

She nods. 'Dad is going to stay while I get better. We found out about help, and where I need to go to get it. It's going to take a long time, and be very difficult. But every time I want to give up or give in I'm going to think of you.' She brushes my fringe out of my eyes. 'My incredible, beautiful, amazing daughter.'

'I thought you hated me being gay,' I say.

'I don't hate you, I never could. I hate the world sometimes, and I hate myself a lot. But never you, or Gracie. And I swear I won't let you down again.'

'And neither will I,' Dad says.

And I look from one of them to the other and for the first time in a very long time, I think I might actually feel normal.

Because this crazy-ginger-haired girl who plays the drums and dreams of falling in love with the perfect woman, that *is* normal for me.

Normal, you see, is whatever you want it to be.

42

It's very early in the morning, and I don't have to go to school today, nobody does. Because school is shut and the police are all over it. And none of that matters as the three of us head towards the hospital determined to get there for as soon as they will let us see her.

She's propped up in bed, and there's a TV on, not that she's watching it, instead her eyes are on Jackie, and Jackie is returning her gaze, mother and daughter just looking at each other as the rose-gold light of the dawn gilds every surface, making it the happiest and most beautiful thing that I have ever seen.

The bandages have gone, there's a diagonal line of stitches that traces its way across her face.

Max waves us in, and slowly we file into the room.

'All right, loser?' Rose is the first to speak.

'Throat's a bit sore,' Naomi says. 'Could murder a pint.'

Jackie smiles and cries at the same time, and we crowd round her. I'm grinning like an idiot, with no idea what to say.

'We'll go outside for a minute,' Jackie says, looking up

at Max who nods. 'But just for a minute, she needs her rest, she's got a lot of recovering to do.'

'OK,' I say, taking Jackie's seat when she gets up.

'I'm really glad you're not dead,' I say to Nai.

'Me too . . . ' She looks from me to Rose and Leo. 'The doctors didn't want Mum to tell me what you'd all been up to, they thought it might stress me out or some shit, but Mum knew that I'd want to know. She knew how much it would mean to me, I think . . .'

It's impossible to imagine what's going on inside her head, but her eyes are full of tears and pain.

'I can't talk about what happened, I don't want to think about it, not yet. Not ever. And I know the next few months are going to be hard, but they will be OK, with Mum and Dad, and you lot, if you will still be my mates.'

'Course we will,' I say.

'Fuck yeah,' Rose adds.

'Like anything else was ever possible.' Leo smiles at her.

'Good.' Naomi sinks back into the pillow. 'Now could you leave me alone please, I'm sick of the sight of you.'

'We'll be back later.' I kiss her gently on the top of her head.

'We'll bring DVDs,' Rose offers.

'And chocolate,' Leo adds. And just as we get to the door we hear her say,

'Guys?'

Turning around we look at her.

'I fucking love you,' she says.

I see Ash in the corridor, sleeping across three chairs, and I stop.

'Fancy going for breakfast?' Rose asks us. 'I'm not

really in the mood to be alone. My treat, I lifted Amanda's card on my way out.'

'Yeah, sure, but I'll catch you up, OK?' I say.

Rose and Leo look at each other, like they know something I don't. But they are wrong. This time I know.

'Hey, Ash?' I touch her on the shoulder, startled when her eyes fly open at once. 'Oh, I thought you were asleep.'

'I just had my eyes closed, still can't sleep, too wired.'

She sits up, and I take a seat opposite her.

'It's going to be hard,' she says. 'Going back to normal. Almost impossible after everything we've done together.'

'Yeah, about that,' I say. 'Look, I'm going to say something now, which might freak you about a bit, and I just want you to know that if it does, that's cool. I'm kind of used to that reaction, and it doesn't change our friendship in any way, because I'll just repress all of my emotions and pretend they don't exist but the thing is, the thing I want to say to you is . . . '

'Red.' Ash gets up from where she is sitting and comes and sits next to me.

'Yeah?' I say bracing myself for the worst.

'You know what you should do?' Ash asks me, the hint of a smile playing on her lips.

'What?' I whisper.

'You should just shut up and kiss me.'

Six months later . . .

It's freezing cold, first thing in the morning, and frost glitters all the way along the bridge, setting it alight with sparkles. Our breath mists in the air as we walk, six of us, tucking our fingers under our arms to keep them warm.

Standing back, I watch as Ashira takes Naomi by the arm, and guides her slowly to the bridge.

It's been a long six months of recovery for her body, her heart and her mind, a recovery that is a long way from over. There's a scar that runs diagonally across her face, which one day, the surgeons say, they can make all but invisible, but Naomi says she isn't ready to let it go yet, she says it's part of her. Just like the semi-circle tattoo on her arm that will form a key part of Smith's trial when it finally happens. The police said they could document it, and she could have it removed or covered up with something else, but Naomi said no. She said she'd keep it until she knew for sure that Smith, and every other man he was in contact with, had been put away.

We've come here today, to the bridge where they found

her, to say thank you for the chance that fate gave to us, that one glimmer of luck in all the darkness that saved her life and gave her back to us. Our belief in each other.

I smile as the sisters step forward with a bunch of bright orange Gerbera, and leaning over the railing, they throw them into the dark, slowly churning water one after the other. Then Leo, with his white daisies, and holding onto his hand, Rose.

Together they pick the petals from the flowers, and let some of them fall, some of them fly, carried up by the wind towards the winter sun for a few moments, before falling down like confetti. Rose wraps her arms around Leo's waist, and he drops a kiss on the top of her head, holding her close.

She's still never mentioned the words he said to her back then, before it all kicked off. They've never talked about it again, but there is a change between them. A promise that says when the time is right, I'm yours.

Leckraj is next with a single red rose, and casts a long, loving look at Naomi as he lets it go. There was this awkward moment, when Nai first came back into the rehearsal room, and he was already there, early as usual, when I thought we were going to have to actually fire him. But before anyone could say anything, he whipped a sheet off an electric piano he'd set up in the corner.

'Did I ever tell you that I also play keyboard?' he said.

My turn.

I take my irises and walking forward I drop each one of the three long stems into the river.

'For the past,
For the now,
For the future.'

I smile at Naomi, and she reaches for me, pulling me into a long hug.

When she finally lets me go, Ash is waiting for me.

She holds out her hand and I take it, stepping into her arms as we kiss in the cold bright air, the heat between our bodies creating something like our own private slice of summer.

'So,' Leo says with his arm around Rose and we look out at the city stretched out right around us. 'What do we do next?'

I look at my friends, and I smile.

'Whatever we want,' I say.

Q&A with Cara Delevingne

Where did the idea for *Mirror, Mirror* come from? What inspired you?

I really wanted to write a novel that showed an uncensored picture of how difficult and painful it can be to become an adult. There's so much pressure on young people to be perfect, but I wanted to show that whoever you are, if you are happy with yourself then you *are* perfect.

Besides being the name of the band, mirror image/ reflection is an important metaphor throughout the novel. Tell us more about what you're trying to convey.

There is always more than one version of anyone, like reflections in a hall of mirrors. There's the perfect, filtered online version; the school or work version; the version that our friends recognise; and the one true version, that all too often we keep to ourselves. The message in *Mirror, Mirror* is that you only need one version of you, the version that is true to who you are.

You're someone who has a massive following online, and social media plays a key role in how our protagonists investigate Naomi's fate. Are you saying that social media is a force for good?

It can be a great force for good, but it can also be dangerous. What I love about social media is being able to connect with my followers and share my life with them. And it's a great way for people to find out who they are, find their tribe and make connections. On the other hand, the desire to try and appear to have a flawless life can be overwhelming, and it can make vulnerable people even more vulnerable. The key is to be smart and safe online.

All of our teen protagonists struggle with their sense of identity; is this something you've come up against?

Yes of course. I think struggling with one's identity is what makes us human. Finding deeper connections with others is what makes us happy, what we get up for in the morning. All of these things give us a better sense of who we are, but that's also something that is almost impossible to put in words. It's more of a feeling.

There are lots of strong characters in the book. Who did you connect with the most?

I connect with all of them in one way or another, because I think we've all been where they've been at some point in our lives. Red is feeling isolated and going through a period of self-discovery, Rose is outwardly invincible but inwardly vulnerable and damaged, and Leo was up against the pressure of his circumstances, and what other people expect him to be like, because of who he is.

There are a lot of really great twists throughout *Mirror, Mirror*! Did you know how the story was going to end? Or did it surprise you?

I always knew how the story was going to end because I wanted these great characters to find the strength within themselves to overcome the obstacles in their way. I truly believe that anyone can do the same with a little bit of self-belief.

Can readers expect to read more about the lives of Red, Leo, Naomi and Rose? Will there be a follow-up?

There's definitely so much more story to tell for these characters, so there certainly could be a follow-up. But you'll have to wait a bit longer to find out!